ALl
FROM

You hold in your hands one of the schlockiest, most over-the-top science fiction novels ever written. Yet for all its absurdities, it reads like a fun night at a drive-in movie theater—you just can't put it down. Huge flying eyes appear out of nowhere, hypnotizing thousands of helpless people and turning them into mindless zombie slaves! What do they want from the Earth? The answer is simple…pure atomic destruction! Only a bitter research scientist and his pal have a ghost of a chance of coming up with a way to save the Earth.

If this sounds like a juicy grade B science fiction film, believe us…it reads like one, too. "The Flying Eyes" is not a sci-fi tale you will soon forget—sit back and enjoy the ride!

FOR A COMPLETE SECOND NOVEL, TURN TO PAGE 143

CAST OF CHARACTERS

LINC HOSLER
He was the one man who had the power to resist the mental powers of the alien eyes, but did he have the courage to use it?

KELLY ADAMS
Could she ever make up her mind and love just one of the two men she was fond of—before the aliens killed all three of them?

WES ROWE
He was Linc Hosler's best friend, and he was willing to sacrifice his life not only to save him, but to save the rest of humanity, too.

IVERSON
Head of an atomic research laboratory, he had to decide on a plan of action that might cost thousands of human lives.

COLONEL STANLEY
Like all military men he wanted quick, decisive action, even if it meant the destruction of an entire city.

COLLINS
He came up with a surefire way to get rid of the alien Eyes—drop an A-bomb on the whole town!

HENDRICKS
This scientist was the first person to return from the alien Eyes' lair, deep inside the Earth. But was he friend or foe?

THE FLYING EYES

By
J. HUNTER HOLLY

ARMCHAIR FICTION
PO Box 4369, Medford, Oregon   97501-0168

*The original text of this novel was first
published by Monarch books*

Copyright 2012, by Gregory J. Luce
All Rights Reserved

*For more information about Armchair Books and products, visit our
website at...*

www.armchairfiction.com

Or email us at...

armchairfiction@yahoo.com

CHAPTER ONE

THE STRIDENT CALL of brass instruments and the thump-thump-thump of bass drums bloomed out across the college football field. The crowd shouted and clapped as the band paraded to the fifty-yard line, but Lincoln Hosler could only piece the scene together from the sound of it. Below the grandstand, down in the shadows of the seats where the sun only arced through from the ramp holes, he waited in a long, impatient line, as impatient as the rest, and doubting the real need for hot dogs and coffee.

Glorified messenger boy was all he was; fetch and carry, chauffeur the car, buy the tickets. He had invited Kelly to this game. She had accepted him. But Wes was always there, too. He could never shake Wes. The three of them together; that was how it always had been, and how it probably always would be.

He moved up, nearing the counter where hot dogs turned on miniature spits and giant coffee urns dribbled brown liquid into cups. He didn't like this day. The sun was out, the stadium was colorful, the atmosphere was exciting with the ball game, but he didn't like the day.

He scratched his head and laughed at himself. He had been trouble-shooter at the Space Research Lab too long. He saw unrest in everything. Even in his day off.

He reached the counter and ordered three hot dogs and three coffees, then dutifully followed instructions with the mustard and ketchup. As he spread Wes's, he wondered why it was bothering him so much? He had known and accepted the score long ago. Kelly was a bone, an attractive bone tossed between himself and Wes, and they had to fight to come out top dog. But he had little to fight with. In anything else, any crisis at the lab—strikebreaking, fear, nerves, danger—he was purely confident. But with Kelly and Wes, he knew he was second best. Wes had polish and charm, a dark, lean handsomeness that women admired. He had none of those things. His own blondness was the screwed-up sort—nose too big, eyes too palely blue, body strong and tall, but brawny.

He picked up the cardboard tray and headed for the ramp, striding upward into the sunlight. As he climbed to his seat, and saw Kelly and Wes together, he shoved the resentment aside and managed a smile.

His seat was on the aisle, and he plunked himself down on it. "Lunch is served," he said, picking up the hot dogs one at a time and passing them out. "Mustard for Kelly—mustard and ketchup for Wes—the works for me."

"You didn't put onions on yours?" Kelly made a face. Even a face was becoming to her, Linc thought. Her black hair gleamed in the sun and her eyes were an unbelievable shade of green. "I'll have to put Wes between you and me and let him bear the brunt of it."

"Not me," Wes protested. "I'm not that gallant."

The band was just filing back into the stands, and a shout rose as the home team came storming out of the pit.

"Was it a good show?" Linc asked around a bite of hot dog.

"Fine," Kelly answered. "What we saw of it."

"What do you mean?"

Kelly's eyes were teasing, and Linc didn't know whether to smile with her or let the resentment build again.

"We were talking most of the time," Wes explained. "There was an article in the morning paper that needed some discussion."

Wes always knew what to say and when to say it. It was part of his polish—like his education, his books and his dog. He was an expert at handling people. Personnel Manager, they called him, but the better title would have been Genius Pacifier, Temperament Sorter, Spreader of Salve.

"Did you see the article, Linc?" Kelly wasn't teasing any more.

"I didn't read the paper."

"It was weird," she said. "It seems that two days ago a lot of people here in town heard a terrible roaring sound, and rushed outdoors to see what it was, and saw a great lighted thing zooming through the sky. It was low, and looked like it might be coming down."

"And," Linc added in a mocking tone, "it scared the daylights out of the idiots because they thought we were shooting things off at the lab."

"You always have a ready answer, and no imagination," Kelly complained, "I should have known better than to mention it."

"It doesn't take imagination to see lights rocketing through the sky, Kelly," Linc defended himself. "It only takes idiocy—a bunch of nuts in town seeing their own fears made manifest. They're all scared of the lab. You know that. They're scared of our reactor and our research. If they saw a shooting star, they'd be sure it was a bomb we'd made to gobble them all up."

"No one said anything about a bomb!" Kelly was stubborn. "They only reported what they saw. They don't have your cocksuredness about everything!" Kelly stood up.

"Where are you going?" Linc asked her. "You're not mad?"

"No, I'm not mad. Just disgusted. Wes managed to discuss the article without making me feel like a moron. Anyway, I'm just going across the aisle. I see some friends and I want to say hello. Let me by, please?"

He stood to let her pass, liking her scowl, yet uneasy with it because all of the little fury in it was directed at him.

When she was out of earshot, Wes said, "You got the Kelly Adams temper up that time, friend. You should have stepped a little more softly. That article frightened her. If you had paid attention to the way she was talking, you might have seen that fact. You've got a black mood on?"

"I guess so. I feel tense. I have all day."

"You should have stayed to watch the halftime show and relaxed a bit," Wes offered. "It was quite a spectacle."

"I had other things to do, remember? I had to play butler."

"Now, wait just a minute." Wes bounced the challenge back. "You offered to go after the coffee. What's the matter with you, Linc? You act like you want to fight. We're friends too long for that."

It was true. They had shared the same lab-rented house for two years now, and if he had any friend in the world, it was Wes. But he couldn't shake the belligerence that had grown in the dimness beneath the stands. Things had to break soon. He had to know soon.

"It's Kelly, isn't it?" Wes asked when he didn't answer.

"Kelly—and me," Linc admitted. "I always seem to be running around after her, buying her things, fetching things while you sit beside her and make time. Things have got to change. We've both known her for a year now, and it's time one of us moved ahead and one of us moved back."

"Kelly doesn't want a clear road. She wants things just the way they are."

"*You* want things the way they are."

Wes absorbed the barb without anger. "If you think she's choosing between us, you're wrong. She's merely sitting in the middle, enjoying the show, and grasping everything she can get from both of us. Kelly actually wants a millionaire. But she hasn't got the courage to break free, throw everything she has in the ring, and go where the millionaires are, so she sticks with us. Two gullible, free-spending fools are better than one."

Linc winced at the stark description. "And they call you a gentleman. Those are terrible things to say about her."

"Even if they're true?"

"Let's not talk about it any more, all right?"

Wes was shaking his head, surprised. "At least I can finally claim proof that you're more than the machine you're reputed to be. There's a hole in your ego, after all—a chip in your armor."

"And I don't like it either."

"You should be glad of it, Linc. No one can be as indestructible or as all-fired right as you make everyone think you are. Sometimes weaknesses win friends, where strengths win enemies."

"Have I ever said I wanted friends?"

"Thanks." Wes turned his gaze away.

"You know what I mean. Friends tie you down with responsibilities. You try to give and take, and pretty soon you find that the taking has ceased and you're only giving. You give until you give your guts out, and when you're worn down to nothing, the so-called friends leave you in the hole. I've seen it happen. My mother—poor as a slum widow can be—starving herself for us kids, and for the neighbors' kids when she could, giving *them* meat and *us* meat, and what did she get in return? Anemia, an early grave, and sweet smiles of thanks.

"I'm alone—free unto myself—and that's the way I want it. You go ahead and love humanity, Wes. You were raised and educated for it. I love Linc Hosler—I work for Linc Hosler—and I do a great job of it. That's enough for me."

"Except Kelly. You'd like to take from Kelly—to tie yourself down there."

"So that's different. A man and a woman—that's different."

Wes said soberly, "You make me feel as though I should pull out, break the triangle and say, 'Take Kelly and God bless.' But I can't, Linc, because there isn't any triangle to break. I don't love Kelly and she doesn't love me. She doesn't love you either. So I'm sticking around as long as Kelly seems inclined to have me."

Linc's answer was drowned in the roar of the crowd as it came to its feet to watch the second half kickoff. Kelly returned to settle in her place, so there was nothing to do but drop the argument.

The visiting team was forced to punt on State's forty-five, and State buckled down to a series of first downs, heading for the goal line. Between plays, Linc glanced about the stadium, enjoying the color and spectacle of the people—the reds, yellows, and oranges of fall clothes, the plaid car robes, the swish and flutter of mums.

Overhead, there was another show going on. Birds zoomed across the pure blue of the sky, shrieking and calling with shrill voices that could be heard clearly when the cheering section was quiet. It was an odd sight. From a few birds, the number grew to an uncountable horde. They flew fast, beating on by the stadium as though something was following close behind and they wanted to get away. Around Linc other people were noticing, too, but only fleetingly. State had reached the eight with goal to go, and there was no time to watch birds.

When Linc looked skyward again after the touchdown, the air was clear. No birds and no clouds. Kelly was smiling beside him, and all the strangeness of the sight was gone.

A few moments later, Wes reached across and touched Linc's arm, pointing to a small formation, high, high up, coming in over the stadium. "What kind of birds do you suppose those are?" Wes asked. "They've got a queer look to them."

It was difficult to be sure at that distance, but the flight of the birds was almost still—there was no visible wing beat. Linc lifted his binoculars and swung them to bear in on the formation. As he set the focus, his fingers tightened around the glasses and his body stiffened. It was too incredible and he knew he was mistaken.

"Here, Wes," he said quickly and handed the binoculars over. "You look."

Wes repeated the procedure. When he turned back, his face was blank, not even a question wrinkled it.

"They're not birds," Wes's answer was shaky. "They look like—"

"Give me the binoculars." Linc raised the glasses again and looked closely at the approaching flight. It was coming fast, and angling down toward the stadium. He thrust his incredulity aside and faced the facts as he saw them. The members of the flight were not birds. They were *eyes!*

Visible, bodiless eyes!

As they zoomed closer, he made out lashes on them, and the colors of them—blue, and brown, and pale green. Revulsion and disbelief rocked through him and he got to his feet, swallowing back sudden nausea.

"Let's get out of here!" he hissed at Wes.

He grabbed Kelly's hand and jerked her up. There was no doubt now. The Eyes were dropping down in a headlong dive, and they were clear even without the glasses. He watched them with an awe that was so close to terror that he couldn't turn away. They sailed in, the sunlight reflecting bright from their centers, their lashes closing quickly in monstrous blinks.

One prolonged shout passed through the stadium as other people saw the things and pointed upward. And then silence. The great bowl, with its tiers of carefully ordered people, was drenched in a dead silence. The football was punted on the field with a dull thud. It flew—and fell unnoticed as the teams craned their necks to look above their heads.

There were eight of the things—eight Eyes—and they came down level with the top row of seats, and circled over the field. They sank lower. Eight of them—each a foot long.

Kelly's clenched hand bit into Linc's, but she didn't move either. He couldn't find the strength to stir his feet. He could only wait, and stare, and scarcely breathe in the mute silence.

Something was happening to the Eyes. They hovered there, and suddenly they were larger. They were expanding—slowly spreading outward and upward, their pale-colored irises bloating into dull, expressionless balls, blankly gazing, moving almost imperceptibly from side to side as they surveyed the crowd.

Linc's field of vision narrowed as something compelled him to watch the one nearest him. It grew from one foot to three; it blinked and bloomed to five feet, then to six. Six feet long and three feet high, it hovered over the fifty-yard line and stared back at him. He met that stare helplessly, too frightened to resist it.

Across the stadium, a movement jerked his attention from the Eye. A whole section of people stood, all at once, as though pulled up simultaneously by invisible strings. They stood, they turned, and the top row of them filed out to the ramp, and then the second, and the third, until all of them were in motion. Behind them, on the seats, lay the bright flecks of blankets and coats, abandoned.

"They walk like mummies." Kelly's low voice sounded loud in the quiet. "Like zombies."

In the end zone, a section of students rose up and started to walk. Linc looked back to the Eye hovering on the fifty-yard line and its watery blueness penetrated through him to his bones.

"We've got to get out of here," he whispered.

Around him, other people had reached the same frantic decision to flee, and they jumped up and started for the ramps. Their gait was a quick walk—stiff-legged, hurrying, but afraid to hurry too much. The pace steadily increased as the horror over the field penetrated the senses. Bodiless Eyes—nothing behind them—only huge eyeballs and great sweeping lashes. Linc led Kelly and Wes into the fast-moving line of people.

Then, beside him, a woman shoved. Her face peered up into his and her eyes were glassy with a sheer, deep terror. Her mouth was stiff as she tried to form words. She pushed at him, and when he refused to relinquish his place, she opened her mouth and screeched, "They're coming after us! Let me out!" Her cries rose to hysteria. "Let me by! They're coming after us!"

He let her through, but he knew it was too late. A great shock like an electric charge swept through the gathered people and they broke their controlled gait to mill for a moment, and then to run. Shouts broke out, and clawing hands grasped at Linc to push him out of the way. He hurried Kelly forward, having to run to keep his balance in the crush of terror. The thunder of a thousand running feet poured into his ears, and the ordered tiers of the stadium broke into a squirming mass of mingled colors.

"Hang on to me!" he ordered Kelly, and started down the ramp.

People stumbled on the incline and fell forward, caught short by the billowing mass of people in front of them. The faces he saw were purest ice-panic in wide, terrified eyes and brutal, mean strength in frantic muscles. Elbows crashed into his ribs and the screams were piercing after the dead silence.

At the foot of the ramp, under the stands, they met the bigger crowd pouring down from the other exits. A great tangle formed around him, and he shouldered forward, using his elbows and knees.

To his right, a woman went down, sprawling against the retreating legs of the people before her.

"Help me!" she cried, and her arms flailed upward to Linc.

He grabbed for her, but a shove from behind sent him forward and his hand barely brushed hers. Then she was behind him, still crying for help. The crowd closed over her. Her head dashed forward under the impact of a foot, and he couldn't see her any more.

Everywhere people were being trampled. Men ran with their children held high over their heads to keep them from the pounding feet.

He saw the arches of the stadium supports and knew freedom lay that way. He rammed up to the gateway, stopped a moment to make sure Kelly and Wes were with him, and when he tried to move, the fat stomach of a giant man barreled into him.

"Get out of the way!" the man cursed, and an elbow crashed against Linc's head and he was thrown off balance. He went down to one knee. A foot landed on his bent leg and pain shot up his thigh. He toppled forward, scrambling to catch hold of something before he was ground to pulp beneath the mass of running feet. Kelly's hand was strong, holding him up from behind, and then

Wes's arm was under his shoulder and was lifting him forward, through the gate. When he regained his feet, he never broke pace.

Everyone was running under the blue sky. The crowd thinned, but the speed of it was a headlong flight aimed at the parked cars. Wes was even with him now, and together they pulled Kelly along, dashing for the red bulk of his car. He pulled the door open and shoved Kelly into the back, then got under the wheel. The engine started without a miss, but there was nowhere to go. Traffic was piled up before him. A parked car blocked him from the rear, and a line of honking, roaring cars defied his escape forward.

He craned around, and as he looked toward the stadium, he saw a double line of people, calmly walking in the center of the crazed flight of the rest. They walked as though they didn't see the terror, didn't share it, or care about it. Beside them, people ran and fell; above them, men who had tried to climb down the outside of the stadium walls tumbled howling onto the cement; but the marchers looked neither left nor right. They simply walked.

Over the stadium, a shape appeared, and a great Eye came sailing over the wall, down the line of people, clearing their heads by inches, and fell into place before them. It hovered there and moved along backward, leading them in their strange march, through the parking lot, toward the river, then turned to move parallel to the water. The people followed, and the parking lot suddenly heaved as cars, despite the lack of room, roared forward. The crunch of metal on metal and the breaking of glass were added to the frantic blast of horns.

Linc couldn't sit still any longer. The panic around him fed his own, and he put the car into reverse and rammed into the one parked behind him, pushing it back. He maneuvered forward again, then back, until there was room for him to move into a lane comparatively free of cars. He swerved in and out, taking chances he knew he couldn't afford, but making each one pay.

As he neared the river, the cars creeping ahead of him were a slow-running snake. Then the one directly before him stopped. The doors opened and two people emerged, their faces free of panic, their bodies almost limp. They left the car doors open and walked off at a slow pace toward the river, where the two Eyes had taken up hovering positions. More cars stopped, and more people crawled out to join the strange march. The abandoned cars blocked traffic, but there was only one between Linc and freedom. The rest of his particular line had gained the road.

"I'll get it," Wes shouted and jumped out. He ran forward and leaned in the driver's side of the other car, turned the wheel, and motioned for Linc to push. Linc edged up and gave it a firm shove. It wheeled off to the side. He stepped hard on the accelerator and raced for the clear space. He paused for Wes, then took off at full speed for the road, heading away from the river.

The river route was the shorter into town, but he had seen what was happening down there. The dead-marching people were crossing the road, and cars were backed up waiting for a passage through that never came. The people paid no attention to honkings or shouts. One car raced through them, knocking down six people and running them over, but others filled their places.

"I'm turning off to take side streets home," Linc said. "Everybody else will want to stay on the main route."

At the first side street, he blasted his horn and cut recklessly across the path of the oncoming cars. His tires squealed as he took the corner at seventy, but he beat the nearest car by a taillight and the street ahead of him was clear.

He sped past houses where people had come onto their porches to investigate the noises coming from the stadium. It wouldn't be long before the question on their faces would turn to panic, too. Home seemed the only safety in the world, and he had to reach it before his hard-pressed sanity revolted and fled to a safety of its own.

CHAPTER TWO

THE WHITE FRAME HOUSE the lab had rented and then given to Wes and Linc, stood on a quiet street, shaded by elms and maples. But the peace that usually comforted Linc when he saw it wasn't there today. It no longer looked like home. Now it was simply a refuge.

He wheeled the car into the drive, and with Wes's help, got Kelly into the house. She was trembling, her slim body alive with fear. She made no sound except a rapid gasping for breath.

They sat her down on the couch, and Linc poured a brandy, holding it to her lips and helping her drink. Wes watched anxiously until she began to sob, then he simply sat down and patted the head of his spotted, mongrel dog.

"Do you want a drink?" Linc asked him.

Wes shook his head.

"Well, I do." He swallowed the rest of Kelly's brandy, embarrassed at the tremor of his own hands. He circled her with one arm. "Please, Kelly. It's all right now." He looked to Wes. "What shall I do with her?"

"Let her cry it out," Wes said. "It's the best way." He stood up and headed out of the room, the dog walking beside him.

"Where are you going?" Linc called.

"To feed Ichabod. His supper is overdue and he has a hungry look. Haven't you, old fellow?"

The dog lopped out his tongue and whined under his breath. "See?" Wes smiled. "He agrees."

Linc watched him go helplessly. Wes invariably turned to his dog for comfort, carrying on one-sided conversations with the mongrel. Linc had never cared much for the animal. The energy Wes spent on him seemed a waste.

"Kelly?" he asked, and turned her face up to his own. She looked like a frightened child, her green eyes red-rimmed.

"Where's the old Irish?" he asked her. "Come on, honey, take a deep breath and pull yourself together."

"Give her a few minutes," Wes called from the kitchen. "We all need a chance to calm down."

"But we can't waste time rallying our nerves," Linc protested. "We've got to find out what's happening and make plans."

"What plans?" Kelly cried. "What were those things, Linc? What were they doing to those people? Did you see them? They walked as though they were dead."

She broke off shivering, and Linc left her, unable to bear the impatience of listening to her cry, while incapable of doing anything about it.

"Let's get some news," he growled, and snapped on the radio.

Ichabod waddled back into the room, and Wes followed, to resume patting the dog's head. A lethargy had settled over him, and Linc felt suddenly alone. Kelly was hysterical. Wes was numb, and he was alone with the terrible need for action.

The radio sputtered to life with the frantic voice of an announcer:

"...and people are following them—where, no one knows—why, no one knows. They just follow. The giant Eyes are sailing out from the stadium. Two of them are in the downtown shopping area and two more at the Recreation Center. The city has gone wild. There has been no damage estimate of anything. There is no one sane enough to estimate. And still people follow the Eyes. I've seen them, ladies and gentlemen. Right now, looking out of the window here on top of the Garner Building. I can see one of them. It's a great, blue Eye—just an Eye—and it hovers above the street and blinks its giant lids and stirs up papers on the street with the sweep of its lashes. There's something ominous in it aside from its immensity—something that looks out of it, weird and foreign. It has no expression. It is just pure horror, and it—"

Linc snapped the set off angrily. "That guy should be horse-whipped for putting out a broadcast like that. He's scaring hundreds of people to death who haven't even seen the things."

Wes's tone was gentler. "He has one of the things staring him in the face and he's letting out his fear in words."

Linc turned in annoyance and strode to the window and looked out at the quiet street. Birds whistled and fluttered in the trees. The neighbor's cat sat on the porch, washing its face with an orange paw, oblivious to anything out of the ordinary. It was impossible to believe what he had seen less than an hour ago when he viewed it from this vantagepoint. It was impossible, and the memory of it was so distorted with fear and frenzy that he welcomed the doubts that assailed him. Unanswered questions—mysteries—always infuriated him. The world was a sensible, ordered place with an answer for everything, if sane men would only search for it. There had to be an answer for this, too.

He swung from the window. "We've let ourselves be made fools of. We saw something unusual, and we panicked and built it all out of proportion. We were too blind with panic even to know what we saw."

"I know what I saw," Kelly said huskily. "A little girl— somebody stepped on her face."

"Don't focus on those things! They were the result, not the cause. I'm talking about those eyes. Our own panic made them grow, made them appear menacing."

"We saw them before the panic started," Wes argued.

"I wonder. Maybe the panic really started the first second you pointed them out. You know what terror can do. Light a match in a crowded theater—make a little smoke and smell—then yell 'Fire!' and people will stampede. They'll run and crush each other, and later report that they saw flames jumping, when there was nothing there but a little smoke and somebody yelling."

Wes was doubtful. "Then what do you think it was?"

"I don't know." Linc turned away. "But unless we suppose it was something perfectly normal, and examine it from that viewpoint, we'll never get anywhere except deeper in fear. Eyes. What could they have been? Machines? A publicity stunt? Big balloons, sent over the stadium? Or what about mass hallucination?"

"No!" Kelly's shout quavered with her voice. "Balloons or hallucinations don't make people walk like zombies."

"And the announcer on the radio?" Linc asked. "Hallucination is contagious—fear is contagious."

"I can't go along with you," Wes answered. "Everything you say about the psychology of terror is true. I admit that, but this was something else again. This terror had a basis."

"Look out the window!" Linc commanded. "Where's the terror on Colt Street? It hasn't spread here yet, and it won't, if somebody has the sense to muzzle that announcer."

"The *Eyes* haven't spread here either. You're reaching too hard, Linc. You want this thing explained, so you're explaining it any way you can."

"I'll prove it to you," Linc said. "I'm going to the lab. Iverson has probably started to figure it out already."

"You can't go outside!" Kelly stood up. "You're not foolhardy enough to go out there with those Eyes?"

"You stay here and let Wes hold your hand. You'll be safe. I've got to move."

He started for the door, but Wes was quickly beside him. "If you feel you have to go, then I'll go with you."

Linc looked at him, his dark eyes and well-planed face, and all he could manage was a nod of consent. He went through the door and toward the car, admitting that he was angry and argumentative because he was mad at himself. As for Kelly, he was sure she would be safe in the house, and just as sure that she wouldn't venture out.

As he pulled open the car door, the neighbor's orange cat suddenly darted from the porch, beneath the car, and out the other side, headed for the shelter of its hiding place under the back shed. Inside the house, Ichabod set up a howl. Wes looked at Linc over the roof of the car, his eyes questioning.

The question was swiftly answered. A stirring of the fall-colored leaves drew their attention upward, and there, sailing over Colt Street was the six-foot length of an Eye. The skin of the lids was a monstrous rubbery mass, the pores visible holes, and the lash-hairs were as big around as matchsticks at the roots.

"Do you want to go back?" Wes asked in a low voice.

The Eye had passed their house, and now the back of it was visible. Linc's heart sank as all of his speculations were ruled out. The Eye wasn't a fake. The back of it was horror enough to make him clutch his stomach in an effort to hold it down. It was the back of an eye: bloody membrane and nerves—skinless, unprotected horror.

"We've got to go," he told Wes. "Now we've *got* to go!"

Wes's answer was simply to get into the car. "Take the side streets," he said, "and don't go through the campus."

"I'll go the country way," Linc agreed, and sped down Colt Street, away from the thing that was drifting off behind them.

The clustered buildings of the Space Research Lab sat alone on a poorly landscaped piece of property out beyond the campus. The biggest building housed the reactor and the artificial gravity research room. Smaller buildings beside it were offices and specialized labs. It looked innocuous sitting there behind its chain-link fence. There was nothing in its appearance to generate the

18

suspicion the townspeople held toward the place. But they still held it.

The parking lot was full, but there was no activity around the buildings.

"Everybody's probably in Iverson's office," Wes said.

Jan Iverson's office was in the administration building, and their heels jarred loudly on the concrete floor as they entered. Linc respected Iverson. As the project's head, he had a frustrating job. He was pure scientist—the artificial gravity project was his life, and all he wanted was to work on it, but he was saddled with the headaches of administration besides. He had to listen, to judge, to approve or disapprove the grumblings and snap ideas of fifty men. Wes was his human bulldozer, Linc his Maginot Line against crisis. Whatever peace and chance to work he had came from them.

As they entered his office, Iverson rose, a relief on his face that was gratifying. He said, "I was sure you'd come."

Linc glanced over the assembly. There were only three others present: Bennet, Myers and Tony Collins. Collins he could do without. A wiry, hawk-faced man, Collins hated Linc's guts and wanted Linc's job. Everybody knew it. But "assistant" Collins stayed.

"Have you seen 'them' firsthand?" Iverson asked.

"We were at the game," Linc explained.

"Then you had the best chance of any of us to observe. What conclusions have you reached?"

Wes laughed sourly. "We came out here to see if *you* had reached any conclusions."

"Oh." Iverson's hope fell. "In other words, you two know just as much as we do—which is nothing."

"Not even a guess?" Linc asked Iverson. "You must have been getting reports."

"Reports we've got by the dozen," Collins said. "The things are all over the place. They've even sailed over here a couple of times. Wherever people are gathered, the Eyes gather, too. They took an estimated seventy-five people out of the Zoo alone."

"What about Washington?" Linc asked.

"I called them first thing, of course," Iverson sighed. "This thing is local from all appearances. At least it's local so far.

They're sending someone out—they wanted to know if we're going to need the National Guard. I suppose we should expect trouble, but it's up to the governor to declare martial law."

There was a hopelessness in Iverson's voice, and in the faces of the rest of them, that jarred Linc. To look at them, anyone would think a battle had already been lost, when actually no counter offensive had been started. "And everybody around here is just going to sit down and give up, is that it?" he snapped.

"I suppose you've got it figured out already," Collins said, a slight sneer on his face.

"No," Linc challenged Collins' thrust honestly. "But once I get my hands on enough facts, I will. Reports of where the Eyes are and what they're doing aren't enough. Where did they come from? Where are they taking the people they seem to be capturing?"

"We have some knowledge of that," Iverson told him. "One of the boys went out in a helicopter and followed a line of people going north, out of town. They disappeared into the woods out there—on the game preserve—and from what he could see, there was something big and dark down among the trees. Something like a pit. He didn't get a good look, and we had no chance to question him because he didn't make it back. He was talking, reporting, and then he said an Eye had spotted him and was coming up fast, and...that was all. He must have gone down."

Linc absorbed the information and it was somehow more menacing knowing that it had been not knowing. Something huge and black down inside the woods—something like a pit. It made his skin crawl. They should have discovered more, because with this fractional description the imagination was free to run wild and create atrocities and horrors that he prayed wouldn't prove to be true. Lines of people—zombie-like people—following the naked, flying Eyes down the road, into the trees; and something big and black, and perhaps pit-like, waiting there for them. To do what?

"What's being done?" he asked, steering himself back to the solid ground of action.

"This isn't our worry," Collins said. "It belongs to the local officials, to the government."

"The Eyes are over *our* buildings, so it belongs to us," Linc slammed back. "We can't sit around and wait for the government to move. This is a government lab. We've got a high concentration of intelligence here, and we're under a firm obligation to use it."

"Linc's right," Wes backed him up. "We have the best chance of anybody, locally."

The others rallied at Linc's show of firmness. He had seen that reaction before. If he spoke calmly and surely, they all thought he had a plan and waited for him to explain it. But this time they were wrong. This time he had no plan and could only sit mute before them.

CHAPTER THREE

IT GREW DARK, and Bennet and Myers left the office. Wes went into the empty cafeteria and spread some sandwiches for the remaining four of them. Linc paced the room, listened to Iverson's end of phone calls, and ate sandwiches without tasting them. Collins watched him jealously. Linc could see the wiry man's brain working, trying to come up with a plan before another was offered.

Outside, on the brightly-lit grounds, there was only quiet. Linc felt cut off—away from the important events, away from the action, the experience of the people. Iverson was waiting for him to voice an idea, but he was too remote from the problem to touch on one; the telephone reports were half-truth only, the rest distorted by terror.

He came back from the window, decided. "I've got to go out. Maybe seeing for myself, I can get a clearer picture. I don't like these hysterical reports. I need facts."

"I should think you could apply your rule without ever seeing the real thing," Collins said, "You're always pushing down my suggestions with, 'The simplest solution is the best solution.' I shouldn't think you'd need firsthand experience to come up with one."

"Did I ever tell you that you should jump in feet first without facts?"

"Please, gentlemen," Iverson interrupted them, "I won't have dissension in my own house when we're trying to *save* that house.

I'd rather you didn't go out, Linc, but if you feel you must, I won't argue with you."

"Thanks, Doc. I'll try to make it only an hour or two."

"Do you want company?" Wes asked. "I'd like the ride."

"I'll bet you're just crazy for it." Linc grinned, then nodded. "I'll be glad to have you along." He headed for the door.

The side streets they traveled were deserted. The lamps lit the cement in little pools and thrust their radiance upward into the trees, making splotches of orange and yellow and red out of the fall-turned leaves. It was a beautiful time of year, the time Linc liked best. The time of crispness and new energy, wind, and wild leaves swirling; the time when a man could hear himself make a sound upon the earth as he walked through the crackle of leaves. But it was robbed of that feeling tonight. Because this was the time of something else—of monstrous things with unholy stares, sailing against the sky, hovering with the falling leaves.

This journey was incredible, too. People should all have been home, cowering, perhaps peering from their windows. Yet the reports said they were downtown—having come out of curiosity, out of fear and the need for the strength of numbers, and then finding too late that they were caught in traffic jams.

Linc pulled to the curb two blocks from the main street. As he got out of the car, he caught the sound of shouting and the blare of horns. Grand Street made a brightness ahead of them, and they strode toward it, shoulder to shoulder. All Linc could see of the thoroughfare was a tight-packed line of cars. Occasionally the figure of a man or woman hurried across the intersection. But there were no Eyes.

They took the last block at a slow lope. As they rounded the corner onto Grand. Linc thought, "Now we'll see," and drew in his breath to face the unexpected.

But it was too unexpected. He stopped in mid-stride and groped for the glass show window of the store nearest him, bumping into Wes, dragging the other man back with him. Ten feet away—ten feet away and two feet above the ground—hovered the hideous oval of an Eye. It had widened in startled surprise as he came into view, and now, as he skittered sideways, the blue iris followed him, rolling sideways between the lids until red appeared at the corners.

They stood, backs to the wall, huddled together. Linc couldn't force his legs to move. His knees were limp and he feared he would fall. Something pulled at him that he didn't understand. But it was compelling and powerful, and the urge of it revolted him until fear was a taste in his mouth, and the acid of it jolted him back to sense.

"Cross the street!" he hissed at Wes, and took off at a dead run. As he edged between the cars and climbed over the hoods of others, he cursed himself for a fool. He should have gone back around the corner, back to safety. Why had he chosen to stay?

He stopped in the shelter of a doorway and Wes panted up beside him. Wes was no longer a tanned, gentle giant of a man. His face was dead white and his lips gray. He pointed toward the center of town, and Linc stepped out of the shelter to see.

The street, itself, was a tangle of stalled cars, some climbing the backs of others, wrecked and abandoned. Glass gleamed broken on the cement, and water ran in streams into the gutters. People sat in some of the cars, their heads visible in the streetlights and the flash of neon signs. More people ran among them, or clamored up and down the sidewalks, or peered frozen from the shops.

And over the street, caught here and there in the light, were six Eyes. They glided back and forth with an even beat as though they were breathing. They sailed up and down the street, turning their whole enormous bulk, tilting downward to gaze into the cars and the stores. Their blinking was a vast closing and opening. Their bodiless rolling was a horror against nature. They moved quickly, tipping, and coming low. The streetlights caught them and were reflected in their depths and the glint was almost phosphorescent, alien and eerie.

The fantastic scene went on for blocks. The Eyes bobbed and sailed, flushing people out of hiding places. In the street, a man tried to gain the safety of a car, an Eye close behind him. A woman in the car struck his grasping hand with the steel spike of a shoe, rolled up the window and locked her door. The man ran on, but the Eye stayed over his head. As he came to a black sedan, a little girl cried and ran from her hiding place, another man behind her. The father caught the child but the Eye had fastened on him now. It swung low, its lashes brushing the child's head. He pushed the child through the car window, reached in the back and pulled out an umbrella, and climbed to the roof of the sedan. The Eye rose up even with his face and he slashed at it with the umbrella; short, vicious stabs. The Eye recoiled, blinking rapidly. The man slashed again, and as the Eye turned away, its interest shifted to a group of four people creeping along behind its back, and went after them.

"Look down at the corner," Wes said into Linc's ear.

Collected in a side street at the intersection was a crowd—a large crowd of fifty or sixty people. And they didn't seem frightened. Linc walked closer to get a better view until he was only a few stores away from them. They stood together, yet apart, their shoulders limp, their hands at their sides, and their eyes glazed over in a hard stare. He had seen them before, only then they were walking double file, and being run down by impatient cars. They belonged to the Eyes. And they, in turn, would walk into the fields and the woods until they came to that black thing down among the trees.

The six Eyes were still sailing up and down the street, passing from light to light, glowing red or blue or green from the neon. Here and there, he saw a person brought up short, go limp, and follow the glide of an Eye, to join the group at the corner.

"Have you seen enough?" he asked Wes.

"Too much," Wes's voice was hoarse. "Look out!"

Linc ducked just in time to miss being caught by the rushing lashes of one of the Eyes. As he regained his feet, the Eye stopped and swiveled to come back for him. Wes's hand was strong on his arm, pulling him out into the street, and he broke away from the watery stare of the six-foot thing, dodging between the cars. They gained the other side. The Eye didn't follow.

He ran around the corner, into the dimness of the side street. Wes's feet sounded beside him, and he didn't stop running until he reached his car. Underneath his revulsion and terror were the facts he had gathered, and in them somewhere had to be something to provide him with an answer.

They reported to Iverson, then went down the corridor to a smaller office where they could have some privacy out of Collins' line of fire. Linc gulped the coffee Wes heated and said nothing, trying to get his thoughts under control.

There was one thing on Linc's mind he could now be rid of. He said, "Wes, this afternoon at the game, and then at the house—all that arguing I did—I want to apologize."

"There's no need for that, and you know it. You have a crooked idea of friendship if you think that every little difference of opinion needs forgiveness."

"Nevertheless, I felt like a fool when you overlooked it and came along with me. Nobody else offered to come. You keep jolting me, you know? What I said this afternoon about friends and the obligations they create, I guess if I'm honest with myself those are the easy ways I've used to soothe my own rejections. You're the first man who has ever put up with me long enough to see if there is anything inside me to be friendly with."

Wes was grinning, "I managed to get by your ugly face, if that's what you mean."

"Okay," Linc surrendered, "I won't say any more."

"I think Kelly's beginning to soften you up a bit."

"Could be," Linc agreed, "I hope she's all right there alone."

"She's got Ichabod, and from the sound of him when we left, he's not likely to cower from those things. Like that man downtown, he'd probably face an Eye and bark his heart out at it."

That man downtown. Linc remembered him as he fought the Eye with the umbrella. Raw courage. That man was probably an average guy, a father with a little girl; and the little girl was probably an average brat most of the time; but at that particular moment she had become priceless, and he had been valiant in his fight to save her. And he had saved her. The Eye had moved off. True, it had gone after bigger game, but the thrusts had made it retreat.

"The simplest solution." And it was so simple that he had overlooked it!

"I see that trouble-shooting expression on your face," Wes commented. "Have you got an idea?"

He nodded. "Even simple enough to satisfy Collins. Let's get Iverson down here and I'll lay it out."

Iverson came alone. Collins had gone home, confident that nothing would be settled tonight. Iverson's face was gaunt with weariness. "I've just had a call from the mayor," he said. "Martial law has been declared. The governor's here, and the National Guard is coming."

"We can use the soldiers, but why the martial law? People need protection from the Eyes, not from each other," Wes said.

"Things have changed since you left downtown. The people have run amuck. They're breaking into stores. Can you imagine it? With those Eyes hanging over them, they're looting. There isn't a store left intact on Grand Street. I'll never understand human beings if I live to be six hundred."

"It's all born of the same thing," Wes said. "Sanity is gone, so they follow any impulse. There will be mobs, too. Any leader in a storm."

Iverson said, "You called me down here, Linc. What do you have in mind?"

"The obvious, Doc. We must attack. Fight. Destroy the Eyes before they take more people out to that place in the woods."

"But how? If it could be done, someone would have started it by now."

"You haven't seen those Eyes up close. You don't understand what they do to a man. You don't have any inclination to fight—you either want to vomit or run. I'll bet no one has attempted to fight them except one little man with an umbrella. We were close to them—and I found out one thing for sure. They are not machines. I don't know what they are, but they're not machinery. They are eyes. And they're like human eyes. Therefore, they should be as vulnerable as human eyes."

"Right," Wes said. "Nothing's more vulnerable than an eye. It has no armor—nothing but a blink to protect it." He was suddenly out of the lethargy and eager over Linc's idea.

Linc hurried on to convince Iverson. "'They're big—anyone could hit them, with a bullet, a shotgun, an arrow, anything. I don't know how they live so I can't say such a wound would kill them, but blinded, they'd be harmless and we could dispose of them."

Iverson's head jerked up, his weariness gone. "Yes. Yes." He smiled slightly as he visualized the battle in his mind.

"The only problem is," Linc said, "we have to find people who are willing to go up against them. It will take courage—more than most men have except when it's forced on them. Then who?"

Iverson was quick with the answer. "We'll wait for the National Guard. They'll act under orders."

"I don't think we can wait. When will they get here?"

"Tomorrow or the next day. The roads into town have to be cleared. If they can't clear them, they'll have to come through the fields. The highways are just masses of wrecked cars."

"Then we can't wait. Every hour that we delay means more people given up to that black thing in the woods. I couldn't sit here with a workable plan knowing they were being led away."

Iverson bobbed his head. "You're right—as usual."

"Then where do we get the men?" Wes asked. "Police?"

"That's a good possibility. Police," Linc answered, "and maybe some of the R.O.T.C. students from the campus. They know how to handle weapons. Then, of course, there are us."

"I think we can probably pick our own ground," Wes said. "The Eyes will undoubtedly come anyplace they see a crowd."

Iverson stood up. "You two go ahead and plan a strategy. I'll make the calls to the police and students. I think I carry enough weight around here to get them. In fact, I know I do—I've got the whole reactor behind me for blackmail."

He left, and Linc pulled out a piece of paper and bent with Wes over the desk, setting up a plan of action. Tomorrow morning, with the first light, he would win back his beautiful time of the year by wrenching it violently away from the ungodly things that had stolen it.

CHAPTER FOUR

DAWN HAD CLIMBED two hours up the sky, and the sun slanted through the east windows of the lab. The assembled men were restless—forty of them, shifting about, fingering their rifles and shotguns with eager hands. Linc waited close to Wes for

Iverson to join them and give the final word. The excitement inside him was a bubbling, a churning in his stomach.

This morning would be his. A real fight, a hand-to-hand battle—this kind of action he knew backward and forward, and the feel and taste of it, the pending wildness of it, were spurs that made his feet want to stride outside on their own will, made his voice want to come up shouting.

"I think we're going to do it." Wes's voice was thick with enthusiasm. "Look at those men, Linc. They're like tigers, every one of them. I think we're going to do it this morning."

Linc glanced over the forty men again, a frown edging between his blue eyes. "Some of those kids are so blatantly kids. Nineteen, twenty. I wish Iverson could have enlisted some seniors, at least. I worry about them."

"Don't," Wes said. "They're eager. They'll be your best men this morning. Just wait and see."

Iverson's entrance interrupted them. "Are we all set?"

"All set," Linc nodded.

"Good. Then we'll move out in ten minutes. You men will go out in a group, so that we can lure the Eyes simply by our show of numbers. The police first, and then the students." He lowered his voice and addressed Linc directly. "We'll follow behind, at a safe distance."

Linc glanced up quickly to meet the old man's gaze. "What do you mean, safe distance? You've got this all wrong, Doc, if you think I'm here to be an observer, or some back-line general. I've brought my gun, and I'm going to fight."

Iverson shook his head. "You're not going to fire one shot. The lab needs you. If this doesn't work then who knows, maybe the whole town needs you for another try. However it is, you're not going to join the fight. No one from the Lab is to engage in combat. And for once, I won't stomach any arguments. Argue, and you're out altogether. Understood?"

Iverson stepped away before Linc could protest. He faced the men and began to outline the plan.

"I don't like this," Linc said to Wes. "I don't like to be counted out of something I planned myself."

"We have no choice. Who knows." Wes tried to joke the scowl off Linc's face, "maybe we can get rich by selling our observations to the Sunday magazines."

A moment later, the quiet was broken by the sharp shuffling of eighty feet. The men were moving out. Linc reached for his gun, but Wes's hand closed over his arm, and he laid it back down. "Okay," Linc grunted, "so I'm out—put to pasture—an observer. Let's go. I guess *our* battle group is forming over there."

He indicated Iverson and the knot of lab men who had formed around him. None of them had guns, and their empty hands were nervously clenching and unclenching.

The morning was warm, the Indian summer sun lying on Linc's shoulders like a sweater. He stayed beside Wes, walking along the concrete of the parking lot, then across trimmed grass, through the crackle of fallen leaves. The students and police were well in advance, already off the lab grounds, onto the brushy weed growth of the open meadow.

A wooded area loomed a thousand feet ahead of them, and a pheasant took flight at their approach, its bright head glinting metallic green in the sunshine. Everything was strangely quiet. Somewhere in the forest, a flicker sounded its jungle cry, warming up for its journey south to tropical forests.

Fifteen minutes had passed, and the guns in the hands of the men had dropped from the ready position. Conversations had sprung up, carried to Linc's hearing by the breeze that rustled the leaves and parachuted others to the ground.

"I guess the Eyes are late sleepers," chuckled Myers, "and just can't get themselves open this early."

Linc winced at the levity; yet he felt an answering laugh within himself. Relief? He didn't know. There was as yet nothing to be relieved about. Maybe the battle wouldn't be fought and no men would die this morning; but there would be another morning.

With a whir of wings that shattered the morning stillness, the forest suddenly erupted, spewing forth birds of all sizes. They soared up from the trees, a cloud of them, noisy flaps that were crows, and whirring flutters that were warblers. Joining in a crowded sky, they drove straight over the approaching men and off toward the lab. Their calls were loud, and the men stopped still, startled by the sudden activity.

Squirrels, which had been nibbling along the edge of the woods, suddenly were dashing headlong into the dimness, making for cover, and rabbits leaped after them.

Then, up and over the highest elm came the skin and ball of a giant Eye. It sailed up in a great swoop, clearing the forest, and arcing down for the field.

"There's another one." Wes grabbed his arm. "To the west."

They came in a steady dive, now, eight of them—oval obscenities, wide-open, staring in a challenge that sent quivers of gooseflesh down Linc's back. They banked and rolled and settled groundward with a swaying motion from side to side.

"When are the fools going to open fire?" Hendricks cursed. "They'll come right through to us, if they're not stopped!"

The Eyes were nearly over the heads of the fighting force, and just as Linc opened his mouth to scream orders, the guns jerked up and spat orange fire into the morning. The simultaneous explosion of forty guns was a thunder in his ears.

The Eye Linc was watching shot upward twenty feet in a convulsive jerk, hung there for an instant, then started a wobbling descent. There were two holes in it. It skimmed the heads of the men, coming for Linc's group. Tears streamed out of the corners of it, dripping to the ground like a trail of rain. And as it neared Linc, blood started to come, seeping from the holes, mixed with fluid.

Wes was pulling him down, trying to make him crouch with the rest of them, but the sight of the Eye bearing down, bleeding and dying, held him frozen. It halted fifty feet away, ten feet above the ground, soaking the land and the leaves beneath it with red. A glaze came over it as though it had drawn into itself, and as its life ebbed before him, he cursed it, eager to watch it die.

But the glaze that spread across it reached the bullet holes and the blood congealed on the edges of them. The glaze continued to spread, and before his horrified sight, the sides of the holes firmed up, drew themselves together from a gaping hole to a red line, and then the line changed color, the fresh purple of a scar fading to a gray that softened out until it was gone from sight.

The Eye was whole again—healed and whole—and it gazed at him with the same empty, alien expression he had seen before. He stared back, into the iris that was bigger than his head, accepting its challenge. There was a pull upon him, a bodily pull, drawing him closer to it, compelling him to walk into it. He wanted to rip it apart with his hands; he wanted to rid the world of the sight of it. He stepped forward.

"You idiot!" Wes was upon him, knocking him down. "Get away from here. You haven't got a gun!"

Linc regained his feet and ran with Wes, sidetracking to go around the Eye. As he passed Hendricks, he heard the man muttering to himself, "They heal themselves. They congeal and heal, repeal the hole and make it whole."

Linc paused in his flight to grab Hendricks and pull him along. The reactor technician was out of his mind, his own eyes glazed, not with the healing power of the Eyes, but with madness.

The three of them ran from the stare of the Eye, and found themselves in the middle of the melee. Around them the Eyes bobbed and swooped, and the ground was slippery with their blood. But they were healed over. The men were no longer a fighting unit, but a panicked horde of individuals. Bullets rained upward, piercing their targets, and the targets shot skyward, wounded and bleeding, only to return to the fight healed. And always, there was that pull, that constant pull upon Linc that impelled him to approach.

Students bumped into him, their guns discharging uselessly. Others fired volleys at the empty air. The field had changed from order to chaos, with the cries and screams of maddened minds.

Streaming blood from one of the Eyes fell on Linc and soaked into his shirt. Close by, a student jerked straight. His body stiffened, then went limp, and his gun fell from his open hands. He walked through the mob of running, whirling men, oblivious to the noise and jumble. An Eye sailed backward before him, the sun glinting on its healing surface. As Linc watched it the pull caressed him again, and grew from a caress to a tug. Another man, a policeman, joined the zombie student, and the Eye took him, too.

Linc broke from the tug of the thing. Sweat from his own body was mingling with the now cold blood of the Eye on his shirt.

"To hell with Iverson's orders!" he yelled to Wes. "We've got to fight them off!"

He dashed for the student's abandoned gun and raised it to his shoulder, blasting away at the Eye that had now gathered four men and was leading them out of the battle toward the field beside the woods. He saw the searing tear as his shot hit home, smack in the middle of the Eye.

"Bull's-eye!" he shouted in triumph, and let go another blast. But the Eye bobbed upward, evading, and even as it did, he saw the wound he had made in it glazing over, the flow of blood halting, the sides of the hole growing together and scarring over.

"Wes!" He swiveled to find his friend. "What are we going to do?"

But Wes didn't hear. He was yards away, a gun raised, shooting at another of the giants.

The sound of gunfire grew less and less. The circle around Linc broke, cascading outward as men took flight. Those who did not flee stood in their places—numb, alone, unaware. Hendricks was one of them. He wasn't muttering any more.

Linc refused to run. The battle was useless against a self-healing opponent, but he wouldn't run. These men, these boys, were here because of him, and he had to cover their flight. He shot upward, missing or hitting, it hardly mattered which, but the hits were at least a delaying action. The Eyes were massed over him and their seepings and weepings splashed over him, in his hair, on his face, but he wouldn't run. Men in flight went limp and shuffled away, but he ignored them. Whatever Iverson said, this was his fight, after all. The Eyes wouldn't get him.

Wes backed into him, also fighting. Together, he and Wes would battle for the world. Then Wes's hands were on his shoulders, shaking him, and Wes's desperate shouts hit his ears.

"Linc! Come to your senses, Linc! It's no use! We've got to get out!"

Linc heard, but couldn't understand; then Wes's shaking dashed sweat into his eyes and with the sting of it he came back to himself. There was no force left on the field. The battle was done.

"Where's Iverson?" Linc gasped, frightened. Nothing must happen to the old man. "Where are the rest of our own men?"

"Iverson has gone back to the lab. Come on, Linc. Please!"

Six Eyes were circling the bloody ground; two Eyes were escorting twenty men away.

"All right," Linc surrendered. "Retreat—run!"

He swung in beside Wes, blind with exhaustion, and twenty steps further on, stumbled over the body of a dead boy. He was riddled with bullet holes, caught in one of the frenzied volleys of his companions. Linc scrambled up and went on. Behind him, the pull on his back told him that the Eyes were coming, giving chase over the field, eager to add to their line of zombies.

Collins was holding the door wide when they reached the lab.

"We're the last," Wes told him. "Shut it!"

Collins bolted the door. "Iverson and the other men are down in the assembly room," he said.

"Iverson—and how many others?" Linc asked.

"I'm not sure," Collins answered. "About twenty, maybe less."

Twenty, maybe less, out of forty-six! Linc met Wes's glance, then strode away. He went into Iverson's office and closed the blinds tight to bar the scene outside. He could see the field and the Eyes hovering beyond the window, waiting.

He closed the blinds and slumped into a chair, aware of the ache in his body, of the exhaustion, and the filth that was all over him. He shuddered.

"Don't think about it," Wes said. "Not right now."

"But it was such a disaster, Wes. Such a fool play. All of those boys—those men. If we could have won just a tiny victory… But as it is, their loss was senseless. It accomplished nothing. I just gave their lives away."

"You can't take all the blame. If you're determined to place guilt, then I'm guilty, too. So is Iverson."

Wes was trying to give him relief, but he couldn't accept relief, not yet, not with the horror still so close. Collins, coming through the door, was a welcome interruption.

"What were you guys doing out there?" Collins asked harshly. "I got here and found nobody at work, and when I went outside I saw you out there. What was that supposed to be—the 'simplest solution'? Shoot 'em up? Fight fire with fire?"

The barbs hit Linc full force. "And where were you? If you saw what was happening, why didn't you come out and help?"

"Thanks for your usual vote of confidence," Collins slashed back. "I saw, all right; and I saw ahead and knew what was going to happen, so I stayed here. If I hadn't been here, Iverson wouldn't have made it back. An Eye almost got him. I pulled him in. Maybe you think Iverson's just another puppet to play with, but I hold him higher than that. So does the government. He's a man who can't be replaced."

"So?" Linc could think of no retort, "I already know that."

"Then why did you take such a chance with him?"

"Because we thought it would work," Wes said. "An attack on a vulnerable eye—we thought it would work. So did Iverson."

"Somebody should have consulted me," Collins said in a nasty tone. "I could have told you what would happen. I saw a guy poke a stick right through one of those things last night, and I saw the thing heal itself up."

Linc knew then that it wasn't only a futile fight, but a senseless fight. He had sent men out when they didn't have a chance, and he could have known it if he had taken the trouble to find out.

"Where were you to be consulted?" he shouted at Collins, needing to take the self-recrimination out on somebody. "You gave up last night, and went home. And then when you got the information about the healing capacity of the Eyes, you didn't even report it?"

"Okay, so I went home. But would you have consulted me if I had been standing right next to you?" Collins' eyes were sparking. "That's not the way you work, Hosler. Not Lincoln Hosler. He's the whole show, the whole department. You don't use your assistants, and you know it. You've never made use of me. You wouldn't have last night."

"I haven't made use of you because there's nothing in you worth making use of!" Linc let it come.

"Linc." Wes stepped between them. "Now isn't the time."

"Now is the time! I'm standing here, covered with blood and drippings from those ungodly things, and he dares to accuse me of stupidity. Of murdering those men who went to carry out my plan, I won't stand it!"

"You don't have to stand it," Iverson said from the door. "I've heard enough, Collins. Anything you're saying about Linc, you're also saying about me. Remember that. Now—with that fact in mind—do you still wish to charge him with incompetence?"

Collins looked at the floor. "I'm sorry, sir. The tension—the heat of the moment."

"We'll forget it, then," Iverson turned to face Linc's belligerence. "You're a mess, boy," he said, and it was both gruff and gentle. "Take a shower, wash that blood out of your hair, and go home. We'll give this over to the National Guard this afternoon."

"You're not giving up on it?" Linc asked.

"I'm not giving up," Iverson said. "But you need rest. So do I. So does Wes. Look at him, Linc. Double the mess he is, and you've got a good picture of yourself."

Linc glanced at Wes. He was a shambles of a man. His face was dirty with mud and caked with fluid; blood streaked it, and his eyes stood out like marbles in a dark hole. His clothes were matted and caked, and Linc saw that the man was utterly exhausted.

He gave in to Iverson on the strength of Wes. He headed for the door, then turned back. "I'm not going to give up, Doc. I was out there, and I felt what they can do to a man beyond the horror they generate, and I'm not going to give up until I see them destroyed. It's too personal now. I have to finish it."

Wes grasped his arm and led him down to the locker room where hot showers waited, and a clean change of clothes.

CHAPTER FIVE

KELLY WAS AT THE HOUSE, doing her best to make the rooms cheerful. She had the drapes drawn and the lights on, creating a cozy world of cushions and carpets. But Linc wasn't able to enjoy it. Wes relaxed in the big chair, Ichabod at his feet, a pipe in his mouth. Linc roamed from living room to kitchen.

Kelly was cooking dinner. The housekeeper hadn't returned after her departure on the day of the game. Kelly turned from the stove, eyeing Linc, and there was something in her expression that made him realize she wasn't offering solace, but asking it. "You can help me cut up stuff for the salad, if you like."

"Don't bother with anything fancy, Kel."

"Don't be melodramatic. There's no sense in going without food just because you're worried. And I'd like company. I've waited in this house, keeping busy simply because I had to, and now I'd like some friendly talk."

She wanted lightness, gaiety, to counteract the bitterness and fear of the long day she had spent waiting. She wanted him to be a rock for her to cling to. A week ago, he would have been anything in the world for her, but not tonight. He was too exhausted.

"The things I have on my mind don't make very gay conversation," he said.

"Then go back to Wes. Let me cook in peace."

He went to her, wanting the feel of her, the comfort of another human body close and safe with his. He put his arms around her, forcing her to stop the stirring motion. But she squirmed away. "For heaven's sake, Linc, not now. What do you think I am?"

"My girl, maybe?"

She ignored his statement. "I'm not here to be mauled. I don't want to be mauled. Go pet Ichabod if that's what you want."

He was too tired to play games. He spoke his mind, "Why do you keep coming around if you don't even want my touch on you? You're no prude, Kelly. Why don't you ever let me near? You've got to make up your mind someday."

"Does it have to be today? You pick the worst imaginable times for your lovemaking. You have no sense of timing—no sense of delicacy. If you think I'll fly into your arms just because I'm frightened, you're dead wrong. I might need comfort, but not that kind."

He left the kitchen before he said anything more and made a worse shambles than there already was between them.

Wes was staring into the flames of the fireplace, deep in his own thoughts. From the look of him, no one would guess that just hours before he had been on a bloody field, fighting horror.

"You sit there like nothing had happened," Linc complained. "How do you manage it?"

"Maybe it's because I know what to put on my conscience and what to toss away."

"And what is that supposed to mean?"

"You're letting this morning's fiasco eat you up. You have to put it out of your mind—forget it—and start fresh."

"I know that." Linc rubbed his head, as though the physical action could clear away the muddle from his mind. "But those boys—I told Iverson they were too young!" His voice was rising, repeating the anger he had thrust at Collins. "Almost none of them came back, do you realize that? Two dead of gunshot wounds, and fifteen taken away by the Eyes. I didn't go with the Eyes. You didn't go, but those boys did. And they're all lost because, as Collins said, I picked the simplest solution I could find and rushed into it without weighing the consequences."

"Don't heap yourself high with blame, Linc. It doesn't belong on you. You fought your guts out this morning. You were the last to leave the field."

"But how can I reconcile—"

"I've made some cocktails," Kelly said from the door. "I want everybody to drink deep and liven up."

She handed the glasses around, and Linc gulped his down.

"Ichabod is great company," she was saying to Wes. "Now I know why you talk to him all the time. He does answer, in his own way. I may steal him and take him home with me."

"Nope," Wes smiled. "A man's woman and his dog are sacred to him. They're untouchable."

"The dog part, anyway," she answered. Her eyes sparkled brightly, perhaps too brightly to be genuine, and certainly too brightly for Linc to stomach. "If you had a woman," she asked Wes, "would she actually mean that much to you? Would she be untouchable?"

"In theory, yes. I can't say in practice, because I've never had a woman."

"Don't I know it! Maybe we can change all that one day. If there ever *is* another day—free from the Eyes." She frowned. "I've felt so guilty and useless, running about, cleaning house, while you two were fighting for my life."

Wes reached out and touched her hand. "But there was nothing better you could do."

"Thank you," she murmured.

The moment between them was close and warm. Linc averted his eyes. He hadn't been able to say things like that to her. Wes always knew the right words, and he took advantage of the fact.

Then Kelly's dark gaze was on him. "Linc just sits here like a gloomy bear. He won't even talk to us."

"If my company is that dampening, I'll remove it." Linc stood.

"For heaven's sake, don't go stiff on us," Wes told him. "Kelly was only trying to tease you out of the mood."

"I guess I just don't understand teasing at a time like this," he answered somewhat nastily.

Wes withdrew his hand from Kelly's grasp, and his face was full of the kindness he always offered. "If you've got things on your mind, friend, talk about them. Let us listen and help."

"Yes, talk if you must." Kelly was watching him, too. "I thought this was just one of your moods. I didn't realize you were really troubled."

He wanted to accept her offer, to make use of her sudden concern, but he threw it aside, because he didn't know how to use it. "There's nothing to talk about. I'm going to make a sandwich, and then I'm going to bed. You two have fun."

He left the room, torn within himself. On the one hand, he had done what he knew Kelly wanted; but on the other he had thrown them together again. He always threw them together. Wes spent more time with Kelly than he did. Wes might say that it was time he didn't want, but he never refused it.

As he sliced the meat, he could hear them in the living room, their voices low, talking and laughing. And piled on top of the other great failures of the day, this one exploded all out of proportion until he finally found a scapegoat for his anger and disappointment: Wes, the professed friend who took every opportunity to stab him in the back, and in the exact spot where he knew it would hurt most.

It was dark outside, ten o'clock dark, when a knock sounded on his bedroom door. He raised up from the pillow where he hadn't found even the peace of a nap, and called, "Come in."

It was Wes.

"Has Kelly gone home?" Linc asked.

"No. She's going to stay the night—in the housekeeper's room. She's too frightened to go home. People have gone crazy, Linc. They're looting private homes now, and a girl isn't safe alone."

"Are you sure she's safe here?"

Wes glanced up quickly, estimating the meaning behind the words.

"You two were laughing it up pretty heavy down there. With her staying in the house—"

"Now, wait just a minute..." Wes's face was red. "Just because you—"

"Just because I nothing. You hand me a long line about not caring a damn for Kelly, but you latch onto her quick enough whenever you get the chance."

"She wanted comfort, and you refused to give it, so I did. One human being to another. No more."

"You must be a saint. Do you know that? You're so full of compassion and philosophy, you must be a saint."

Wes sighed. "A minute ago, I was a heel, and now I'm a saint. Make up your mind, Linc. Which is it?"

"Time will tell that. Meanwhile, I think I'll sleep downstairs where I can keep an eye on her door."

Wes's hands were clenched, and the same fighting look Linc had seen in him this morning stared back at him now. "I'd like to knock your head off," Wes growled. "I've taken a lot from you—making excuses, trying to find something in you to like, but I guess I was wrong, Collins and the men at the lab have you pegged. You're an egotist—an overbearing, swaggering egotist, so sure of yourself and your own cockeyed judgments that you stink. Your trouble is you don't know how to accept a friend. I thought last night maybe you'd learned, but you only made it sound good. When it comes down to it, you're still alone, and want it that way."

Linc's own hands were clenching into fists. He wanted to make physical contact. It seemed a certain, sure relief.

Wes backed off two steps and said, "I'm not going to fight with you. It's not worth it—not over this accusation. You'd win, anyway. I'm no match for you physically, but if you measure by heart or decency—then, friend, you fall so short it's pitiful. And all because of that woman. She'll ruin you yet, Linc. She's got you by the tail and she'll turn you inside out, if you're not careful."

He strode from the room and slammed the door behind him. Linc sat on the edge of the bed, his fists still clenched in unvented anger. He threw himself across the bed. The hell with Wes and Kelly. The Eyes were more important. He had been wrong this morning, dead wrong, and the realization threw him. He felt unsure of himself and he had to remedy that. Unless he was competent in his work, nothing would ever matter again. He'd find a way to destroy the Eyes yet. He'd find a way to redeem himself.

Two days passed. The National Guard moved in and was beginning to contain the town. But the Eyes remained.

Linc spent the days mostly alone, wrapped in depression. Kelly was gone, and the atmosphere in the house was strained, constantly edging on a near fight between the two men.

On the third morning, the dim ringing of the phone brought Linc out of a fitful sleep, and he dressed and went down to the kitchen. Wes was there, drinking coffee.

"Was that the phone?" Linc asked.

"It was," Wes answered. "Iverson with the latest news."

Wes's short tone sent Linc to the stove, where he plopped some margarine into a frying pan and dumped in two eggs. Wes knew what he wanted. He could volunteer the information.

"The National Guard has been nosing around, asking for information on the hole in the woods," Wes opened up.

"It is a hole then?"

"It is. A big one. The people go down into it. And they don't come back up. Some of the observers don't make it back either."

"But it is a hole." Linc was glad of the confirmation. If it was a hole, a known thing, then his nightmarish imaginings could be cast aside. "Has it always been there?"

"The farmers in the area and the game warden out there say it just 'appeared.' There's talk about an explosion out that way, the same night the light was reported streaking over town. The light you called an idiot's hallucination."

"So I was wrong again," he said. "And you're pleased to be able to prove it to me."

"Iverson has a straight line to Washington now. They're sending somebody out." Wes refused to take the bait and add fuel to the quarrel. "But nobody has a solution. No protection has been found. The Eyes are still leading people away."

Linc put his plate on the table and poured himself a cup of coffee, "I thought I'd go in to the lab today."

"Iverson says there's no need. Nothing's going on out there. I'm staying here. I don't see much sense in running back and forth when there's nothing to be accomplished."

"That's fine with me. I guess the last few days have proved that we were never meant to be a team anyway. A little crisis, and we tear out each other's throats."

The lab was being run by a skeleton crew. None of the project work was going on, but a certain number of men had to be there to keep tabs on the reactor.

Iverson glanced up from his paper-strewn desk, "I told Wes there wasn't any need for you to come," he said.

"I know. But you're here, so why not me?"

"I won't say I'm not glad, but I really don't see what good you can do. Things are getting worse. That's all the news there is."

"I saw the soldiers. Sooner or later they'll calm the place down."

"I don't know, Linc. The panic's spreading. People are jumping the gun all over the county. Everyone's afraid the Eyes will widen their activities and the towns around here are turning into ghost towns. People are running. So, in the long run, if we should need them to help, they won't be there."

"Maybe they're smart. The Eyes might spread."

"Don't even think that." Iverson shuddered. "If they can make such a shambles here, what could they do to the whole country? I'm at my wits' end, Linc. Washington seems to be holding us responsible for some solution. They're sending a man out, yes, but they expect us to have something to tell him. Of course, they have some ideas of their own. They think the attack was a good plan and they want the Guard to try it again."

"Oh, no!" It was Linc's turn to shudder. The first failure had been his fault, and another failure would reflect on him, too—still his idea, still his guilt. "They wouldn't have any more chance than we did."

"Washington thinks they would. Where we could only inflict small, single wounds, the Guard will have big weapons. They can blow the things apart."

"And they can turn into zombies just as easily as those boys."

Iverson stared at him, his face ashen. "I don't suppose you've been outside of town—out toward the hole?"

"No. Why?"

"It's a sight you wouldn't easily forget. The soldiers drove me out there in a Jeep. The roads are crammed with people—four rows deep—all lost to us, all zombies. How do they do it, Linc?" Iverson's voice rose in desperation. "What do they do, and how?"

"I've been working that over in my mind for two days. The answer is obvious: hypnosis."

"You're not serious..." Iverson was shaking his head.

"Don't slough it off before you've given it a chance. I was out on that field with them and downtown with them. I felt their pull. It's so strong it's like a physical tug. I resisted it—I was angry and I resisted, but I felt it drawing me."

"Yet you resisted it."

"That's the proof of my point. I've got a strong will, Doc. I impose it on everybody, so you should know. And that strong will saved me. It saved the others who returned. The boys—the unformed, groping boys—didn't have a chance. The Eyes hypnotized them before they knew what to resist."

Iverson was quiet, staring at his hands. "If you're right, how can they be stopped? How can we fight such a thing? It's beyond our power."

"You've overlooked the main point, Doc. If the Eyes can hypnotize, then there must be a mentality behind them. Right?"

"I suppose I knew that already. They act intelligently."

"Then what we should do is try to reach that mentality and study it. Maybe in that way we can discover how to destroy them."

"You're leading up to something."

"The only thing I can think of as our next action. I want to capture an Eye, Dr. Iverson. I want to capture one and study it— inside and out."

Iverson showed no enthusiasm. He didn't show much of anything.

"Should I take your silence to be disapproval?" Linc asked.

"No. You make sense, as usual, but the idea is so tenuous—it depends on so many 'ifs.' How will you capture one? How will you study it? Even if you do, will it work? I can't help but feel the Guard has the right idea. Blow them apart and rid our skies of them."

Linc sat back. He had expected more appreciation of his suggestion. "At least give me your permission to try."

"Well—" Iverson's answer was cut short by the clang of bells and a siren wail. He sat bolt upright in his chair. Linc was already on his feet. The bells were the external alarm on the reactor. Something was wrong in the atomic pile.

Iverson grabbed up his direct line to the reactor and spat questions into the phone. "Where? Why aren't they inside? Who?"

When he hung up, he hissed at Linc, "Somebody's in the reactor. He hit the guard over the head and broke in. He's sending the pile crazy. It's going to go sky-high!"

CHAPTER SIX

LINC RACED OUT of the administration building and across the grass toward the reactor. A man was waving frantically at the entrance. Blood seeped down his neck from a cut on his head.

"Who's inside?" Linc fired the question.

"I don't know! Everybody left for coffee, and this guy must have sneaked up behind me. I felt the blow—then nothing. When I woke up, the alarms were sounding. Is she going to blow?"

"Pray!" Linc ran inside, making for the locker room and the radiation suits. The bells were continuous explosions against his eardrums, and lights flashed in the corridors, yellow lights, danger lights. He pulled open the first locker he reached, yanked out the suit, and struggled to get it on. But the light over the door changed from yellow to red, and there was no time. It was now or never. If he had a chance of saving the pile at all, he had to move now.

He grabbed up a lapel radiation indicator and stuck it in his pocket. It was already turning color, warning of danger. He took off down the hall again, heading through the maze of corridors toward the building center and the pile itself. Fear trembled inside him as the lights flashed and the bells clanged.

He rounded the last corner leading to the main room, and stopped. Ahead of him, lit by the flashing red of the warning lights, moved the slim figure of a man. It halted, too, and they faced each other for a brief second. Then the man darted sideways into another hallway. Linc took out after him. He didn't know how to operate the reactor, but the man, the cause of the danger, could be removed.

He turned the corner and saw the fleeing figure ahead of him. He pushed himself into a sprint. The hall was dark, bursting with red flashes, and they two were alone, hunter and hunted, both running through the tangible tension of impending atomic disaster.

With a great leap, Linc was on the man, pulling him down from behind. He fell on top of him, but the man rolled free and regained his feet. Linc was up, and before he even identified the face in front of him, his fist was crashing into it. The man fought back, and a fistful of knuckles caught Linc's jaw. The wall close to his back kept him from falling, and he thrust himself forward, hitting and slashing wildly, overpowering his target with the sheer fury of his attack. Finally, the man went limp before him, and sank down the wall to collapse on the floor.

Linc forced air into his lungs and ran back down the hall. Whether he knew how to stop the reaction or not, he had to try. He threw open the door to the main room, and stopped. The room was full of radiation-suited technicians, already working to deaden the build-up, lowering the leads into place to stem the frantic circular dash of destruction.

"Get out of here!" somebody yelled at him. "You need a suit!"

Linc suddenly realized his vulnerability and panic washed over him, a great hot wave from his solar plexus, taking his breath and hazing his vision. He caught hold of himself and hurried out. He stopped for the unconscious body of the man he had caught and beaten, and lugged him up over his shoulders. He carried him to the nearest exit, out into the clean air, and dropped him onto the grass.

He stood there, trembling. Had he gotten too much radiation? Had it already started to eat at him? He thrust a shaky hand into his pocket and pulled out the lapel indicator. Already, over the door, the lights had changed back to flashing yellow. He held the indicator up, afraid to acknowledge what he was sure he would see.

But it was all right. It hadn't reached the critical point.

He had gotten out in time. The sigh that roared out of him came from deep in his soul.

The man at his feet stirred, and Linc looked at him closely, peering beneath the smeared dirt that darkened the face. It was a familiar face that stared up into his—Hendricks.

"Hendricks!" Linc knelt, but Hendricks didn't hear. He was conscious, but his eyes were dull, glazed over. Linc recalled the last time he had seen the man—the morning of the fight, walking away with the Eyes. From the look of him, Hendricks still belonged to the Eyes. He was still hypnotized, still under their power.

Linc faced the impact of what that meant. Hendricks had been *sent* to blow the reactor, sent to destroy the lab. Why?

That *why* was the most important thing in the world. Someone ran up beside him, the technician, Bennet. "We got it under control," he panted. "It's going to be all right." Bennet knelt quickly beside Hendricks and peered into his face, rubbed his head and hair. "There's something wrong with him."

"He's still a zombie."

"I don't mean that. He's sick. Sick to death, by the look of him."

Linc searched vainly for the symptoms Bennet had seen. "A disease?"

"Radiation sickness. That's how it appears to me."

"From his stay in the reactor?" Linc was doubtful.

"Must be."

"But I got out all right."

"He was inside longer, and closer to the pile than you were."

Linc rose. "I'll get a doctor. Iverson will probably want him treated here. A case of radiation sickness would only add to the panic downtown."

He strode away. Hendricks' illness would be turned over to men who were competent in that area. For himself, he had to move ahead with his own plans. And he had to make certain that no more reactor technicians were lost to the Eyes. Their diabolical use of Hendricks, and Hendricks' special knowledge, was sure warning of what they would do with any more they managed to lure away.

Hendricks was dead. Linc's brief nap was broken by that news. Hendricks was dead. In addition, a certain Colonel Stanley had arrived from Washington, and the National Guard had gone out to battle the Eyes.

It was Wes who stood over him and pelted off the sentences. "This colonel wants both of us in on the briefings."

"So now we're going to have briefings and be military," Linc sighed, "I take it then that Iverson hasn't given permission for my plan."

"No. He told me about it, but he hasn't decided. I imagine his decision depends on what the Guard accomplishes."

"Which will be nothing." He ran his hand across his blond hair to put it back in place. "Did Hendricks come out of his trance long enough to talk?"

"No. He just died. That's a mystery, too. He shouldn't have died so fast—not from the effects of the reactor. But it was radiation that killed him, all right."

Linc shook his head. "If we try to solve them all, we'll bury ourselves. First things first. Let's go meet the brass."

Colonel Stanley was waiting with Iverson and Collins. He was a short man, muscular and tense. He strode about like a cock rooster and demanded attention. It was clear that he intended to add discipline to the fight, and win it through sheer routine.

"Glad to meet you," he said when Linc and Wes were introduced. "If you'll please sit down, I'll fill you in on what Washington has discovered.

"First off," Stanley's clipped words dominated the quiet, "this is a local phenomenon you're experiencing. Whether or not it will spread, is something we're concerned with, since there is every indication that it will. Following down the line of facts, we know that your phenomenon started with a roaring light that passed over your city, followed by an explosion in the woods.

"Investigation has shown that your roaring light wasn't the only one of its kind. Two weeks previous, a similar phenomenon was seen over our Western testing grounds. A week previous to that, the Russian bomb-test sites reported the same occurrence. Consequently, we can expect what has happened here to be duplicated at either of these two places, or almost anywhere else.

"Confidentially, I may tell you that Washington is frantic, and requires that something be done to stop it immediately. Something is being done right now. Our National Guard is at this moment engaging the Eyes, and this afternoon will see the end of them."

"And if it doesn't?" Linc asked.

Stanley clearly didn't like the remark. "I see no reason to doubt that it will, and no reason to jump ahead of ourselves. One thing at a time, please. One tactic at a time."

"Has Dr. Iverson explained my idea to you?" Linc asked.

"Yes," Stanley said, "and it has merit. But it won't be necessary."

"Merit?" Collins cut in. "It's preposterous. The Eyes can't be captured and contained. Such an idea assumes that the Eyes are complete, live beings that can be pounced upon and taken captive. And that is ridiculous."

"Then what are they?" Linc demanded.

Collins shrugged. "Two possibilities enter my mind. One, they are some kind of machines—remotely controlled machines. Two, they are merely manifestations, created by a power operating somewhere else entirely. If they have the mental power to hypnotize masses of people, then why couldn't they also cause hallucinations?"

"Well?" Colonel Stanley turned quickly on Linc, jarring him out of his intended retort. "What do you have to say to that?"

"Nothing much. Collins may be right. I've had the same thoughts myself. However, I do know that the Eyes are solid matter. I saw them shot. I saw them break open. I saw them bleed. I'm not prepared to go any further than that. But I'd like to attempt to capture one, and then we'd know, wouldn't we?"

"Quite so. I like the way your mind works, Hosler," Stanley said. "You go after concrete proof of your contentions—none of this scientific jabberwocky. However, I still stay that you're premature and too pessimistic. This afternoon is going to tell the story. Our fighting men will be the answer, mark my words."

A hesitant rap on the door swung him round. He always seemed to be pivoting. "Come in," he called.

A young lieutenant entered, a National Guardsman, and he was dirty, disheveled and haunted-looking. He didn't salute the rank of the man before him, and even Stanley didn't object.

Linc gave the soldier his chair and waited for the words he knew were coming. The Lieutenant's voice was low as though he was afraid to speak above a whisper.

"We went out as ordered, sir. Out into the country, into an open field. We had high-powered rifles and two field pieces. We waited. And they came." A shiver passed through him with the remembering. "It was a rout, sir. We tried. We shot them to pieces; we shot holes right through them—the big guns blew them into jagged bits—*but the bits came back together again! They came back together and they healed up and they—*"

"Take it easy." Linc placed his hands on the boy's shoulders. "Somebody get him a drink."

The soldier swallowed the water convulsively.

"How many did you lose?" Colonel Stanley asked.

"Over half," the boy answered. "Over half."

"There's your answer," Linc said to the colonel. "There's your end to the phenomenon. Now do I get my chance?"

Stanley was too stunned to answer. But Iverson said, "It may be all we have. At least it would be something to do while we're looking for a new idea."

Slowly Stanley nodded his head. "All right, we'll try it. But no one from this lab must be in on it. It's too dangerous, after what happened with that man Hendricks."

"That's impossible," Iverson protested. "Any such study of an Eye is scientific work. And aside from our men here there is no one else. Any possible civilian scientists in the area are hiding. People won't come out of their houses any more. They caught on quickly that the Eyes only attack groups of people and leave individuals alone. No one will volunteer, and this has to be a voluntary effort."

"It's my idea," Linc said, "and if it's tried at all, I intend to try it. Collins can come along with me."

"No." Collins was fast with his refusal. "I'm not going out in the open and dare one of those things to climb into a cage. That's suicide, zombie-style. Count me out."

Linc suddenly felt alone. He couldn't manage it alone—not this. He needed someone, and he had to admit it.

"You've forgotten me all of a sudden." Wes stood up. "That's no way to keep a friend—by overlooking him."

Wes was offering to help and to mend their quarrel all in one. Linc was almost too ashamed to answer, but he had to answer, and to express his deep-felt thanks in that answer. He glanced at the floor and said, "There's no one I'd rather have with me."

"Then it's settled." Stanley ignored the emotions in the room. "You two have a try at this while Iverson and Collins put their heads together with me and try to come up with something else."

Even as the colonel was talking, Linc was aware that he had made an important discovery. He needed Wes and Wes's friendship. But he wouldn't have had it if Wes hadn't been a big enough man to make the first move—time and again to make the first move. He had a lot to learn from the quiet, bookish man. He hoped he was given the time and the chance to learn it.

CHAPTER SEVEN

THE ROOM LINC APPROPRIATED for their workshop was in the administration building. It was just adequate to hold the workbench, desk and three chairs that crammed it. They opened the window to clear out the musty odor, and Wes swept the floor.

"What's first?" Wes asked between swishes of the broom.

Linc sat down in one of the chairs. "Something to contain the Eye, once we have it. A box, a cage? If a cage, then out of what materials?"

Wes paused in the sweeping. "The obvious answer is wire or chain link, but in order to have a good view of it, one side should be glass."

"Good. I'll order the stuff."

"If you just poke around in the storeroom, you'll probably find what we need without waiting for deliveries. I doubt if there's anyone to deliver, anyway."

They went down the hall to the large room at the end. It was crammed with materials, ordered and unused, thrust into storage and forgotten. They searched through it, sneezing in the dust, and it was nightfall by the time they had found everything they required.

Linc was driven by the need for speed, yet knew that when the cage was completed he would have to face the larger problem of the capture. How could they capture an Eye? The answer depended upon being able to incapacitate it long enough to get it into the cage. Nothing from his experience seemed to meet the requirements.

As the cage took shape, a tall rectangular frame—top, bottom, and three sides covered with fencing, the other waiting for Wes's glass—he made a conscious effort to think the problem through. What he needed was a simple idea—something that would work because it was simple, and had few parts to go haywire.

The Eyes appeared to be like normal human eyes; they wept when stung and bled when wounded. Therefore, they could be blinded. And whether it sounded too simple or not, tear gas might be the instrument for that blinding. Tear gas bombs, smothering it in fumes, should incapacitate an Eye long enough for them to get their hands on it.

He told Wes, and Wes agreed that it sounded logical. "But what do we do with it once it's blinded?" Wes asked. There was a crawly look on his face. "I don't think I could muster the courage to touch one of those things. To touch it and carry it—what would an Eye feel like to touch?"

Linc shivered. "Ughhh. I hadn't considered that."

"So what do we do?"

"Find some other way to maneuver it into the cage. Something to pull or push it."

"Pulling sounds best to me. They float, so if we could get something around it and pull, it ought to float along behind us."

Even as Wes talked, the picture he created took form in Linc's mind, and the tool they needed was there in the picture. "A net," Linc said. "We'll get a big net, and while the thing is blinded by the gas, we'll throw the net over it and pull it in."

Wes sighed a loud sigh of relief. "Here's the glass." He fitted it into the slots. "It sounds crazy—going after an Eye with tear gas and a net—but at least it's a plan. When I volunteered, I doubted if you'd ever figure it out."

"You volunteered for more than either of us expected. Frankly, I thought Iverson would grab my idea, then give it to some poor fools to carry out, and I'd have to bear the guilt of their failure."

"He gave it to two poor fools, all right. Linc Hosler and Wesley Rowe—two fools in the traditional pattern."

Morning came brightly and they left the house three-strong, because Ichabod refused to be locked behind. He had been alone too much since the departure of the housekeeper and demanded companionship.

"I haven't heard of the Eyes attacking animals," Wes said, as he put the dog between them on the front seat. "He'll be safe."

The dog was nervous and eager, bumping Linc's arm with his busy nose. It was the last thing Linc needed, but he made no comment.

They had driven home in the lab's pick-up truck, and now it clattered down Colt Street, disturbing the morning silence. Linc thought they must make a strange sight: two men and a dog, a rattly truck, and on that truck, covered with a tarpaulin, an eight-foot cage, empty and waiting. They were going out to do battle like men armed with sticks against cannons. The tear gas bombs were in a box that Wes held, two gas masks on top of them. The net lay folded beside the cage.

Linc took the deserted roads into the country. The farms they saw were devoid of activity; they might as well have been dead farms. Linc was headed in the direction of the game preserve and the "hole," but minutes passed and they were still alone. There was no Eye in sight.

The sun had climbed to ten o'clock and still they moved alone down the road, making a clear target, but unchallenged. Linc's hands were sweaty as the minutes ticked by without release from tension.

"Why don't they come?" he hissed at Wes. "Do we have to go right up to their den?"

"Let's not try that." Wes's hand was on Ichabod's head, taking his own nerves out in the comfort of his dog. "Maybe we're not juicy enough prey. One truck—two men—they go for bigger numbers."

"They've got to go for us!"

"Take it easy. You'll get yourself so worked up you'll panic when we do find one."

The fields at their side were high with weeds, and looming ahead was a small wooded area, bright-colored against the sky. Linc tried to see its beauty, the red torches of maples, and the higher yellow of elms. He tried to relax in it. Too much tension could lose a battle, and this would be a battle so dangerous that he must have all his wits about him. If there *was* a battle.

As they neared the woods, Ichabod stiffened. His busy nose ceased its probing and pointed, quivering, straight ahead. There was an almost imperceptible growl in his throat, and Linc's foot stamped on the brake in reaction to the sense of danger.

Up and over the trees, a shadow came, and resolved into the distended form of a giant Eye. It was blue—a watery blue—and it slithered its iris from side to side, sweeping the ground.

Wes's hand closed over Linc's arm, and Wes was a shaft of stiffness to match his dog. The Eye zoomed higher and sailed on. Its blank gaze touched the truck and swept past. It wasn't going to bother with them. It was going to leave them behind.

Frantically, Linc leaped from the truck. This was his chance, and he was missing it. He hit the ground and started yelling and waving his hands in the air. "You devil!" he shouted. "You dirty, slimy devil. Come down and fight! Come down!"

The Eye swerved in the air to peer at him, and he waved harder and cursed it. If it could be angered, he would anger it.

The Eye moved closer, and he continued with his dares, his flaring insults. The Eye leveled off, picked up speed, and came at him. He jumped back into the truck and stepped on the accelerator.

Wes yelled, "We didn't come to run away from it."

"I've got to find some cover," Linc explained quickly. "I've got to force it down to our level."

He maneuvered the truck off the road, and into the trees. The Eye couldn't approach from the sky now, but would be forced to come down into the small clearing ahead. It had to come down—so they could get the net around it.

He climbed out of the truck and Wes came to stand beside him, proffering a gas mask and two bombs. Linc took them, readying himself for the moment. Everything was quiet. There wasn't even the sound of a bird in the woods. Overhead, he knew there was a shadow sailing, and the monstrous thing that cast it, but here they were in a world alone. The moment had come, and he was afraid.

A movement through the leaves dragged his attention forward and up. Into the clearing before them, beneath the leaves, edged a pinkish lower lid, then a white iris, and then the watery blue of the Eye he had cursed. It sank down, more and more of it visible until it was all there, hovering two feet above the ground, staring at them with the blankness of its alien sense.

Linc hated it violently in that moment. Its ugliness, its monstrosity, was a blight upon the earth. He hated it, but he couldn't move. It fascinated him, it awed him, and it paralyzed him. Wes was silent beside him, and together they stared at the thing that had come down into their trees.

Ichabod barked wildly from the truck and the sharp yaps pierced through Linc's consciousness, shocking him back to reality. He felt the tear gas bombs hard in his hand. He raised them slowly, ready to throw, his left hand fumbling with the mask for his own protection. As the Eye settled, making no move except great, hypnotic blinks, he tightened the muscles of his arm.

"Now!" he screamed to Wes, and heaved his bombs straight at the thing in the path. They hit and burst, and two spurts from Wes's hand rose beside them. Linc pulled on his mask, started forward, and stopped. The whole clearing was obscured by the fog of the gas. The Eye was invisible behind it. Wes pushed one end of the net into his waiting grasp, but still he stood.

"Come on," Wes called. "We'll lose our chance."

Linc stumbled forward into the smog, trying to hurry, yet trying to keep his feet in the blur. Then he couldn't stand the suspense another moment. He ran headlong into the mist, the tug on the other end of the net telling him that Wes was keeping pace.

The mist cleared briefly and something brushed his face, something soft and hairy, and he cried out and jumped backward. In the momentary clearness, he saw the thing that had touched him—the Eye, its great lashes twitching, water running from it to wet the ground. He had almost run straight into it.

"Go to the left," he yelled at Wes.

Linc ran to the right, past the place where he knew the Eye to be, although he could no longer see it through the mist. He seemed to run for miles before he felt the pull of the net as it hit the Eye and circled it. He cut in then, to meet Wes, and they came together in the fog, joining their hands and the ends of the net, only sure of the capture by the tugging of the mesh and the pulling bulge it made behind them.

"Hurry," Wes's whisper was shaky. "Go back through the trees."

"Be careful!" Linc called. "Don't get away from me."

They moved quickly but carefully, pulling the net and the floating weight of the Eye in a circle, back through the woods and out of the tear gas. When they reached the open air, they turned to look at what they were dragging.

Behind them, wrapped in the mesh, the Eye floated, bulging, unable to blink because of the restraining material, dripping great drops of water on the leaves in a sodden trail. It was still blinded, and it looked for once completely helpless, with no hands to wipe away its tears.

At the truck they separated, each proceeding down a different side, aiming the Eye and the net at the cage. The door was open for the thing, and they maneuvered it up. The net shoved it partway inside, but the back of it stuck out.

"Give it a jerk," Wes said.

They tried jerking the net, but it didn't work. The Eye still protruded. Linc fastened his end of the net around the side mirror at the front of the truck, then ran back to the Eye. He took a deep breath to hold his stomach from retching, and said, "I'm going to shove it in. When you see it go, come around and free the net from the cage so I can close the door. Got that?"

"Got it," Wes answered. "Be careful."

Linc braced himself, put his hands out, and closing his eyes against the horror, and steeling himself against the touch, he shoved.

The thing was warm under his hands, warm and wet, and a shudder raced up his wrists and down his back. He jumped backward, letting Wes run between him and the truck with the free net, then he slammed the cage shut and fastened the lock.

He stood there panting. It was done. The Eye was in the cage, still weeping, still blinded, its back to them as it faced the glass wall. Wes trembled as he reached for the tarp to throw over it.

"Let's get it to the lab," he said to Linc, "before I'm sick."

Linc climbed into the truck. Wes immediately gave Ichabod a great hug. "You saved us, old fellow," Wes said to the dog. "Your barking saved us, and we've got our Eye."

But could they keep it? Linc wondered as he sped away from the trees. Now that they had it, would Collins prove to be right? Would it seep away from them somehow? Or would it stay in the cage?

Linc swung into the lab parking lot. Bennet was walking through, and Linc called, "Would you give us a hand here?"

Bennet approached warily. "Have you got what I think you have? Did you bring back...*an Eye?*"

"We brought one. Help us get the cage into our lab."

"O—okay." Bennet's reluctance was only too plain. "But don't take the cover off. I'd rather not see the thing, if you don't mind."

When they lifted the cage down, it was no heavier full than it had been empty. Was the Eye gone then? "Wait a minute," he ordered, and lifted his side of the tarp. He had to know.

But the Eye was still inside. It rested inside. It rested there, floating a few inches above the floor of the cage, adding no weight to the enclosure.

They carried the cage into the lab and placed it on the workbench.

Bennet left in a hurry, but Myers quickly replaced him. Myers was more eager, more confident, and he came in as fast as Bennet had gone out.

"You got it," Myers said. "Collins has bet all day that you'd come back empty-handed. I put my money on you, Hosler. I've seen Collins lose too many bets before." He walked around the bench where the cage sat. "Is it in there? Really locked up in there?"

"It is," Linc answered. "Do you want to see it?"

He expected Myers to run, but the technician fooled him. "That's why I came. Who's going to do the unveiling?"

"I will," Linc said. He caught the tarp in both hands and swiftly jerked it off the cage.

And there it was. Watery blue, still red and moist, it hovered in the cage, peering out through the glass wall, straight at them. There was blankness in it, and that was all. Its great lids blinked and fluttered, covering the blankness for a brief second and then showing it again. There seemed little menace about it. Something in it was gone.

Linc turned away. "At least we know one answer. It can be caged. So it must be a being unto itself. A living, separate eye."

"It looks pretty harmless, all of a sudden," Wes commented. "I expected some try at retaliation, but it just sits there."

"Fascinating," Myers mumbled. He was watching the Eye intently.

Linc sat down. He had done it. He had formed a plan of action against the Eyes and carried it through successfully. And judging by the Eye's new docility, he felt the study of it wouldn't be hard.

"I guess we make a decent team after all," Wes was saying. "The three of us—Ichabod, you and me. Only, Ichabod deserves the medal. There wouldn't have been any you and me without him."

Linc was about to answer when Myers' strange movements caught his eye. The technician was standing before the cage, intent on it one moment, then he stiffened so quickly that his head jerked backward on his shoulders. He stood like a steel man for a count of three, and went limp. Before Linc could reach him, he was walking for the door—walking like a dead man, a zombie.

Linc spun him around, but there was no sense in his eyes, no vibrant life in his body. Linc let him go, and Myers opened the outside door, and proceeded across the grounds toward the open fields.

Linc turned to find Wes staring at him in pale shock.

The thing in the cage sat unmoving, barely blinking, and utterly blank. But it wasn't harmless. It was as deadly and dangerous as ever, and now all its danger was caged inside the lab, inside this tiny room.

Linc threw the tarp over the cage, covering the stare and the danger with it. It wasn't so easy, after all. Before they could even begin to study the thing, they had to find some way to resist its hypnotic power.

"We'd better report Myers," Wes said.

Linc nodded. "And then go home. I don't want to hear Collins' accusations—not tonight. They'd probably be justified this time."

"Are you blaming yourself for Myers, too?"

"No. Just for the stupidity of thinking that if caged, the Eye would suddenly lose its ability to hypnotize."

"Courage and the will to try are not stupidity," Wes corrected him. "Even if it comes to nothing, no one can take the credit of trying away from us. Go get Ichabod and put him in the car. I'll tell Iverson about Myers and meet you outside. Our friend here," he indicated the cage, "can just cool his eyeball till morning."

CHAPTER EIGHT

WES BROILED the steaks, for once leaving Linc alone in the living room with Kelly. She was nervous, constantly busy with something. Linc mixed cocktails and put one into her hand.

"Relax, Kel," he said.

"I can't. It's been an awful day." She asked, unexpectedly. "Linc, do you think I should get a gun?"

"Why?"

"To protect myself. You're not at home all day, so you don't realize what's going on. I'm not safe in my apartment. Even the soldiers can't stop the looting. If I had a gun, I'd feel more secure."

"You mean that people are looting private homes?"

"All over town."

"But that wouldn't include your apartment," he said. "You have no silver, no furs, nothing to be looted."

"They're not after jewels. They're after food. People are hungry, and they're afraid to go to the markets because if they did, that would make a crowd, and the Eyes would come after them. In order to get food, they have to rob private houses. Yours is a good target. You have a big freezer. You're loaded with meat."

"Do you actually mean that you'd shoot a man who came to steal a piece of beef? That you'd shoot him over a bit of meat?"

"What else could I do?"

"Give it to him, of course."

"Would you empty your freezer to every man who came to your door?" She was incredulous.

"I would. I wouldn't shoot him! I'd talk to him and—"

"You don't understand. These men aren't reasonable. You can't talk to them. They come armed, and you can't hold conversations with them. They scare me to death, Linc. They haven't hit my apartment yet, but they've been all over the neighborhood. You look out of your window and see your neighbors, people you've known for years, and wonder which one of them it will be? Which one of them will break into your kitchen and steal the little food you have, and kill you if you don't give it over willingly? The world has gone crazy and there's no place safe."

Kelly had changed. The sureness had left her gaze; the belligerence, the "don't touch me" attitude, was replaced with a softer, more pliant expression. He felt more the man with her, and less the best available flunky.

Her hand reached out to close over his, and her grasp was slightly desperate, and awfully willing. She was turning to him, not to Wes.

"I have such faith in you," she said. "You're a strong person— a sure person. Will you keep your eye on me a little?"

"I thought I was doing that."

"You haven't been. You haven't called me, you haven't once checked on me to see if I was even alive."

"I was sure you were all right, or I would have been on your doorstep all the time. You know that."

"Do I?" Her face was near and soft.

This was his moment, and he started to take it, then drew back. She was offering the comfort she had refused before, but now he was too keyed up to take it. He said, breaking the new mood she was building, "Wes hasn't called either?"

"Once," she admitted. "But Wes is different. In this danger, Wes isn't you, and can never be you. You'll be the winner, the safe one."

He drew back. "And is that why you've come to me like this? Because you think I'm your best protection?"

She stiffened again. "That's a terrible thing to say. Maybe the danger has opened my eyes. Didn't you even consider that?"

He had changed her pliant mood to anger again. Always anger between them. "I'm sorry. I didn't mean that. I jump at things because I'm jumpy inside. Can we call a truce?"

"Not a truce. A whole treaty. Kelly promises not to fly off at everything Lincoln Hosler mistakenly says, and Linc promises not to doubt Kelly Adams' motives. Agreed?"

"Agreed," he smiled. It was new and good, this warmth between them.

"Soup's on," Wes called from the kitchen. "Get in here, you two, or Ichabod and I will eat it all ourselves."

"That man and his dog," Linc grunted as he got to his feet. "I sometimes think he believes Ichabod to be more human than I am."

"Ichabod is master of the world," Kelly laughed. "Of Wes's world, anyway. Our trouble is, we're not little spotted dogs."

Night was dark around the windows, and Linc awoke screaming. He thrashed his arms, beating back the nightmare monsters that pursued him, then sat bolt upright.

The sleeping pill hadn't worked. Nothing, it seemed, could chase the Eyes from his mind, awake or sleeping. They had come after him in his dreams, sailing, hovering, brushing him with their lashes, and he had fought up out of the stupor, nullifying the drug to gain consciousness. Now he couldn't close his eyes again—not when there were other Eyes waiting on the near side of oblivion.

He drew on his robe and went into the hall, not wanting to wake Wes. But Wes popped his head out of his door.

"Going down for coffee?" Wes asked.

"Couldn't you sleep either?"

"Not too well. And those last few howls of yours finished what I did manage. Let's have something to eat."

Wes started the coffee, and cut two pieces of pie. The click of Ichabod's feet on the linoleum announced the dog's arrival, and Wes opened the refrigerator to get some meat. The animal wolfed it down greedily.

"If we don't stop these middle-of-the-night parleys, Ichabod's going to get too fat," Wes said.

"This parley wasn't planned. It just couldn't be helped."

"Your trouble is, you expect an answer to pop right up in front of you. You've always worked that way. Nobody is as fast as you are with a direct solution, but this time is different, Linc. You're not dealing with men and man-made crises. You're dealing with something alien. You can't expect to find an answer out of your store of experience this time. So quit pushing yourself."

"How can I quit pushing?" Linc asked loudly. "We went out and risked our lives to catch that Eye, and now we can't even get near it. I'm not used to being so indecisive, and it's eating holes in me. I'd like to march into that room and stand up to that thing and face it out—but I don't think I could do it."

"With your strong will, you just might."

"No. Myers made it back from the fight, remember—he was strong enough not to give in that day. But it still got him. Caged, it got him, where free it couldn't. Yet will power should have something to do with it, if it's hypnosis as we know hypnosis. If the Eyes haven't got a special force that we can't even imagine, then a strong will should be able to withstand their pull. You think that, and hope with it, and then you come right back to the fact that if you're wrong, you're also a zombie.

"The crisis point comes when you stare straight at them. If you avoid their gaze and are strong enough, they're less able to reach you. But we're supposed to study that thing, so how can we avoid its gaze?"

Wes was quiet, then he murmured the thoughts that were at the heart of his own worry. "What do you suppose they do with the people they take, Linc? After they go into that hole, what do they do with them? Why do they want them?"

Linc shook his head. "Hendricks came back out of the hole. He was all right, except for being in a trance. But you can bet they do something with them, and that Hendricks was an exception because of his special abilities with the reactor. I haven't even been able to guess why they wanted the reactor blown."

Ichabod whined under his breath, begging for more meat. "We might have found out firsthand what the Eyes do, if it hadn't been for you, old fellow." Wes patted the dog. "You jarred us back to our senses just in time."

"Just in time," Linc echoed, and his tone jumped from desperation to eagerness. "Just in time! Don't you see the possibilities that fact opens up? A man can be brought back from the edge if there's someone there to bring him back."

"And how does that help us?"

"It's all based on one big 'IF.' If an Eye can only hypnotize by having the person look directly at it, then why couldn't two people team up and defeat it, just as Ichabod did yesterday? One of us could look at the thing, study the thing, while the other man kept his attention off of it and only concentrated on his partner."

"I see. And at the first sign of trance in the partner, the man could pull him away, jar him out of it. But such short moments of study wouldn't get us anywhere. We need prolonged time."

Linc sat back again, deflated. It had sounded good—now it didn't. Then he brightened a bit. "Isn't it possible that with experience and practice we could learn to fight off the hypnosis?

Learn what it takes to stand against it and not be hypnotized? If that were so, then we could have our prolonged time for study."

Wes made no comment.

"What do you think?" Linc asked. He had again come up with something and he ached to try it, but it depended on Wes.

"It would be dangerous," Wes said. "If it doesn't work, then it means that one of us will definitely be taken by the Eye."

"Yes?"

"I see." Wes sighed this time. "You've found another possibility, and you're hot on it. So…I guess we try it out."

Linc lit into his pie so his gratitude wouldn't show blatantly. Wes was willing to help him. Wes was his only confederate, and Wes knew it, and dangerous or not, foolish or not, Wes was willing to help. At this moment, and in this place, he realized something he should have known long ago, but something that had needed crisis to show him; that Wes was a once-in-lifetime friend; that Lincoln Hosler was not a man unto himself, after all; that he needed loyalty and friendship as much as the next man, and that accepting it wasn't a weakness, but a goodness.

The little lab room was charged with high-voltage tension. Linc was almost ready to reach for the tarpaulin and uncover the monster that hovered beneath it. He had insisted in being the first to try, letting Wes be his back-guard, to pull him away to safety.

"Are you ready?" Linc asked.

"Any time you are."

"Then come close to me, and remember—not one glance at the Eye. Not even a peek."

Wes's hand came out and gripped Linc's arm strongly. Linc could feel the warm exhalation of his friend's breath hitting his cheek.

"I'm going to do it now," Linc said.

He reached for the tarp, paused to gather himself against the storm of battle he expected, and raised the cloth.

The Eye was open. It rolled its watery blueness to focus on him, and then it was still…staring. The gaze of it was newly malevolent, newly evil this morning, and Linc held himself from recoiling. He breathed deeply and evenly, keeping his store of oxygen high, and stared back into the great iris, looking for a soul, looking for sense. All of his wits were collected into a ball inside him, a ball that made up his will not to succumb, and he stared back with a dare, a challenge to the hideous thing to take him.

But nothing happened.

His mind was calm, yet swirling slightly with mental effort. The swirls were just at the edge of consciousness, but close enough so that he was aware of them. Swirls and shadows, and misty visions that wanted to come through and be recognized. He breathed deeply again and set them sailing off. He didn't want them. He wanted a meeting of mentalities, not shadows. He forced his own conscious thoughts to the foreground and concentrated on those alone.

Still nothing happened. He was too tense, trying too hard. He couldn't succeed this way. He was blocking the contact through his own great effort. He had to relax, to be more pliant, if he was even to approach his goal.

The shadows and swirlings were coming back and he must relax and look at them and sort them out. He gave way now, accepting them back, ready to make use of them, more comfortable with the relaxing. There was only himself and the blue of the Eye.

And then the world tilted and went out of kilter and he was falling sideways. The Eye was disappearing and he had to flail his arms to catch himself. A hardness clutched at him and he fell against it. A smell of shaving lotion hit his nose and he pushed on through to full awareness.

He looked up, and there was Wes's face, peering anxiously into his, searching for the sense in his eyes as he had searched in the monstrous one.

"Linc?" Wes was calling his name. "Do you hear me?"

"I hear," Linc answered. "I hear, Wes."

He let Wes help him to a chair and set him down. He shivered once, and covered his face with his hands, shutting away the last of the shadows. When he glanced up again, he was smiling.

"It worked," he said softly. "It worked—I was almost gone, but you pulled me back in time." As he started to explain, jubilation mingled with relief. "And I learned, Wes. Now I know what to resist. The shadows and the swirls of smoke and the obscure visions that you want to grasp and see—those are the things to resist. The call to relax—that is a great thing to resist." Wes was still watching him soberly. "Be jubilant!" Linc stood and grasped Wes's shoulders. "We've won! We've found the way. With practice, we can grow strong enough to stand alone, and break through to the truth. Don't you see?"

Wes's lips parted slightly, then his quick smile broke through his concern. "Anything you say, Linc. I think you actually run the world."

CHAPTER NINE

MORNING TICKED AWAY into afternoon, and they stayed in the Lab, taking turns with the Eye. They promised themselves that they would work until each could stand alone, without the other to pull him away, without the need to be pulled away.

But at two o'clock a knock sounded on the door and Iverson stepped in. He came three steps forward, then two steps back, as he spotted the eye floating in its cage.

"Oh," Iverson grunted, "I didn't know you had it uncovered."

"Come on in," Linc said. "I'll put the tarp over it." He covered the Eye.

"Ugly thing, isn't it," Iverson asked, suppressing a grimace. "And so big."

"We're whittling it down to size," Wes said proudly.

"Do you really think so?" Iverson sounded doubtful. He drew a great breath. "I don't want either of you to take this as a personal slight or rejection, but the situation around town is getting so bad—neighbor against neighbor, the whole population hiding and sneaking and stealing—that we can't wait. Panic is spreading. The rest of the state is nervous, ready to explode at the first rumor of the Eyes heading out to them, and the country, as a whole, is jumpy. We've had to hire extra men just to keep the reporters out of here. Something has to be done, and done now."

"We're working as fast as we can," Linc protested.

"On *your* plan, yes. But we can't wait for one plan. We have to try every idea that comes along. Colonel Stanley and the National

Guard have come up with one and we're putting it into operation this afternoon. In one hour, to be exact."

"If it has soldiers in it, then I take it it's fighting," Linc stated. "Are you and Stanley actually going to let them risk their lives again?"

Iverson waved him down. "You jump too fast, Linc. The new effort might work. Stanley has incorporated one of your own ideas into it. You caught your Eye with tear gas. Well, this fight is going to be with tear gas. The guard is going to attack the hole, and get inside it. With the Eyes incapacitated, maybe they can be destroyed."

"So they're going to fight at three o'clock. Why did you bother to tell us?"

"I thought you'd like to come along—to observe. If anything does go wrong, then what you see will help with your own planning. You can always use information. And you've never seen the hole, have you?"

"No," Linc admitted.

"Then come see it with me."

Linc looked to Wes, and the other man shrugged. "Why not? We can get a look and watch the Guard's effort at the same time."

"Good." Iverson took Wes's acceptance as agreement for both of them. "We'll have to leave right away. I have a car ready."

They drove along the edge of town, headed for open country. The driver turned for the game preserve, and Iverson said, "We're not going in close. We'll be standing off. I've brought binoculars."

"If we're going at all, we may as well go in," Linc sputtered.

"I'm following Stanley's orders," Iverson replied. "This is his show, and his command. If we ever have one of our own, I'll expect him to abide by our say-so."

The car swung into a narrow lane. There were slight hills here, rolling and wooded, and they passed through brush, hearing the scrape of branches on the fenders. Ahead rose the tower of a fire-spotting station, and when they left the car, Iverson led them up to the small room that served as home and office for the watcher. Linc moved to the big glass windows, looking for the place where the hole would be, black and eerie in the trees.

"To the north," Iverson directed him.

He looked northward, and it wasn't hard to spot. From this height, the worn path the zombie people had followed was visible from the road to the place it stopped inside the forest. And the hole crouched at the end of it—black and featureless. It wasn't just a hole now, because there were no people on the path and no activity. But as he watched, the mouth of the hole changed from stillness to movement, and the distended shape of an Eye sailed up out of it. Then another. They hovered above the clearing.

He squinted and saw movement inside the woods, too. Soldiers. The National Guard, moving up for their fight.

"It's time," Iverson said. "They should be starting."

The words were barely uttered when the exploding mist of gas rose from the face of the hole, and the woods came alive with the running, gas-masked figures of Guardsmen. They dashed forward, and Linc grabbed the binoculars to get a close look. The two Eyes which had been hovering were bobbing up and down, weeping and spinning in the gas. A breeze was spreading the gas low, enveloping the soldiers. It spread, clearing the mouth of the hole, and close behind it, as it left an open space, came the Eyes in force. Blue, brown, green, they zoomed up and through the smoky wisps. Eight of them, quick and deadly.

The woods blazed with gunfire, and the battle repeated itself before Linc's sickened gaze. There were just too many Eyes. The soldiers had no chance. They advanced bravely, but Linc could see the impending result so clearly that he wanted to shout to them to run.

The Eyes were above the gas, obscured from the soldiers' vision, aligning themselves for their own attack. As the gas cleared in one area, and the Guardsmen became visible to them, the Eyes tipped forward, staring at the ground, ignoring the wounds inflicted on them, and one by one the soldiers fled, or limply dropped their weapons and walked into the hole. Five went down into the blackness, then ten more, and Linc swung away from the view.

"They're losing half their men!" he shouted at Iverson. "You should have stopped Stanley. When you fail with a method once, you don't keep trying it again and again and throwing men away."

Iverson was peering through his own binoculars. His face was white and his lips moved in silent words. "Poor devils," the words finally came to voice. "Poor, poor devils. Eight Eyes. They can't fight eight Eyes. And more coming in from town."

Linc swallowed the pity he felt for the soldiers and growled, "Let's go, Iverson. Now that we've seen what we came to see, allow us to get back to our own work. Every minute away is a minute too much."

Daylight shadowed into night and bloomed into day again, as Linc and Wes worked the clock around. Two days gone in the strain of practice, another day started. But they were learning. On Linc's last turn, he had stood against the Eye for a half-hour, giving up from fatigue and not as a result of Wes's saving tug. Wes had managed to fight for fifteen minutes.

Linc was before the cage, using his will against the will of the Eye, when Collins came in. He didn't knock, he just walked in and stood, watching the silent fight. As Linc noticed him, he withdrew from the Eye.

"What was that all about?" Collins asked.

"You'd never understand," Linc answered.

"Oh? So what do you have to show for three days closed in this room?" Collins wanted to know. "What have you accomplished?"

"That will become apparent as we progress," Linc said. "But right at this moment, we know more about the Eyes and their power than anyone else on Earth."

"What good does knowledge do?" Collins asked cockily. "Are you trying to understand them? To get to know them so you can take them to the negotiating table?"

"You're very funny," Linc answered. "How you can be such a wit at such a time is more than I can understand."

Collins smiled and sat down. "I'm not worried any more. While you've been shut away in here, I've been using my head, and things are coming my way."

"That business with the tear gas and the Guard wasn't your brain work, was it?" Wes asked him.

"No. That was strictly soldiering. I told Stanley it wasn't drastic enough. Halfway measures aren't going to win this fight. Neither is staring at an Eye and giving it human qualities. Now, *my* plan is simple—that part is for you, Linc—and completely workable. It will finish the job in minutes."

"Okay," Wes was saying, "let's hear it."

Collins set his sharp face in arrogant lines and his voice dropped a pitch as he explained. "Guns don't work. Tear gas doesn't work. Field pieces don't work. But we've been forgetting our biggest weapon. A nuclear bomb. A bomb dropped right on that stinking hole while the Eyes are inside it, and in one explosion we rid ourselves of them forever. They couldn't survive that."

Linc was silent. There was something wrong with Collins' scheme, but he couldn't quite chase it down.

Wes said it for him. "Impossible! There are thousands of people down in that hole, Collins—thousands of innocent, helpless people. You'd get the Eyes, but what about the people?"

Collins was quick with his answer. "They've been considered. They'll have to be sacrificed. The few for the many in this case. There are thousands now, but if they die, and the Eyes die with them, that will save millions. They'll have to be sacrificed."

Wes leaned back, white with the idea of wholesale murder done in the name of goodness and prevention.

"Don't worry about it, Wes," Linc said. "Collins has overlooked a major point." He addressed his assistant now, glad to be able to pierce his bubble of egotism. "You can't detonate a bomb out there anymore than we could let the reactor go when Hendricks tried to set it off. A bomb would kill the town, the campus."

"That has been considered, too," Collins answered. "If we put the plan into effect—and I'm sure we will—then the area will be evacuated."

Linc shook his head. The scheme was so full of holes that it was almost laughable. "Evacuation is ridiculous. Try it, and you won't be evacuating people out of the area, you'll be evacuating people *to the Eyes*. They pounce on groups. They pick them to pieces."

"And a slow evacuation?" Collins asked.

"To be slow enough to escape the Eyes, it would take weeks. You've really fumbled the ball this time."

Collins stood up. "Tear it apart all you like, Hosler. It still will be done. Iverson and Stanley are coming to it fast. *I've* got their ears now. You've wasted too much time in here. If the evacuation has to be slow, then it will be slow, but it will be done."

"We don't have the time!" Linc was exasperated. Why did he have to point everything out, explain everything to men who were supposed to know? "Those Eyes want something. The devil only knows what—but they want something, and soon they're going to make a new move."

"And what are you going to do about it? Have you accomplished anything here?"

"All right, tell me what *your* investigation has discovered. Do you know what the Eyes are? Where they come from? If there will be more coming? Or what they do with the people they take away?"

"If we can destroy them, who cares where they come from, or why? And if more appear, we'll destroy them, too. As for the people Wes is so worried about, there is a theory going around that there aren't any people down in that hole."

"We've seen them go in," Wes countered.

"But not come out," Collins said. "How many could get in that hole? How much room is there in it? It would be overflowing by now, if they were still there."

"Then where does the current theory say they are?" Linc was biting.

Collins' eyes pierced into his and one word hissed out between his lips: "Eaten!"

Wes whirled away to stare out of the window. Linc recoiled, too, at the memory of Myers walking from the lab. Eaten? He had never considered it. But it was a possibility. Eaten—Myers and the rest. No.

"You're crazy," he spat at Collins. "This Eye, here in this cage—it hasn't taken food of any kind. And it hasn't grown weak without it."

"Have you offered it anything?" Collins was snide.

Linc couldn't answer that, because he hadn't offered it anything. He hadn't even considered it. What would an Eye eat?

The whole subject was fantastic and revolting. *How* would an Eye eat?

Collins was chuckling at his consternation. "I've finally stumped you, haven't I?" he said to Linc. "Finally, I knew it could be done." He turned for the door, glancing again at the Eye in the cage. "You two stay here and play with your pet. Stanley and Iverson and I will fight the battle."

The door slammed behind him, and Linc spat out a curse. Yet, being honest, he had to consider what Collins had said and consider it seriously. The one point—the dimension of the hole and the number of people who had gone into it—made it necessary to consider. Where were those people? Why weren't they overflowing the black pit inside the woods?

CHAPTER TEN

IT WASN'T EVEN A FULL DAY before the news seeped through the lab that Collins' plan had been approved and set in motion. Evacuation was started—slow evacuation that sent cars out on the roads one at a time. How long it would take to complete, Linc couldn't guess, but the idea of a bomb falling on the people trapped in the hole spurred him to find some alternative action.

Wes came back from the cafeteria with four sandwiches and two steaming coffees. He plunked them on the desk, gave a peevish glance at the Eye, which they never covered any more, and let loose.

"You were right, Linc. Four hundred yards apart—they space the evacuating cars four hundred yards apart—and the people go out, hopeful for the first time in days, and the Eyes pick them off one by one."

"The single cars?" Linc asked.

"Enough singles finally make a group, and they're clever, Linc. A car goes down the road, swerves off into the ditch, and the people get out, zombie-style. Another car comes, and it repeats the action. When the Eyes have a group gathered, they lead them off to the hole. This time they were clever enough to force the drivers off the road, to avoid the traffic jams that would stop the flow of people coming to them."

"The evacuation has been called off, of course."

"Not yet! People are still going out, and still being taken. I don't know what the brass is thinking of. I tried to talk to Iverson. He wouldn't listen. And Stanley—this lab has split wide-open, taken two sides, and Stanley is with Collins. That puts the weight there. What are we going to do now?" Wes was almost frantic. The picture of hopeful people being sent out to horror, and then ultimately bombed to nothingness was too much for him to stomach. "We've got to show Iverson that Collins is wrong."

"There's only one possible way. We'll use the time it takes them to come to their senses to prove what's going on in that hole. If someone could actually find out what is down there, what goes on in that pit, the bomb business could be decided—one way or the other. We've got to get into that hole, and get out again with a report. That's the only way."

Wes didn't doubt it for a moment. He only doubted the possibility of doing it. "Half of the scouts who go out to watch the place don't even make it back, Linc. The National Guard has the hole ringed with men, and some of them get taken."

"You sound discouraged," Linc chided, "and you have no right to be. Not now. Our work has finally paid off. You and I can do what no other men have a chance of doing. Wes, what would it take to go into that hole and come back out?"

"Guts," Wes said. "And not even guts would do it. Only a free mind. You go in hypnotized and come out hypnotized, like Hendricks, so guts wouldn't do you an iota of good."

"*If* you're hypnotized. We've learned not to be. Don't you see? We can stand against the Eyes. We've done it right here in this room. We could go down into that hole, have a look around, and come back out, free agents. It would take more than we've managed so far, a lot of fighting against the hypnosis, but it could be done."

"The Eyes would spot us among their zombies."

"Not if we walked like zombies. Who would see a zombie among zombies? We go out on the road, drive our car into the ditch, and walk away like the rest of the people do. Then, fighting against the hypnosis—fighting like hell—we get ourselves into that hole and out again."

Wes pursed his lips. "You keep saying 'we.' It shouldn't be 'we.' Only one of us should try it, so that if he fails, the other will be left. If we're so unique, Linc, then one of us has to be preserved."

"But the idea as a whole—what do you think?"

"I think it's good. It's smart, and most importantly, it's human. I'd do anything to save those poor wretches from vaporization in an A-bomb."

"Then it only remains to decide which one of us will go."

"Let me." Wes was quick with the decision. "I don't kid myself that I'm as necessary as you are. If I'm lost, you'll still be here to think up something else. If you were lost, I'd founder."

"Those aren't good enough reasons, Wes. The one of us who is most able should go. And I think that's me. I've stood out against the Eye for forty-five minutes. You've only managed a half-hour."

"But this is different. This is all or nothing. A man musters extra strength in this kind of situation."

Linc didn't want to argue. Not about this—not about life and death. He knew he was best qualified. He had to go. But he postponed the decision.

"Let's wait a while to decide. Let's think about it without hurrying. All right?"

Wes nodded his assent.

"Then," Linc added, "I'm going home. If it's me, I need some rest. I can use the change of scene and the quiet anyway."

"Go ahead. Just be sure to feed Ichabod. I put his plate in the refrigerator. Let it warm up before you give it to him."

"He'll tell me what to do," Linc smiled. "I'll be back by four. Maybe earlier. Think this over carefully, Wes. Don't let your nerves and your conscience get the better of your judgment."

Linc's key opened the front door, and he was surprised that Ichabod didn't come bounding to meet him. He made his way to the kitchen, and discovered the reason. Kelly was there, puttering, doing up their breakfast dishes, and the dog was content in her company. His plate was on the floor, already empty.

"Hi," Kelly called. "Are you alone?"

"Wes stayed at the lab."

"I should have known. If he had come, Ichabod would have deserted me. He's a loyal little devil."

"How did you get in?" Linc asked.

"Wes gave me a key."

Linc cleared his throat meaningfully, softening it with a grin.

"No," Kelly laughed. "It was just that I was afraid, and so he gave me the key. My apartment seems spookier than this house. Maybe because Ichabod's here; or maybe because there are people so close to me there. Isn't it funny? It used to be that I felt secure knowing there were people in the rooms below me. Now I'm more afraid of the people than I am of the Eyes."

"That will soon change."

"I know," she said. "I'm on the list for evacuation in five days. I can't wait to get out. When are you scheduled?"

"Never. No one's getting away. The Eyes are capturing every evacuee."

"Oh, no!" Kelly's reaction was more than he had expected. She went pale, and clutched the sink. "Then we just have to stay here and hide from each other forever?"

"Not that either. Pour that coffee you're brewing and I'll tell you about it."

She did as he said silently. When she was seated across from him, and the coffee was creamed and cooling, he laid the plan out. She listened, but didn't comprehend the good of it, only the danger.

"Which one of you is going?" she asked.

"I am."

"No. It shouldn't be you. Wes wants to go—let him."

"I can't, Kelly. He's not as well prepared."

"That's just your egotism showing. You never think anyone else can do the job as well as you. I don't think I could stand it, Linc—if you didn't come back."

"Come on, Kelly," he scoffed. "This concern isn't flattering to you. You haven't made a choice between Wes and me. It couldn't matter to you which of us went."

"You never give me credit, do you? Maybe the last days have changed things for me. Maybe I have made a choice. This danger, Linc, changes a woman. She suddenly finds that she does need someone, and things come into focus, and she knows who that someone is."

"Just by the magic formula of how well he can protect her?"

"Is that wrong? Does it matter what yardstick I used, just so long as I used it and you were the one to measure up?"

There was the ring of dishonesty about what she said, and Linc hated himself for hearing it. Kelly was beautiful at this moment, with her green eyes worried, her hand pleading with him. Two weeks before, he could have asked for nothing else from her. Now he wondered.

"Linc, you love me. You've never said it, but I know. I've been a fool to keep you distant—a fool to resist. I'm not resisting any more." She came around to his side of the table, and she was tall and slim as he looked up at her. "Or," she murmured, "are you just a man who likes the chase, and who backs off after he has won?"

He saw through her game. She was turning on the sex. She had never used it on him before, except teasingly; and although he knew this entire sequence was deliberate, he didn't care.

He stood and drew her against him, and she didn't pull away. She came into his arms, pliant and past flirtation. He kissed her, and she answered it, and it was sweet—as sweet as he imagined it would be in the days when he had waited for her to answer him and not simply *allow* his kisses.

"Let Wes go," she whispered. "Don't tear yourself away from me, now that we've found each other."

"But, Kelly—"

Her fingers came up to quiver against his lips and halt the protest. "Wes wants to go, Linc. He's just as capable as you are. If you'd be honest with yourself, you'd know it. Let him do this, if it means so much to him. And you stay here with me, if I mean anything to you."

She was making sense. Even over the emotions that the touch of her raised in him, he knew she was making sense. Wes was just about as capable as he was. And Wes had a mission. A man with a mission always had the better chance of winning. If he himself went, he would be torn—part of him staying with Kelly. Wes had nothing to hinder him—only a humanitarian mission to push him forward.

There was no room for conscience with Kelly in his arms. He had waited too long for her to be there. When he let himself realize it, he rode high on the crest of victory. Wes was a rival no longer, but a man who wanted with all his soul to undertake the zombie trip into the lair of the Eyes and rescue humanity. He couldn't deny Wes what Wes wanted most in the world. Not when what he wanted most is the world was just now being given to him. He would let Wes decide. If Wes still wanted to go, Wes would go.

"I hope," he whispered to her, "you haven't discovered my weak spot, and are playing on it."

"You don't have a weak spot, darling."

Ichabod was snuffing around their feet, but Linc stopped hearing, as Kelly's mouth tilted upward, waiting for his again. He met her mouth with his own, and the decision was made.

At three-thirty, a car pulled into the drive. Wes got out of it. He was anxious, his nerves rawly showing for the first time since Linc had known him. "I simply couldn't wait any longer," he explained, stemming the eager yaps of Ichabod. "We can't put this action off, Linc. All the time we spend choosing up sides allows more people to be taken into that hole—put more there for Collins to destroy."

"I know," Linc answered. "That's been on my mind, too."

"Then what have you decided? Which one of us is going?"

Kelly's eyes flashed to Linc, and he shifted. "It's not my decision alone, you know, Wes. It's up to both of us."

"But, knowing you, you'll make it," Wes grinned.

"And you? Have you thought about it further? Have you really thought it out?"

"All afternoon. But I couldn't do much thinking through my impatience. We've got to get moving. I still want to go, if that's what you're getting at. After you left the lab, I went up against the Eye all by myself. I fought it for thirty-five minutes before I had to quit—and then I quit of my own accord. That was intense concentration, face to face. This job won't be that way. It will be an evasion tactic."

"It won't be any picnic." Linc couldn't bring himself to voice his decision yet.

"Who expects a picnic?" Wes came forward two steps. "Please Linc, don't waste any more time. Who is it to be?"

Kelly's taut gaze was on him again, and he answered, "If you want it this badly, Wes, what can I say?"

"You mean you'll let me be the first to go?"

Linc nodded, strongly aware that he might be making the wrong choice. "You can go. I'll play backstop this time."

Wes grasped his arms, smiling and flushed, "I never once believed you'd agree. Now that it's settled, I'm going to get started right away—before dark. I can't wait through another night. By the way, I didn't mention a word to Iverson or anybody else. Should we notify them?"

"No. If we ask for permission, we'll only get more arguments. We'll go this one alone."

"That's what I thought, too. Well—" Wes swiveled awkwardly in the center of the floor. "—I may as well get going."

"Right now?" Kelly was startled.

"I want to reach the hole before dark."

"Not yet." Linc said, feeling a sudden need to hold his friend back, "we have to plan this first. Set a specific course of action."

"We did all that this morning. There's nothing to plan. I drive out, pose as a zombie, go to the hole, and from there on, planning won't help me anyway. Besides, there isn't time. Iverson may call off the slow evacuation and speed things up, since the Eyes are getting the people anyway."

"Where did you hear that news?"

"At the lab. It's all confusion out there. Rumors are flying thicker than the Eyes. So I'm going...going now. No more arguments...okay?"

Kelly crossed to Wes and hugged him close. "I didn't realize it would be so soon. Take care, and don't throw yourself away in the name of heroism. Turn back if you see you can't make it."

Wes kissed her lightly on the cheek, then took Linc's hand in a strong clasp. "Let's leave it like this—I'll be back, if I can get back, by tomorrow night. That gives me plenty of leeway. So, tomorrow night by dusk—or never. All clear?"

"Take it easy. And bring back what we need—friend."

Wes walked to the door. "Take care of Ichabod for me, won't you? I'm entrusting him to you. And don't worry. I'll see you tomorrow for supper."

He went out, the car door slammed, and he was gone.

Linc was numb. It had happened so quickly. There had been no hesitation, no lingering farewell. It was over already, and it had barely begun. But Wes hadn't wanted to wait. He had made up his mind to do it, and he was doing it.

Linc looked to Kelly, and she echoed his numbness. "He could at least have had dinner," she said. There was fear in her eyes, and a doubt that hadn't been there before. But Wes was gone, and there was nothing either of them could do about it except wait.

They waited in the house, together, but alone, too tense to take sympathy from each other. The joy Linc had known a few hours before was submerged in worry.

Night passed and in the morning the sun was hidden behind a heavy overcast. Outside the windows, Colt Street was in full glory as the trees outlined themselves and their fiery colors against the dark sky. But there was no word.

Linc went to the lab after breakfast to check on his caged Eye. He stopped to see no one, and when Iverson shot a question at him from down the hall, he mumbled words he knew would be incoherent, but would sound like an answer, and hurried out. He didn't want to be questioned. When Wes returned, successful, that would be soon enough for revelation.

When he reached home again, Kelly was in the living room with the vacuum cleaner, dumping ashtray debris and rubbish into a paper bag.

"I've never seen such a mess. Remind me never to include a man in my housekeeping."

"I thought that was just about settled yesterday."

"Only on the condition that you promise more consideration than this. For instance, when you get mail, dump the envelopes in the wastebasket, not on the coffee table. And cigarette packages, and match books, and newspapers. In two weeks, you wouldn't be able to climb over the mountain of papers you'd have in here."

Linc watched her work, trying to drain contentment from it. It was a good moment. Kelly's new relationship with him made it good. And yet he couldn't relish it. There was too much on his mind to let contentment in: the Eyes, the one Eye imprisoned in the cage, and Wes. Most of all Wes. He kept imagining what Wes was doing at any given moment. He mentally placed him deep inside the hole, but the background of the picture was so uncertain, so nebulous, that he could go no further. Only Wes could fill in that background. It wouldn't be too many hours before Wes would be home.

"I'm cooking tonight," Kelly interrupted his thoughts. "Fried chicken and candied sweet potatoes."

"Wes's favorites?"

"Yes. He'll deserve anything he wants after today."

Caught up again in his own thoughts, it didn't seem long before Kelly had finished the housework and was in the kitchen, banging pots and pans about. He looked out of the windows, and Colt Street was darkening. The street lamps were on, and the trees were shadowed. Dusk. He listened for the sound of the car—but there was nothing.

"Give him time," Linc told himself. "It's still early. Give the man time."

And the time went by. Kelly's special dinner was ready, then held in the warming oven, then dried out and cold. They didn't even nibble at it. At ten o'clock, Linc picked up the phone and dialed the number of the lab.

"Is Wes there, by any chance?" he asked.

The reply was loud in his ear, but Kelly was straining to hear. Linc put the phone back in its cradle and turned to her.

She read the answer in his eyes, and quickly lit a cigarette. "A lot of things could have delayed him," she said.

"Just *one* thing would have been enough."

"Don't believe that, Linc. No Eye in the world could defeat Wes, not in the state he was in. He had the courage of twenty men."

"He went too fast. He was overanxious. I should have known better than to let him go that way. I was a fool."

Kelly snuffed the cigarette out. "Is it all right if I stay the night? Or would you rather—"

"It makes no difference to me. I'm not going to bed anyway. I'm going to stay right here in this chair until Wes comes. And he'd better come! He'd damn well better."

Kelly stood up at his desperate, angry tone. "I'll make some more coffee—in case it's a long wait."

She left the room and Linc was alone with only the sleepy eyes of Wes's little spotted dog. He refused to look at Ichabod. There was only one thing important in Ichabod's world—Wes. And he couldn't stand to think that perhaps Ichabod's world was now empty.

CHAPTER ELEVEN

THE DEADLINE was two days gone; Wes was three days late; but still Linc waited. He stayed alone in the house, and waited. Logically, he knew it was useless, but there was nothing else to do. A nagging thought reminded him of what Wes had said—that if he was lost, he would at least be lost knowing that Linc was alive and able to try something else. He supposed he should be trying something else. But he hadn't the heart.

The radio news reported the evacuation still going on. Stanley had worked out a new method, sending larger groups of people and using all the roads, paved and unpaved, to baffle the Eyes. With so many out at once, the Eyes couldn't get them all. Some got through. Many didn't, but following Collins' rule of the loss of the few for the good of the many, Stanley went ahead with the evacuating-bombing plan.

Twice during the three days, there were footsteps in the driveway, and the back door rattled as someone tested it for entrance. Peering out, he saw a man one time, a woman and boy the next time, all of them dirty and disheveled. The man carried a shotgun; the boy had a crowbar. When the doorknob failed to turn, they prepared to break the lock, but in both cases Ichabod's barking—such a deep bark for a small dog—sent them away.

At noon, the phone rang and he answered it fast. Iverson's voice spewed out of the ear-piece, "Where in the devil have you been, Hosler? I've been making excuses for you until I'm blue in the face. What do you and Wes think you're doing, running out in the middle of the fight?"

"We haven't run out," Linc said.

"Then where have you been?" Iverson had barely asked it when he interrupted himself. "Well, never mind—there's something big happening, and I want you and Wes here to cover it."

"Wes isn't with me."

"Then find him and bring him. But make it in fifteen minutes, understand? This is urgent."

Iverson hung up and Linc stood undecided. Then he dialed Kelly's number and asked her to come, to take over the waiting while he was gone. He scribbled a note for Wes, in case he got back before Kelly arrived, and went out, locking the door behind him. Whatever Iverson wanted, he had to find out. He had sat by long enough. It was time he dove into his work again.

When he went through the gate into the parking lot, a station wagon was waiting, its motor running, and Iverson waved at him to hurry. As he climbed in beside the driver, he glanced back to find Stanley and Collins in the rear.

"What's this all about?" he asked, as the driver revved the car forward, in the direction of open country.

"We don't know much about it ourselves," Iverson said. "Stanley got a call from the National Guard post out by the hole, and—the people are coming out. Great crowds of them, coming up out of the hole."

Coming out? Was this some of Wes's doing? Was that why Wes was so late?

"Where are they going from the hole?" he asked.

"The report said they were just walking away—no Eyes with them, or leading them. We'll soon see."

"I don't like it." Stanley was glowering in the back seat. "It's a new move—probably something to counter our evacuation. They're not simply going to surrender those people. That wouldn't make sense. I tell you, it's a new move, and until we know where it's leading, we're on dangerous ground."

"We should have gotten in there sooner with the bomb," Collins said. "We may have lost our chance. If the people are going, the Eyes may leave, too. We should have acted sooner."

"Thank God we didn't," Iverson sighed. "All those people—I was nearly convinced that they were not in the hole any more. We would have blown them all into ashes."

The driver turned onto the highway that passed near the game preserve, and the car suddenly stopped. "Look ahead," the driver said, and it was half-whisper, half-scream.

There was no road ahead of them. Only a sea of moving forms.

For coming out of the woods half a mile down, and spilling onto the asphault, into the ditches, and halfway across the fields, was a great mass of people. Thousands of them—staggering along, stumbling, holding their hands before them to grope like blind men. They were tattered and filthy, and their stench preceded them on the highway.

They came straight for the car, and the driver backed it around the corner he had taken a moment before. Linc got out, and went to the road. Iverson was beside him, and he heard Stanley's intake of breath. The people were coming straight toward them, fanning out, covering the pavement and field alike. They were pale, and queerly not like people. But Linc walked to meet them—thousands of eyewitnesses to the conditions inside the hole.

The first of them reached him and walked by. He roamed among them, growing sicker with each one he passed. To his right an old woman stumbled, and fell to the ground. She rolled and twisted, moaning animal sounds pouring out of her mouth. He knelt beside her and turned her over. She was covered with black dirt and the red stain of clay from the inside of the pit. Her gray hair was matted on her head, and the cries poured out of her without stopping. He left her. Others stumbled over her and fell, making a pile-up of rolling bodies. There was nothing he could do.

When he moved back into their midst again, he saw others down, vomiting, fainting, crying. A little girl limped by, pulling at her hair. It came out in her hands, great handfuls of it, blond and useless. He closed his eyes and stood still to catch hold of himself, but he was buffeted by the crowd sweeping past him, blindly unaware of barriers, man or tree. The stench of them was overpowering. Linc pulled out his handkerchief and held it over his nose, trying to shut it out.

Now he gazed into their faces, ignoring the desperate state of their bodies. The shock of meeting them eye to eye brought the protecting handkerchief down. There was nothing in these people. He looked at them, but they didn't look back. Their eyes met his, and went through him. Their gaze was empty, devoid of sense or humanity. They were nothing, staring at him with the blank stare of idiots.

He watched them hard, determining if the blankness was the trance of hypnosis or something else. It was something else. They were no longer hypnotized; they were no longer anything to be hypnotized; they were dead shells of human beings, the light and mind gone out of them.

He walked faster, striding through them, trying not to look upon their naked horror, but searching for a pair of eyes with a vestige of sense left in them. The crowd surged about him, a stumbling, falling surge, and he grew dizzy with dodging.

A certain color caught his eye—the soft, gray plaid of a sport jacket—and he ran. That man, off at the edge of the crowd—he had to be Wes. The man's back was to him, but as he neared, he knew it was Wes. And the jacket wasn't as dirty as the others, the figure not so bent or fumbling.

Linc reached him, grabbed him by the shoulders and spun him around. "Wes!" he cried as he met the happily familiar face. "Wes, where—?"

Linc stopped, for the eyes that swept to meet his own were not Wes's eyes. The face was Wes's, the body, the jacket, were Wes's, but Wes was gone out of them all. The shell of the man looked at him and sighed. And that was all.

Linc closed his eyes and cried out, loud and strong against the stench and the shuffling of thousands of feet. He clenched his friend tight and cried with the sighs that breathed out of Wes's lungs.

A hand on his shoulder turned him around fearfully. He didn't want to meet any more idiot eyes. But it was Stanley. And in Stanley's hand was a small radiation counter.

At the sight of Wes, his face fell. "How," was all he said, "did he get here?"

"He's been among them for three days," Linc told him.

"And you didn't report it?"

"I couldn't. He went on my say-so. I had to wait." Linc indicated the counter in Stanley's hand. "What are you doing with that?"

"Following a hunch that turned out to be right. These pitiful, collapsing people are radioactive, Linc. All of them, slightly radioactive. That's why they're dying—radiation sickness. Everyone of them is doomed. Everyone of them is radioactive."

Linc took a firmer hold on Wes.

"Wes, too," Stanley said. "Only not quite so much as the others." He put the counter in his pocket, out of sight. "I figure that Hendricks died of the same cause. It wasn't his proximity to the reactor, as you thought. It was his stay in the hole. And that's why you came away from the reactor all right, while he didn't."

Linc nodded. It made sense, but he didn't want to consider it right now.

"What about the other thing?" he asked Stanley. "What about their minds? Radiation can't account for their mindlessness."

"No, it can't. That's something else again. I don't know yet." Stanley hesitated a moment, then moved away, back through the stumbling stream of dying people that walked the road.

"What will we do with them all?" Linc heard Iverson's voice over the din of moans and cries. "They're dying! What will we do with them?"

Linc tilted his head back and searched the sky. He wanted to see the distorted shape of a flying Eye—to vent his hate, to allay the guilt and grief that burdened his heart. But the sky was empty, and overcast. The Eyes had let these people go. Yet he knew that they were gathering more into the hole, even while they were herding these out.

He took hold of Wes firmly, and steadying him, walked back through the crowd, leading him around the fallen ones, shielding him from the falling, hearing his sighs like cries from his own soul.

He cut out of the stream at the corner, and with the driver's help, lifted Wes into the station wagon. Iverson could worry about the others. Wes was going home.

"It's pure hell," the driver muttered. "A pure hell those things have made. I tried to pick up a little boy but the others tramped over him before I could get there. What's going to happen to us, Mr. Hosler? What are we going to do?"

Back again in the parking lot, Iverson and Stanley helped him shift Wes from the station wagon to his own car. Iverson had work to do—hospitals to call, arrangements to make for the care and final disposition of thousands—but he waited to help with Wes. Linc felt a numbness that penetrated to his bones. He hadn't known grief since childhood, and the weight of it was almost intolerable.

"He was only gone three days," Stanley said. "Maybe we can bring him out of it. Those others have been in there a week or more."

"I'd like to know why he went in the first place—and why you didn't report it three days ago," Iverson was sour.

"Not now," Linc sighed. "Don't light into me now. How much do you think I can stand, old man? Wes is my friend. Let me do what I have to do for him, then tear me to bits if you want. But not now!"

He went around to his side of the car and climbed in, slamming the door on Iverson's low "Sorry. Take all the time you need."

He drove out of the lot and down the streets for home. Wes sat propped beside him, his eyes empty and distant, his only sound the continual sighing. If only the sighing meant there was fight still left in the shell. If only the sighing was a sign that Wes was still struggling against the effects of the Eyes. But such a hope was senseless. Linc knew that whenever he glanced at Wes's dark, blank eyes.

As the asphalt hummed beneath the wheels, he let the damnation come and torture him. He had found one friend—one hard-sought friend—and he had killed him. Selfishly killed him.

He had sent him out unprepared, and what tortures Wes had suffered, what horrors of mind and body he had endured, would remain forever a mystery. But he had done it—on account of Kelly. To have Kelly and feel her warm in his arms, he had killed his friend.

He pulled into the drive and lifted Wes from the car. Kelly already had the door open, and together they carried Wes upstairs and placed him on his bed. With warm, sudsy water, Linc washed the lanky body, dressed Wes gently in pajamas, and tucked him warmly under the covers. When Kelly came back, Wes's dull eyes were closed, and the room looked like any other sickroom.

"Linc?" Kelly's touch was on his arm, fleeting and unsure. "What are you thinking?"

"That he can't even offer me forgiveness."

She didn't answer him, one way or another. She simply stood by the bed, staring at Wes, and she was white and trembling.

"Don't you have anything to say?" he asked loudly. "Why aren't you telling me that it's best this way? That you're happy it's Wes lying there and not me? That you're grateful to have your chosen protector 'safe and sound' and to hell with the rest of the world? You should be here, in my arms, making me forget my conscience again."

She turned a stricken face to him, but still said nothing.

"Well?" he shouted. "Have you got enough love or worth in your whole body and soul to make up for what we did together? Wes is not a man to be easily atoned for. He was worth more than the two of us combined!"

She wavered, swaying on her feet. She took everything he threw at her, but offered no reply.

"Say something!" He cursed her, wanting to make her cry, to sob and pay in part for some of his grief.

In the heavy silence, Ichabod's nails clicked across the floor. The dog jumped onto the bed, peered into Wes's face, licked the man's chin, wagged his little tail—then whined, long and high. His tail drooped, and he jumped from the bed, clicking back out of the room and down the stairs.

Kelly was crying now. Silently, and to herself, she was crying. "Wes is dead to the dog," she said. "Ichabod knows he's not really here any more."

"But he's not dead to us," Linc answered her. "We still have to go through that. It may take days for him to die. And we're going to spend those days taking care of him. Watching him, nursing him, knowing we can't save him, but offering our souls to try."

"Of course, we are," she said softly. "Of course, we are."

CHAPTER TWELVE

LINC SAT IN THE DIM BEDROOM, watching Wes breathe, hearing Wes sigh, bathing Wes's hot forehead with cool, damp cloths. The doctor had come and gone, and now there was only waiting.

The doctor's words still echoed off the empty ceiling. Linc recalled him as he had entered the room—Dr. Ellston, the lab physician and one of Wes's friends. He was a tall man, thin and balding, with a transparent look to his skin and a pinkness that proclaimed frequent scrubbing. His blue eyes were large and intently probing, but after he had examined Wes and sat down with Linc, they lost their intentness, turning to blunt sympathy and frank apology.

"There's not a thing to be done," Ellston had said. "I've worked with radiation cases before, but Wes's condition has gone too far. I can't help him, Linc."

"I didn't expect that you could. But I feel easier knowing that you came and tried."

The doctor let out his breath in a soft exhalation of weariness. "I had just returned to the lab for more supplies when you called. I've spent the last hours in pure hell. They've taken the people who came out of the hole to every available place—the armory, the high schools, the basement of the library—and they overflow every accommodation. And there's nothing to be done for any of them except lead them to shelter, try to make them comfortable, and wait for them to die. Some die on the way."

"Don't their relatives come to claim them?"

"Some do, but it only complicates things. As dying patients, they have to be kept together in some semblance of hospital order. They can't be spread all over town. Anyway, I've learned how it must have been for doctors during the great plagues—when they were surrounded by death and completely helpless to prevent it. These people won't stay in their beds. They wander about, moaning and sighing. It's more like bedlam than a hospital."

For a moment Linc wondered why Ellston was burdening him with these pictures, then realized the reason. By describing the miseries of thousands, he was trying to dwarf the misery of Wes a little. Ellston would have deliberately done that. He was that kind of man.

But now he was gone and the verdict for Wes was pronounced and certain. And Linc was lonely. Sitting by the bed, waiting for death, he was lonely.

It was a new emotion, and it stung sharply. He had never had a friend, or wanted one. Wes was the first—and now, without Wes, he was lonely. It struck home clearly how many times he had sloughed other people off, unsympathetic to what he saw in their faces. Yet how could he blame himself when he hadn't understood?

Along with the loneliness, another emotion grew to stand watch with him. Fear. Every plan he'd followed had failed, and the Eyes still roamed the streets. He could see them on Colt Street whenever he looked out. The time for Collins' bomb was approaching faster now that so many people had emerged from the hole. The people who remained captive numbered only in the hundreds. The number grew every day, but three thousand had come out to walk and crawl down the road with Wes.

Linc wasn't confident anymore. He had failed, and failed greatly, bringing shame with failure, and self-damnation. Whenever he fed Ichabod, or forced himself to fondle the dog and give him some of the affection he so badly missed, he realized again how traitorous he had been, accepting Kelly and letting Wes walk bravely to his doom.

As night closed around the house, and Kelly came to take her turn at the bed watch, Linc drove to the lab. His stomach growled for food, yet he wasn't hungry; his eyes blurred from fatigue, yet he wasn't sleepy. He had promised himself one thing—to rid himself of the fear, the shame and the loneliness. That could be accomplished only one way, through revenge.

He pulled the tarp off the cage and looked into the watery blueness of the Eye. It glowered back at him, and he imagined he could see laughter in it, victory in it. He braced himself and hated it with his soul, and when the shadows and swirls began to form inside his mind, he thrust them off viciously, making the great, distorted thing in the cage blink and recoil. He fought it. Every new thrust, every new pull and tug, met with refusal, violent refusal. His body ached and he felt it from a distance. His mind reeled, and he still pushed on. This Eye had lied to Wes. It had told Wes that he had a chance of withstanding its brothers. It wouldn't lie to him.

When he felt himself swaying from weariness, he looked away from the iris, shuffled to the window, and breathed deep of the cold, fresh air that billowed in. He checked his watch: two hours. Two hours! He had withstood the Eye for two hours, alone, sustaining himself with hatred.

Wes's words echoed in him. Wes's hope for the future had been centered in him, and he had ignored it. For two days he had sat beside the silent bed and forgotten his first duty. He turned from the window. He would ignore it no longer.

"Tomorrow," he said to the Eye. "Tomorrow! Then maybe you'll know what it is to grieve, and suffer, and be defeated. If you can feel at all, you'll know! I'll make you know!"

As he sped through the dark streets, he felt better, uplifted and purposeful. Tomorrow he would go on the journey he should have taken before. Tomorrow he would go into the hole and finish what Wes had started. And take revenge for Wes.

He slammed into the house, more alive than he had been for days, and suddenly hungry. He went straight to the kitchen. He wanted nothing to do with Kelly. Since he had found Wes, he hadn't touched her. He hadn't wanted her touch. It was somehow unclean. It had led to treachery before, and he wouldn't give it the chance again.

He got out the old, dry remains of the fried chicken, poured a tall glass of milk, and sat down at the table. He had barely taken a bite when Kelly came in.

"What are you doing away from Wes?" he demanded.

"Wes is sleeping. I heard you slam the door, and I thought something must be wrong."

"Well, it isn't. For the first time in days, it isn't."

"What do you mean by that?"

"Simply that I've decided on a plan of action, and I'm going to follow it. One way or another, it will atone. If I win, then I'll forgive myself for Wes. If I lose, I'll have followed him and won't need forgiveness."

She gripped the back of the nearest chair. "You sound as though you intend to repeat what Wes did," she murmured, not letting it out in full voice as though she was afraid of it.

"Exactly," he said, "I should have gone in the first place."

"Down into that hole?" Kelly's words were slow and spaced. "Down into that radiation? You can't, Linc. You're crazy even to consider it."

"Let's not begin on that again," he commanded. "It won't work twice. I know exactly what I mean to you. Well, if I don't come back, go out and find yourself a new protector. I'm through with that job anyway. The minute we lose Wes, we lose each other."

"We actually lost each other the minute you *found* Wes!"

"Am I supposed to weep at that? And pity each of us and say we should have another chance?"

"How could we have another chance, when we didn't have one in the beginning? You never trusted me."

"Should I have?" he shouted.

"No," she admitted, "I was using you. Things are different now."

"You can't prove that statement, Kelly, so don't say it."

"All right—shut me out, and play the wronged hero, but I'm human, too. I've seen you change in the last few days. I've seen you grow desperate and fearful and need things you didn't need before."

"I admit it," he said. "I'm not ashamed of it."

"Then why can't you understand that the same things have happened to me? I need things—you—as I've never needed you before. If a person can love out of desperation, then that's what I'm doing." She came over to him and put her arms about his shoulders, making him face her. "I'm not pretending any more. I mean every word I say. I'm pleading with you to stay here and be safe—not to keep me safe this time, but because I want you and need you."

"Take your hands off me, Kelly!" He stood up, shoving her away.

"You blame me, don't you? You think it was my fault that Wes went out and didn't make it back?"

"I'd like to blame you, but I can't. I'm the one who gave in—who was swayed from sense and conscience. One thing I do know, I have brains enough not to make the same mistake again."

"Since when is it a mistake to love someone? Or is that emotion too weakening for you?"

"You won't get around me with sarcasm either." He was stubborn. "You won't get around me at all, so quit trying. Go back to Wes. Whatever share of the blame you did earn needs to be worked out with Wes."

She stared at him hard, and her green eyes were wild and sparking. "If you think I'll ever come to you again—" she began, then stopped. "You're a fool, Linc. An absolute, pitiful fool! You've never felt true emotion in yourself, so you can't recognize it in anybody else. Go ahead and walk into that hole tomorrow. Kill yourself. I'll be the last to mourn."

He heard her feet running up the stairs, and then the creak of old flooring as she went in to Wes. He sat down again and ate the chicken. Perhaps he hadn't been fair to her, but he cared little about it. The debt he owed to Wes excluded everything else.

Morning was cold. Linc could see his breath in the air when he took Ichabod out for his morning walk. It was a good morning, clear and clean, ready to accept his new start. And the natural chill of the air hid the unnatural chill of his bones when he thought about the next hours.

He fortified himself with a heavy breakfast, storing energy for the battle that lay ahead. At nine o'clock, he was ready. He climbed the stairs to Wes's room and went in. As he did, Kelly came out. He walked to the bed and stared down at his friend. Wes was paler, weaker, sighing more frequently. The radiation was eating him alive, and he hadn't much time left.

He took Wes's limp hand in his own and whispered, "Wait for me, friend. Wait for me to come back, because I will come back, with revenge for you and victory for all of us. I promise you that. If I can't win it, then I won't come back at all."

Linc squeezed the hot hand once more, then laid it gently upon the sheet. "I'll see you soon," he said, and left the room.

He passed Kelly at the head of the stairs, and she said nothing. She wished him neither good luck nor bad, and he felt a little empty without it.

He got into his car, drawing his bulky car coat close about him, and reached into the glove compartment for the flimsy weapons he had stored there the night before. Two tear gas bombs. As frail as they were, they might give him a valuable minute at some point or other and mean the difference between success and failure. He put them in his right-hand pocket, and started the car. As he drove off down Colt Street, he noticed Kelly watching him from the upstairs window. She didn't wave.

Just outside the city limits, he swung into line with five other cars, heading out under evacuation orders. He prayed that he had chosen correctly—that his group was one of those to be captured, not one that would manage to get through.

Two miles down the road, an Eye appeared, zooming across the open fields. The cars ahead of him surged forward. He could hear screams and see hands pointing skyward from the cars, and he kept pace. He wanted the capture, but he must pretend to be unwilling.

The car before him suddenly swerved in to the ditch, and stalled halfway up the other side. Following suit, he turned the wheel and swung off the road, feeling the jolt as the car lurched into the ditch and up again, coming to rest at the edge of a barren cornfield. He waited, sitting quietly, taking his cue from those in the other cars. All five of them were off the road, and silent. The doors of a blue sedan opened and three people got out: a man, a woman and an old woman. They stood in the field, limp in the cold sun, waiting.

Linc climbed out of his car, and dropped his hands to his sides, hoping they looked properly limp and insensitive. He let his shoulders droop and his head fall forward. The Eye was now in the cornfield, hovering six feet off the ground, rolling its brown eyeball back and forth, gathering its people in. Clouds and shadows and swirls ebbed around him, and he was familiar with them and fought them but gently. Too strong a resistance would arouse suspicion. The Eye would feel it and recoil, as the one in the lab had done.

The people were walking now, and he joined them, falling into step with the nearest man. They walked blindly, stumbling over the dead rubble of cornstalks, heads down, sightlessly following deeper and deeper into the field.

Linc could see where he was going; he could see the people if he peered up from under his eyelids; and he could see the Eye leading them, bobbing above them one moment, coming to rest the next. It blinked its giant lids and the lashes made a little breeze that ruffled the feather on one of the women's hats.

There were twelve people—men, women and children—in the march beside himself. He made thirteen. He wanted more. Twelve wasn't enough cover.

The corn stubble ended and gave way to tall, browning grass, and their feet made swishing noises as they passed through it. Swish and crunch. Swish and crunch. He focused his mind on the sound, keeping away from the swirls of the Eye.

The swirls eddied stronger and there was a tug at him that almost drew his head up, ready to fight back. He grabbed hold of himself and resumed the limp pose, but resistance was somehow harder. The shadows buffeted at the door of his mind, demanding entrance.

Peeking upward, he saw the reason for the new strength in the hypnotic pull. Another Eye, a green one, had joined his brown captor, and they were sailing together, backward across the grass toward the woods. Following the green Eye was a large mass of people. He estimated thirty at a quick count. He breathed easier. This number would give him safety.

The two groups joined, and headed toward the game preserve. Each step forward brought more swirls to pummel him, as the Eyes gathered, reinforcing each other, and led their herd of the helpless to their lair. He felt like a man on a blind walk, on a walk among the dead. There wasn't a sound around him. Even the birds were silent, having fled before the monstrosities that had taken over their skies. Crunch and swish went the feet of the mob, and that was all. It was eerie and he felt immensely alone, immensely frail. The struggle to keep from succumbing to the hypnotic power grew steadily harder and more desperate.

As long as they weren't aware of him, he was all right. As long as they didn't sense his difference, his immunity, and gang up on him, he would be safe. But he doubted that he could stand against a joint attack. Together, they were too strong.

The sun was two hours in the sky, and his breath ceased to be visible. The day was warming, and he was sweating inside the car coat, sweating from heat, and struggle, and fear. They were approaching a road. Cars were stalled along the sides of it—empty cars.

A woods rose on the other side, and far to his left, another road cut into it. He recognized it and shuddered. This was the road where he had found Wes in that one spurt of joy, and then had sunk into despair when he had turned him around. The game preserve was near. The hole was near. The end of his walk had almost come.

Then he was on the worn path he had seen from the fire tower; the path made by the thousands of zombie feet, walking toward the hole. "A few more minutes," he told himself, "a few more minutes and the hole will open before you, and you'll know."

He fought harder against the shadows that beat at him. It was an almost physical feeling upon his brain; tugging, pulling, drawing him close, flagellating his mind with soft shafts of thought; and he fought it, harder now because it was so concentrated.

Beside him a crack of thunder pealed out, and he jerked erect.

Along the path, both hidden and unhidden were National Guardsmen. They were entrenched here, bravely ringing the mouth of the hole. The thunder had been the crack of a rifle.

He had come into the middle of a foray against the Eyes, and the woods erupted about him into gunshots and yelling. Soldiers popped out from behind trees, and Eyes reeled as they were stung. But he couldn't watch; he couldn't pay attention. He was too engrossed in his own battle against hypnosis.

The fight raged, then subsided as he walked through it, pretending to be unaware. He saw, as the quiet descended, that the group was being joined by more and more uniformed figures. Whatever the Guard had tried this time, they had failed again.

The people in front of him seemed to grow shorter. He hesitated. They weren't growing shorter. They were going down into the earth. They had reached the hole.

Linc braced himself, and took the first of his own steps down the dirt ramp that led from the sunshine to the depths of the pit. There was no longer room for fear in him. It was crowded out by terror and apprehension.

CHAPTER THIRTEEN

THE EARTH slanted under Linc's feet and he journeyed down it toward the approaching blackness. It was a huge ramp that met his steps—fifty feet wide, smoothed over by the thousands of feet that had traversed it previously. Down and down it went, until the sunlight from the rear became dim, and dimmer, and then was gone entirely. Down, down into the innards of the Earth. How far he wondered? And how would he see in the pitch-blackness of inner Earth? The zombie people around him had no need to see. They were being led. He was not. Now he was truly a blind man walking among the dead.

When the light faded entirely, he closed his eyes. He couldn't stand the sense of blindness, couldn't stand to keep them open and see nothing. So he closed them and moved close to the rest of the captives, letting their shoulders, bumping against him, be his guide.

Something touched his eyes—a pressure, a soft hint of vision—and he opened them. It was no longer dark. The ramp and the dirt side walls were lit with a wispy glow, violet and purplish. It grew stronger with each step forward, until he could see again, make out forms, then even the faces of the zombies. It was dull light, but a light that he was thankful for. And ahead the ramp ended.

A sheer wall rose abruptly, marking the ramp's end. The people spread out of their close pack, and as they did, he got a good view of the wall and what made the ramp end.

A huge, metal shape blocked the passage. It was only half-visible, towering above him, the other half embedded in the dirt which had stopped its forward movement.

He studied it as unobtrusively as possible. He couldn't be positive, but the over-all shape of the thing brought to mind a ship of some sort. A spaceship? He recalled the reports of a great roaring light passing over the town, and the explosion in the woods. Then this metal giant had made the light, and the explosion had been its impact and burrowing descent into the Earth.

Someone shoved him and he moved on. The zombie people waited for no one. They plowed ahead, oblivious to anything in their path. He shuffled with them toward the ship, then at the end of the ramp, turned to the right. Before him was a large, natural cavern, and the glow from it was stronger.

As he entered the cavern, the glow bloomed brighter, and still keeping his pose of limpness, he looked up from under his eyelids to find its source.

The discovery was a surprise that sucked out his breath. Over by the wall, glowing brightly so that every movement was outlined, was a semicircle of bloated, shapeless creatures. They were huge and living and they glowed with the violet light, which emanated from their skins, changing shade with their emotion. Beneath the glowing, they were black and shiny, with hides of a slimy leather texture. He counted quickly, and there were nine of them.

Zombies were everywhere. Sitting huddled against the walls, crouching together in groups, they seemed to fill the cavern. Some were filthy from their stay in the dirt—others had only lately arrived. They were all blank-eyed from hypnosis; and some had already taken on the idiot stare of mindlessness that Wes had acquired here in this pit.

He was sickeningly near the circled monsters now. He sank to the floor as the others did, and sat still, staring at the dirt in front of him. Out of the corner of his eye, he had a slant-eyed view of the glowing giants.

Everything they did seemed to be in slow motion; sluggish and heavy, as though they weighed a ton and could not lift their arms. Arms they had—fat, long arms of amorphous shape. And legs they had, of the same appearance. Their ears and mouths were not visible, and as he looked them over, he recoiled and had to forcibly keep his hands from flying—to cover his mouth. Some of the giant things had two eyes. Some of them had only one. Yet the monsters with one had sockets for two—the socket for the missing eye glaring redly, revoltingly empty.

As he continued to watch, one of the flying Eyes floated into the cavern. It hovered, its six-foot length dwarfing Linc beneath it, and then as it had on that first day at the ball game, it began to change size. It shrank, from six to four feet, to two feet, to one. And when it reached the size of about eight inches, it floated away from him, and toward one of the monsters. It stopped before the glowing thing, turned around, and—backed into the empty socket in the thing's face.

It was impossible! Yet he had seen it. One moment the socket had been empty and a six-foot flying Eye had hovered near. The next moment, the socket was full and the flying Eye was filling it. How?

He searched frantically for some rational word that might stem the rise of panic. He found one—teleportation. The glowing creatures had the power not only to hypnotize, but to teleport part of their bodies to another place. To send their eyes out from their sockets, to skim the Earth with their flying Eyes, see with them, and capture with them. The mentality behind the hypnosis, then, was within these grotesque, glowing things. The Eyes were merely their instruments.

Linc closed his eyes against the sickening pull of his stomach. He had to gather strength. The swirls and shadows still waited just beyond his mind, ready to pounce and take him. He renewed his fight against them. And when he had them under control, he kept his eyes shut to give himself a chance to think—to think without constant revulsion at what he saw around him; to think sanely and logically.

The big creatures had obviously come to Earth in the metal spaceship; the flying Eyes were not separate entities, but part of the creatures themselves, teleported over the Earth to bring in captives; when the Eyes were wounded, the creatures who owned them, using their special mental powers, healed them; and the creatures glowed. This last fact brought his thinking up short. The creatures glowed; the violet and purple radiance emanated from their skins as though they were giving it off. But what was it?

He peered again at the zombie people. They were hypnotized now, and soon they would have the radiation sickness. Every one of the people who had returned from this hole, including Wes, was dying of radioactivity. The source of it was here—not in the hole itself, but in the glow of the creatures who inhabited it.

It made sense. These giant sluggish things gave off a constant glow of radiation, which infected their captives and killed them. Sitting here, in the glow, he was soaking up radiation, too. He would die of it, too. Hendricks had been here only a short time—a few days—and Hendricks had died. Wes had been here only three days, and Wes was dying.

He knew, then, that he had to discover whatever there was to discover quickly, and get out. If he stayed in this hole too long, he would perish.

He lifted his head, forgetting the pose. The time was short, anyway, and he had to see. The hypnotic pull was ebbing somewhat. The monsters had their captives, and they could relax, devoting only a small amount of attention to the hypnotizing, using the rest of their energies for something else.

A man rose from the group of new zombies and approached the semicircle of glowing things. He knelt down before them and remained there on his knees. At the far end of the cavern, two Eyes were sailing back and forth. They swayed in the glow of the parent creatures, weirdly violet with flashing lashes, then falling into shadow. Linc could guess where they belonged. The two giant things nearest to him were each minus an eye, lopsided with their single-orbed gaze.

He couldn't stand this place any longer. The blackness of it, the violet glow cutting that blackness, the swaying Eyes, popping in and out of sockets, were too much to bear. He had to get out. He felt the panic and rush inside him, and got up on his knees. The man was still kneeling before the circle of creatures like a sacrifice in some ancient ritual. He had no hope of deciphering that ritual, and he had no time.

He leaped to his feet and ran through the cavern toward the ramp, following the glow backward from its greatest strength to its weakest. He leaped over the tired bodies of the zombie people, pushed others out of his way, toppling them over like dominoes in his wake.

Behind him, he heard a swish of air, and the new harsh pull at his mind told him the Eyes were giving chase. He made the foot of the ramp and veered to climb it. Ahead it was pitch-black. The glow faded partway up, and after that he would have to run blind.

He darted to the wall. Running his hands along the vertical dirt gave him direction. Glancing over his shoulder as he struck the blackness, he saw two Eyes coming after him, still lighted by the glow, purple and staring.

He ran harder, his legs knowing the way out of terror. Faint light washed some of the black away as he neared the sunlight. And finally he could see his path again. The vision gave him an added spurt and he clawed his way on, using his hands against the wall as leverage for his weakened legs.

When he gained the ramp entrance, a shock like a great fist struck his brain and unnatural blackness rushed to engulf him. He fell forward, his fingernails clutching the ground and filling with dirt. He fought and struggled in the prone position. He writhed to his knees and opened his eyes against the hammering that wanted to beat them shut.

He was encircled; the tiny center of a circle of six flying Eyes. They had him cornered, and united they were pounding at his consciousness, beating him into submission. He hated them, and he thrust the hate at them in great stabs, but they were too many. They absorbed the stabs and battled back. His brain was numbing, the swirls and shadows verging into hypnotic visions, and he was deathly tired.

It was an effort just to move. His limbs felt three times their normal weight. With a desperate effort he inched his hand toward his pocket, then into it. He grasped the hard shapes of the tear gas bombs.

He pulled them out slowly, every motion of his muscles an ache along his nerves. Arrowing hatred from his mind at the Eyes, he drew back his hand, and let the bombs fly.

They hit, and the gas bloomed and billowed. He covered his face as the Eyes disappeared into the fog. He tried his legs again. They still wouldn't move. Then, in the middle of the try, they became mobile, and the strain he was putting into them sent him sprawling out of the gas on momentum alone. As he hit the ground, he rolled away from the mist. His eyes burned and watered and he felt that he would choke. But when his body lost its rolling speed, he scrambled to his feet and ran, back along the trail through the woods. If he could just run far enough, he would find help. The National Guard was entrenched here somewhere, and they would help him.

He ran, his thumping feet jarred his body and his overtaxed heart. Saliva seeped out of his mouth, and he was afraid to sample it for fear of finding blood. Still, he ran.

He broke into a clearing, and something bobbed up in front of him. He shrieked once, and fell. Unconsciousness beckoned and he clutched it, not caring any longer where it led him.

The sun was on its early fall journey downward when he awoke. He sat straight up, but hands caught his shoulders and laid him back.

"Take it easy," someone said. "You're all right now."

He looked up into the blurred face of a tall man, and as his foggy vision cleared he saw gray eyes and a smooth skin with tired lines and the flash of ribbons on a uniform blouse.

"National Guard?" he asked.

"Yes. You ran right into us. What was after you anyhow?"

"Eyes."

"Oh," the other man grunted. "No wonder you were so desperate."

"They didn't follow me then?"

"Not into our position, anyway." The man stood up. "My name is Kellroy, Lieutenant Kellroy. Whoever you are, buddy, you look like you've been to hell and back."

"I have. I'm Linc Hosler from the Space Lab."

"And just what were you doing out there?"

"I was in the hole."

Kellroy's expression clearly showed doubt.

"I was," Linc argued, "I went in and came out again. I know what's down there now. I've got to get back and report."

Kellroy still looked doubtful, and Linc didn't blame him. It was a crazy story.

"Look," Linc said, "if you've got a hook-up, get hold of Dr. Iverson or Colonel Stanley. They'll vouch for me."

"Do you know Stanley?"

"Of course. I've been working with him."

"Then do you know about the attack we made the other day against the hole?" Kellroy was pumping him for confirming knowledge.

"I watched the whole thing from the fire tower in the woods. I saw your boys get taken. As a matter of fact, the tear gas was my idea in the first place—only I never intended it to be used that way. It's not a weapon."

Kellroy grunted again. "Tear gas, huh?" he said. "You're not by any chance the guy who captured one of those Eyes, are you?"

"I am. I have it caged in my lab right now."

Kellroy nodded quickly. "Okay. I believe you. If you were anybody else, I'd order you to stay in bed for a while. But with the information you must have, I'll send you to the lab in a jeep. Express."

"Thank heaven I ran into a sensible man," Linc sighed.

"And a scared one. If you've got anything at all to help solve this mess, I want it put to use—and fast. Come on. I'll drive you back myself."

CHAPTER FOURTEEN

IVERSON, STANLEY, KELLROY AND COLLINS gathered close around him as he told the story from start to finish, leaving out none of the fantastic or revolting details. He told them of the dark, and the glow, the empty sockets and the shrinking eyes. He described the queer ritual of the man, and relayed his guesswork about the source of the radiation sickness.

"So you see," he concluded, "the Eyes aren't what we thought at all. Our first guess was actually the right one. They're not complete beings. They're a fantastic part of a fantastic creature. From space—they must be from space."

No one said anything, and he sat back in his chair, giving them time to come around. He felt better. The first thing he had done on hitting the lab was to check himself for radioactivity. He was carrying some, but not enough to harm him. Still, he had taken a shower and scrubbed his skin red to wash away every trace. And now, with night outside and the good, yellow light of electricity about him, the fear was washing away, too.

Stanley said, beginning in the middle of his train of thought, "Then destroying the Eyes alone will do us no good, if it's even possible. There's more to destroy—the creatures themselves."

"Right," Linc answered. "And they're big. Like small whales with arms and legs. I'd guess that they normally go on all fours. I don't see how they could heft their bulk any other way."

"Well," Iverson said, "I guess that settles it. I've been against it from the start, but now I can see that it's the only way."

"What are you talking about?" Linc asked.

"Collins' plan," Iverson met his gaze. "The A-bomb. If we have to destroy those giants to get rid of the Eyes, then the bomb is the only way. The poor people in there with them will just have to die, too."

Of course, Iverson was right. The information he had retrieved from the hole made Collins' plan more feasible. The bomb would not only destroy the Eyes, it would destroy the parents of the Eyes.

Linc searched his conscience to see if he had any compunction against this killing of the innocents, and decided that he didn't. They would die, anyway—slowly and painfully. Then his mind swung to Wes, and he found the compunctions. Wes had given his life to save those people. Whether they died later or not, they shouldn't be slaughtered without a chance. And what of the new ones who walked down the ramp every hour of the day? They could be saved. They shouldn't be bombed.

He stood up, determined to carry on Wes's fight. "Collins' plan is no good. It never has been. Aside from the people in the hole, there's the entire area to consider. The evacuation has been a fiasco. You're sending people out to their doom in flocks. You can't do that and call it a necessity. It's inhuman. No matter what label you give it, it's inhuman."

"Then what do you suggest?" Collins sneered. "You're the hero here. What do you suggest?"

Linc smashed his cigarette out in the ashtray. "It might not be a bad thing if you *remembered* that I'm the hero here. I risked my life, just as Wes did, to get information. I didn't sit here in this safe office and plan to murder thousands of people. I went in with them. Now, I intend to use what I know to find a way to save them."

"But every hour we delay means more lost," Iverson protested. "People are being captured. We can't let that go on either."

"Then stop your stupid evacuation and order people to stay in their houses!" Linc commanded.

"How long do you think it would be before the Eyes started going in after them?" Collins asked.

"Who knows?" Linc didn't let it jar him. "It would at least give us a breather—give us time. I need time to sort things out. One thing I've learned—I don't jump at actions any more. I was responsible for too many deaths through over-eagerness." He turned to Iverson. "Give me your answer, Doc. I want time—a day, maybe two days—but time. Am I going to get it?"

Iverson hesitated and swerved to Stanley. Stanley, in turn, swung to Collins. Collins shrugged. "You know what I think."

Stanley fingered a pencil lying on the desk. "I have to stick with Collins. I'm a military man. I understand weapons and I trust weapons. The bombing plan sounds good to me."

"Doc?" Linc asked the gray-haired man.

Iverson stared out the window, then said whiningly, "I hate to go against you, Linc. I've always known you to be capable in the past, but this situation seems to have you stumped. I can't in good conscience say, 'Okay, take your two days,' while innocent people are constantly being captured. I have to go along with Stanley. The bomb is the best answer. And the sooner, the better."

"All right," Linc said. "Then it's your show. I'll go home and bury my own dead. You bury yours—after you've finished killing them." He strode for the door, angry deep inside, wanting to smash the smirk off Collins' sharp face with equally sharp blows.

"Hosler!" Stanley's voice was harsh with command. "The evacuation will run at least three more days. Isn't that good enough for you? Why do you need special privilege?"

"I never asked for special privilege," Linc shot back. "I only asked for lives. For time when people wouldn't be sent out to die. What's the use of my work when you guys here are undermining any good I might do? Your evacuation has to stop. That's the kind of time I want."

"Then it's settled," Stanley said. "I'm sorry to see you leave us like this."

"And surprised," Iverson added.

"I'm not," Collins said. "Nothing Hosler could do would surprise me. I've worked beside him too long."

"One more crack, Collins," Linc hissed. "Just one more—"

"Before you leave the lab, Linc," Iverson interrupted him, "please turn that Eye you've got caged loose. I don't want it around any more. It's too much of a danger to the staff. It may start reaching out for people. Turn it loose."

"I'm sure it will thank you for its freedom," Linc said, and left the room.

He went to the little lab where he and Wes had battled so hard with the watery-blue monstrosity. He switched on the light. The Eye still floated in the cage. It turned slightly to meet him, and gazed at him blankly.

"I'd like to punch the insides out of you," Linc cursed it. "But you've gotten the thumbs-up sign, you slimy, rotting—"

He stamped to the window and opened it wide, then back to the cage and loosened the lock. The Eye was free, but it didn't move. He picked up the tarp and shook it at the thing, shooing it out, tipping the cage up to spill it out. Still it remained captive.

He put the tarp down, grasped the cage tightly, and pulled. The cage came away, leaving the Eye hovering four inches above the bare workbench, free of the enclosure.

"Now get out of here!" He shooed it again, hitting it with the tarp. He maneuvered it up and finally out, then shut the window and locked it.

He left the little room despondently. It had all been for nothing. All of the energy put into fighting the hypnosis, and all of the danger. Wes had killed himself for nothing, and he had risked death for nothing. Collins and his bomb had won.

Kelly met him at the door. She was hollow-eyed with tiredness, and her voice was husky. "Hurry, Linc. I think Wes—" She broke off and ran for the stairs. Linc followed her quickly, climbing the stairs three at a time.

They went into Wes's room, and he stopped short beside the bed. He had been absent only one day, but the change in Wes was the change of years. His skin was ashen, and his hair ragged and sparse. There was a rattle to his sighing, and the feel of death clouded about him.

"I'm so glad you got here in time," Kelly whispered. "I didn't know if I could face it alone."

"You could have faced it." Linc wasn't kind.

She stared at him, and her chin was quivering and her face begging for a scrap of compassion.

He wanted to respond to her need, feeling an equal one of his own. But the words wouldn't pull themselves free of his throat.

He went closer to the bed. "I'll watch," he said to Kelly. "You go down and get yourself some coffee."

"No. Wes was my friend, too. You never remember that. Everything is always all yours. But he was my friend, too, and I'm going to stay with him."

Linc didn't say anything more. He merely held on to Wes's hand, and waited.

He knew when it was dawn by the coldness that settled in his bones. Dawn was always chill and stark, dismal, before the pink of sunrise, a fearing time, a time for the evils of the world to have one last gallop before they settled back into their holes. And this dawn was more stark, more chill, than usual, because with the coming of it Wes grew cold. His gasps came less and less often; his jaw went slack, and he grew cold.

Then it was done, and it wasn't hard, because his brain and soul were already away, and only his body had to stop its pulsing.

Linc let go of his hand and closed himself inward, not daring to utter a sound. Kelly cried quietly. He put the sheet up and over Wes's face in the age-old ritual of hiding death, then said, "Now—will you make that coffee?"

She left, and her footsteps were soft on the stairs. He heard the click of Ichabod going beside her, and the imagined sight of the little dog was more tearing than the entire night had been. Now, he supposed, Ichabod was his, and as much his duty to care for and comfort as Wes had been.

He denied himself the relief of grief or maudlin thoughts, and joined Kelly in the kitchen. The dog already eating his breakfast and Linc put the cream and sugar on the table as Kelly finished with the coffee.

She sat across from him, yet they were light years apart.

He had to break the silence. "I'm going out as soon as it's a decent hour and arrange for a funeral."

"There aren't any funerals anymore," she said. "No one will go to them. People don't bury their dead. Not with ritual, anyway."

"Wes will have ritual," he said flatly. "I'll find somebody if I have to drag them out by the hair."

"Will we wait the usual three days?"

"No. He's dead now, and who can say what will happen in three days?" He gulped a hot bubble of coffee. "Wes was a Methodist, wasn't he?"

Kelly nodded.

"Then I'll get a Methodist minister." He stood up. "You be ready when I come for you."

"I thought you said you'd wait for a decent hour."

"There isn't any decent hour if people are unwilling. I may as well pull them out of bed, too." He started out of the kitchen. "Play with Ichabod, will you? Throw that toy rat he likes to chase and—Kelly, don't be nervous here alone—I mean..."

"I know what you mean. I'll be fine. Don't worry about it."

He found the rectory, and his knock was loud and brutal on the door. He was prepared to argue, to plead, to be angry, anything to accomplish what he had come to accomplish. He pounded again, and this time the door creaked open and a pale face peered out at him.

"Yes?" the face said.

"Is the minister at home?"

The door opened a bit further and revealed a woman in a bright print housedress. "He's at breakfast," she said.

"I want to see him. May I come in?"

"He's at breakfast."

"So? Does that mean he's unavailable? Since when does breakfast interfere with service to God?"

The woman met his gaze sharply, then stood back and opened the door wide. "Right through that door, and straight ahead to the kitchen," she pointed the way. "It's Dr. Putney. Tell him I sent you in."

He followed her directions and came into the better light of a big kitchen. It was clean and airy, much like his own, and a small man sat at the table, sipping juice and eating toast. He wore horn-rimmed glasses that fell forward on his nose whenever he bent to take a bite, and his hands were pale and delicate.

"Dr. Putney?"

The minister swiveled brown eyes quickly around to rest on Linc, "I am, young man. What can I do for you?"

"I've come to ask for your services. I have a funeral to be held, and I want it Methodist, and I want it today."

The minister went back to his juice, filling time.

"Well?" Linc demanded.

"Sit down. Have something to eat. I don't like to have strangers in my home without offering to break bread with them."

"Thanks just the same, but I didn't come for that. I have a funeral to—"

"I heard you the first time."

"Then why the stalling?"

"It's an unusual request nowadays, young man. I haven't held a funeral in weeks. Not even a Sunday service."

"But you have no reason to refuse?" Linc probed.

"To be honest, I hadn't given it any consideration, because I didn't expect to be asked." He indicated a chair. "Are you sure you won't join me?"

"I haven't the time. I have other arrangements to make. A cemetery lot, a grave to dig, a casket. I came to you first because I thought you would naturally be the easiest to get. As I told the woman who let me in, nothing—not even the Eyes—could interfere with your service to God."

Dr. Putney cleared his throat, and his pale face reddened. "You run right to the heart of things, don't you?"

"I see no point in hiding what I mean in obscure language. You either accept me or refuse. Which is it going to be?"

"What sort of service are you planning?"

"I don't need anything fancy. Just a graveside service."

"That would entail a group of people, out in the open," Putney said, and his voice suddenly trembled.

"It would. It might be dangerous—and it might not. We'd have to take that chance. But, Doctor, if you knew the chance this man took—he wasn't simply a victim of the Eyes. He gave his life trying to fight them. He can't be buried without the proper honors."

"He gave his life, did you say?"

Linc explained the circumstances of Wes's death, and Putney listened quietly. The man's face was expressionless, giving no hint of the thoughts behind it, but when Linc was through, he said, "Well, that decides it, doesn't it? If he was willing to lay down his life for his brother, I certainly can't do any less."

"Then you'll come?"

"Just tell me when you want me, and I'll be there."

"Come with me—now. Maybe I can help to keep you safe. I don't know. I'd like to try."

"That's a fine idea, anyway." Putney rose from the table. "I can help persuade the others you'll need to complete the service. The caretaker at Bladen cemetery is a special friend of mine. If he hasn't been evacuated, I think I can prick his conscience enough to make him prepare the grave."

Linc took the little man in tow, and together they drove the deserted streets. The town was a ghost town. Many of the houses stood empty as the result of the evacuation. Others might as well have been empty, for the people inside were hiding, tight and fearful behind their locked windows and doors.

The first three mortuaries they visited were closed. The fourth was open, but the mortician refused to help. He wouldn't even supply a casket.

The fifth mortuary harbored a man with a heart, and that part of the search was ended. The man's name was Evans, and he was oddly unafraid. He volunteered to take the casket to Linc's house, prepare the body quickly, and be waiting there when they were ready.

Bladen Cemetery presented no problem. Linc had to stand by, on guard for approaching Eyes, while the big, husky caretaker dug into the not yet frozen earth. The grave was deep and waiting when he and the minister left.

Kelly was ready, her coat on, and the hearse was in the driveway. A quick call to the lab brought enough men to act as pallbearers. The funeral began from the house...to the hearse...to the cemetery. There the wind, springing up in the noontime, whipped at them and chilled with its gusts. The leaves fell wildly, the last of them, drifting red and yellow to settle on the brown ones that had withered earlier.

The service over the grave was brief and sharply sad. There was one bouquet of late mums that Kelly had picked from their garden, there were the familiar words that surrounded a death, and then it was over. Linc's chest was tight with pent-up emotion, but he kept himself hard. Iverson stood beside him, and he couldn't even feel anger toward the old man in this situation.

Linc whispered "Good-bye" under his breath, and walked for the car. Kelly fell in beside him, but he couldn't touch her. Even his own journey into the hole couldn't atone for what he had done to Wes, and this place with its tombstones and quiet made him so heavily guilty that he could barely order his feet to walk away from it. He should be there, in that casket, quiet beneath the dark earth. It was because of Kelly, and his own weakness, that he wasn't.

CHAPTER FIFTEEN

LINC WAS AWAKENED out of a fitful sleep by the persistent ring of the phone. He stumbled out of bed and down the stairs, picked it up, and yawned into it, "Yes?"

"Hosler, is that you?" Iverson's voice spewed out at him.

"It's me, but why it's you I don't know. I thought we were through with our association."

"Not quite," Iverson's tone raised, now that he was sure he had the right target, "I want you over here inside the hour. There's a job you didn't clean up."

Iverson hung up with a bang. Linc swore under his breath. He wouldn't go. He had a right to some time, a right to some adjustment after losing Wes. But, even as he shuffled toward the kitchen and coffee, he knew he would go. The day stretched empty before him and he would grasp at anything to fill it. Even Iverson's shaking anger. But he would also take his time.

He fed Ichabod, fed himself, took a shower, and then led the dog outside for his customary morning romp. He saw Ichabod looming as a duty to consume his future. He wished he could find some feeling for the dog—some of what Wes had known—but it wouldn't appear just because he wished it. He liked the spotted dog, and that was all. Any stronger feeling was beyond him.

Once the animal was safely settled in the house, he started the drive to the lab. He would be late twenty minutes, and he drove slowly, obstinately trying to stretch it into a half-hour.

He strode the empty corridors into Iverson's office.

"You're late." Iverson glanced up from his desk sourly.

"I had things to do."

"You have more important things to do here. Come with me. I want to show you the result of your handiwork." Linc followed Iverson into the little room he and Wes had used to study the Eye. Iverson went to the window and pointed outside. "What do you think of that?"

Linc looked, and looked the second time. Outside, six feet from the window, hovered the watery-blue Eye.

"Well?" Iverson said.

"Well, nothing. What am I supposed to say?"

"You're supposed to get rid of it. We've done everything to chase it off, but the damn thing comes right back again, like it's searching for its long-lost mother. I can't figure you, Linc. You really goofed this time. All down the line. That thing hovers out there and endangers every man in the lab. We don't dare walk near it. It just waits. It has already picked off Bennet."

"Oh, no." Linc felt a surge of pity. He liked Bennet.

"I want you to get rid of it. I can't have it about, ready to capture all of my men. We need those men. And as long as it's there, the reactor is in danger. You should have known better."

"Hold on. I tried to chase it off the other night. What can I do that you haven't done?"

"That's what I called you to figure out. You made the mess, so you clean it up."

Iverson was speaking to him in a way that he had no right to do, and Linc felt belligerence rising in himself to match the old man's. He had absorbed the name-calling, had heard himself called a fool in every way but the outright one, and was angry with himself for enduring it.

"You're just making a lot of noise," he said. "Noise and panic and half-baked plans—that's all that's left in this lab. You've forgotten the questions!"

"What questions?"

"Questions like: Why does that Eye stay here? When you drive it off, why does it come back? What does it want? I set it free. If it had wanted freedom, it would have taken it. It hasn't."

"I can see that," Iverson countered.

"Okay, and there are more questions, too. Why did it allow itself to be caged in the first place? That's a question *I* missed. I should have asked it right after I came back from the hole, right after I knew what these Eyes really are. That thing could have shrunk itself and teleported out of that cage at any time. It didn't need to stay a prisoner. So why did it?"

"And you have the answer now?" Iverson perked up a bit.

"The same one I had for the other questions. It didn't fly the coop because it wanted something. The mentality behind it, the brain in whatever bloated monster it came from, wants something. While Wes and I were studying it, it was studying us."

110

Iverson wiped his forehead, shaken by the volume of Linc's voice, and gathering in the new ideas, "I admit, it sounds interesting, but what good does it do us?"

"A lot, if we've got the guts to carry through the next step. To go out there and find out what it wants."

"How?" The old man was incredulous. "The thing can't talk. It could only lead you back to the hole. Maybe that's what it wants anyway. Personal revenge against the man who caged it. I imagine it was tormented aplenty. Now please don't tell me that what this Eye wants is contact. Is that what you're getting at? Contact?"

"I suppose it is," Linc admitted, uneasily.

"Then why haven't the things made a move toward it before? Why only this one, and why only you? Even your reputed egotism can't make you think that you're so different it wants to treat you as an equal!"

"It wouldn't be egotism, if I did think so. Who else has ever stood up to it but Wes and me? Who else has had the guts to face it out? It finally found two men with courage and sense that it could understand, and it wants us back. It didn't want to leave us."

"It left Wes!" Iverson said meanly. As he saw Linc's reaction, he sat down. "I'm sorry for that, Linc. I don't know what's gotten into me. This isn't me, you know that. I've just had too much. Constant bickering, constantly changing plans, all so gigantically opposed to each other that I've had no real choice between them."

"I realize that." Linc accepted the apology. "But if you'd listen to me just once more."

"And if I should go along with you, what would it entail?"

Linc braced himself to bring the words out. They weren't going to lead to anything easy, but it was all he could think of to do.

"Let me go there and see what happens. I don't know what I will do, or what the Eye will do, but I have to try. If I'm wrong, I won't come back, most likely. But if I'm right, this could be the big and final moment in the whole fight."

"I don't like to take the chance with you. Not you."

"Thanks, but where was this vote of confidence the other night when all I was asking for was time?"

"You think I betrayed you, don't you? I didn't. I simply took the course I thought best. I had to go along with Collins' plan."

"You'll still have Collins' plan, if I fail out there. If I succeed, then who knows? Maybe those hundreds of people won't have to be killed, after all. Time is short." He tried to jar Iverson out of his indecision. "Every hour that those people are down in that hole, they're soaking in more radioactivity. They're dying bit by bit while we stand here arguing."

Iverson couldn't make the decision. He was wrung out with deciding. Linc made it for him. "Stay inside," Linc said. "Don't endanger yourself."

He ran for the outside door.

As he came into the air, he wanted to stop. Every sensible nerve in him shouted to stop, to go back, and quit being the fool. This was crazy—crazy from beginning to end. What was he to do when he came upon the Eye? What would the Eye do? He should have thought those points through before he hit Iverson with the grand questions.

But now it was too late to stop, because hovering and swaying before him was the six-foot, watery-blue Eye that he knew so well.

He approached it at a walk. This was the moment, then—his moment—and he didn't want it. But he needed it. His mind was a turmoil of confusion, and all he could do to free himself was face the puzzle and let come what may.

He halted four feet from the Eye. It was low, and at this distance the great iris was level with his face. It stretched away on both sides of him, filling his vision, and it blinked, and watched, and was blank.

Trembling hit him in the knees and he was afraid. But he stood there, alone before it, loosening part of his mind to catch the swirls he knew the Eye would be casting, and keeping the other part tight to protect himself. He held one sentence, swimming in his brain. "Talk to me," he said over and over again. "Talk to me."

It was foolishness, because the Eye couldn't speak; yet he had to bridge the gulf between them with the sense of what he wanted. The Eyes were hypnotists, teleports—why not telepaths, too?

The shadows rose to buffet his brain and the swirls eddied in his mind's eye, round and round, softly hitting against the tight part of his thought and being repelled by the force of will he had developed. He was getting nowhere.

Perhaps… He shuddered, a great rolling tremor that shook his body. He threw back his head and gave himself over to Fate. There was no other way. He had to drop all his defenses if he hoped to make the contact. If this was to be his time to walk away lead-footed, then he would consciously allow it. He hardly cared, anyway.

As he relaxed and threw away his guard, the shadows grew to towering giants and the swirls hit him like a tornado, twisting his mind to dizzy heights and dashing it down again. The Eye blinked. And then he couldn't see it. He was blind with the clouds it was forming on the screen of his brain, and there was only blackness.

He struggled to recapture some of his will to fight the shadows back, but it was too late. The shadows had him, possessed him fully, and he was alone before the Eye, he belonged to the Eye.

The blackness lightened and a moving shape crept in. Visions followed the shape—visions that were unknowable because of their alienness. He couldn't understand.

The visions cleared, and a voice without substance whispered into his mind; it ignored his ears and whispered directly into the grayness of his brain; a voice that wasn't a voice, that didn't really speak, but that put intelligible thoughts into his head. These he could understand. They were stilted, but he could understand them.

"You cannot comprehend my pictures," the whisper painted on his brain. "So I will employ language."

Linc trembled. Was this victory? His vision was clear now, but he no longer wanted to look. He was riveted to the blue of the Eye and it filled him up completely.

"Can you not answer?" the whisper came again.

How? Linc thought. How could he return the whisper?

"That is how," the whisper said. "Just let it form in your mind and I will know."

"Then you are telepaths, too…" Linc was exultant.

"There are few mental powers lost to us. We are all powerful."

The boast brought Linc back out of awe. The situation was weird, and should have been wondrous—this meeting of two alien forms of life, two alien worlds. But he felt only hatred and revulsion, and the strong, strong need to destroy. This was no historic meeting, but a foray. He was here for information.

"You shall have it," the Eye whispered, "I wanted you for the same reason. The time of groping has come to an end. Now we must make contact, and you must hear my demands and comply. Do you wish to question for your information? Or would you rather that I relate?"

"Both," thought Linc. "I have no prepared questions at the moment. Tell me what you need to tell me, then I'll ask."

The Eye swayed, adjusting its position, "I see in your mind that you already know a great deal of the truth. We are from space, yes. We are telepaths, yes. We can teleport, yet what you have seen is not true teleportation. It is extension—more wonderful than the other. It is a matter of removing an organ completely from the body, severing and healing the connections, yet still keeping mental contact; then returning, reconnecting and healing to become whole again." It paused, returning to enumerate its powers. "And we are radioactive, as you suspected. You have done remarkably well in your guessing."

Linc laughed inside himself, a rueful grunt of a laugh. The first praise he had received in all this fight had to come from an Eye itself. From a hated, abominable, killing Eye.

"You are too harsh in your judgment of us." The Eye answered his laughter. "We have only done what we needed to survive. Our history is desperate. Now I will start the relating, giving you facts to digest.

"My people came originally from a planet that was spawned radioactive. We evolved there, on Zine, adjusting and using the radiation as the basis for our life. Zine was barren compared with Earth; yours is heavily crowded with growth, green and animal. All that existed for us was the radioactivity. It is a great commentary on my race that we learned to develop and adapt ourselves to the use of it.

"But then, even as you will do one day, we used up our foodstuff, our radiation source. Only, contrary to your resources, ours was not replaceable. We had accommodated ourselves to accepting the great amounts of radiation our planet cloaked us with, and we couldn't accommodate backward, so we eventually used it up, exhausted it. Thus in the end we had to leave. We migrated in our machines, taking what we could, searching for another radioactive planet. We were separated during those years—one ship from another—until, to my knowledge, there are only nine of us remaining. The nine from my ship. There may be others, of course, but far from here, and it is a sadness to think that they will never find this place and perhaps never save themselves."

"But Earth isn't radioactive!" Linc argued.

"Not in and of itself. But there are belts about it in space that drew us here, and enough radiation in your atmosphere to keep us here, searching for its source. We were gravely disappointed when we found that this source was artificial, that it had to be produced, and that you and your kind were the only ones who could produce it."

"You mean the bombs we tested?"

"The bombs—yes. But they were not enough for us. We have used up most of their remains. Thus we searched further and found this place. Here you constantly create radioactivity. Enough to draw us. You can, as you put it, test more bombs here, for you know the way. This is what we want."

Radioactivity? Linc tried to absorb the vast array of information the Eye was feeding him, and to bring up questions that were to the point, but it was difficult. He wasn't quite himself, quite his own.

"Then you didn't crash here by accident?" he finally asked.

"Of course not. Why should we have an accident? We chose this place and sank our ship into the coolness of the Earth, always to be near this place. We wanted the dark of the ground to protect us. Your gravity is too intense. We can barely move on your Earth. We are too large, and accustomed to far less gravity. It is difficult. Thus to save our energy, we hit on the method of sending our sensory-visual organs about. This requires little energy, whereas if we tried to move ourselves, we would exhaust your meager, artificial supply within hours.

"The horrors you have perpetrated on our defenseless eyes shall not soon be forgotten. But we had to persist in spite of them. We need another—bomb, I think you called it. We need radioactivity. The natural radiation of your planet is enough to keep us alive, but we need freedom of movement, freedom to live comfortably."

"And that's why you sent Hendricks to blow the reactor?" Linc understood now.

"We have searched the minds of countless men for the ones who have the secret of the bombs. He, alone, had it here. But we failed in the new situation and he didn't complete his mission. We want this place—this reactor—to be free to feed us, and the bombs free to feed us. We must have more food."

"This searching of minds—is this what caused those people to return brainless?"

"I suppose it is. We drained the knowledge from them, wiped them clean for what we needed. It is unfortunate that they were changed, but they will grow again."

"They're all dead!" Linc shot back, hatred replacing his docility.

The whisper voice was still, and there was a feeling of shock, followed quickly by a sense that it was, after all, too bad, but necessary.

"Radioactivity kills us," Linc thought on. "You eat it—but it kills us. Just being in the hole with you killed all of those people."

"I see." The whisper was hesitant. "Then I take it you would be opposed to testing all of your bombs at once—to letting us have a huge quantity of food in reserve?"

"You're damn right we'd be opposed. We couldn't do it. It would ruin our world."

"For you, yes, but not, of course, for us."

"And we don't care about you, so that's an easy decision."

"Too quick a decision. You are overlooking our power when you stand here, dwarfed before me, and say you do not care that this pitiful remnant of a great race is lacking comfort."

"I'm forgetting nothing."

"No. I see you aren't," the Eye whispered, "I see in your mind an anger. I do not appreciate threats against my people. Therefore I will counter your threat with another. If we do not have our way, then we will spread ourselves about, and if we die, millions of you will die, too. It will be a death struggle between two races, and we shall win it. We will cover great distances and take millions of you captive. We will sear the minds of all of you! There will be none of you left to run this world. You are an arrogant people, we have seen that. But your arrogance will shrivel before our hypnotic power, and you will all become cringing dead men. All like the ones we released from the hole—mindless idiots!"

Linc's swiftly thought threat had backfired. If the Eyes weren't given their radiation, then they would cast themselves worldwide and do to the minds of millions what they had done to Wes. And there was no way to prevent them, not when they could teleport pieces of themselves, shrink and grow at will, rejoin shattered parts of their bodies.

They needed no physical strength—the power of their mentality was enough to conquer the Earth. The natural radiation of the planet was enough to keep them alive, to keep them conscious; and consciousness was all they needed to sear out the minds of every man, woman and child on Earth. In any such struggle, they would win.

Yet there was hope. There were only nine of them, after all.

"That is a false hope," came his answer. "You are thinking—nine Zines, eighteen Eyes. Why do you presume it must be *Eyes?* All the atoms of a body are one—all cells are one, belonging to one controlling mind. We could send a hand to capture, just as well as an eye. It is not the organ, but the brain behind it that hypnotizes. Therefore, why not separate cells?"

Linc stood mute and stunned. Separate cells? That would mean millions of hypnotizing agents—millions exploding out of the hole all at once to saturate the Earth and capture the minds of every living human being. Millions of cells controlled by each monster. No one could escape that—not a mind or a soul anywhere. The monsters would decompose their bodies, keeping only the brain, and each separate cell would become an agent of hypnotic destruction. In the end, the cells would return to the monsters, rejoin them as the Eyes had done, and the monsters would be whole again.

"In our worldwide search, somewhere we will find the men who control the bombs," the Eye continued, "and with them, we will bring down a rain of radioactivity on your nation, on your world, and feed ourselves."

"What am I supposed to say?" Linc demanded. "If we do as you ask, it will kill us; if we refuse, *you* will kill us. You're leaving us no choice. It's useless for us even to talk."

"Are not nine of us greater than millions of you? Are we not more important? To me, we are."

"Then you've decided and I can't do any more good here."

"Perhaps you can. Perhaps we can compromise for the present. For I must think of our future. The time of reproduction—of splitting ourselves into fours—will soon arrive, and I must think of our regeneration. Our new, divided selves will require food, too. Therefore, I am willing to compromise for the present."

The Eye was smirking with its victory and Linc knew that the compromise was no concession to him or the human race, just a delay against the inevitable day of destruction. But he would accept the delay.

"Give us a bomb within three days, before we lose patience with this subsistence feeding entirely. Then a week later, give us another, and another a week after that, and so on. This is a good plan and a good compromise."

"But it isn't!" Linc objected. "It would be a slower annihilation for us, but still annihilation. We couldn't keep that up for very long without killing ourselves. The expense alone—"

"I see you picturing yourselves as slaves to us. That is of no matter to me. You are slaves to us already. As for the danger to your people, you must work that out among yourselves. This is a compromise, and I am bending a great deal to offer it. You will have to accept. You have no other choice."

Linc was caught between the two impossible choices. He had nothing to say or to think. He was done.

"Good," the Eye answered his unspoken words. "You have realized your position. Now we will accomplish something. We will quit this communication and you will return to your people and arrange for the first bomb. Within three days, remember. And again, two days after that. It will be beautiful to return to full energy. Maybe then we can even overcome this terrible gravity and find our place in the greatness we used to possess. Your Earth will do as our home. We can become used to its crowdedness."

Immediately as the words whispered across his brain, the contact broke, and Linc was himself again, alone beside the lab, staring into the watery-blue of the giant Eye. The Eye was blank and alien, all contact gone. It swayed, then bobbed up, hitting him with the breeze of its wake. It zoomed away toward the woods, leaving him gazing stupidly after it, like the insignificant thing it believed him to be.

He had a report to make—a long report—he thought, as he went doggedly back to Iverson.

So the end of the world had come, and he wondered if it wouldn't actually be better to give them what they wanted—a big bang that shook the globe and killed everyone at once—than to drag it out and perish inch by inch in the fall-out from the monsters' food?

CHAPTER SIXTEEN

THE MEETING in Iverson's office was an echo of the previous ones. Iverson, Stanley and Collins at first listened to his report eagerly, then slowly fell into despondency. When Linc concluded, not even Collins was gloating over the fact that his bombing plan was not only acceptable, but demanded by the Eyes themselves.

"We're lost, aren't we?" Stanley murmured, the discipline and fight gone out of him. No one answered, and he continued, listing points for his own clarification. "If we give them the radiation, it will eventually kill us all. Certainly it will when they have reproduced, dividing into fours. Do you realize that it means thirty-six of them the first time alone? They'll want more radiation—thirty-six need more than nine. The next time there will be one hundred and forty-four, and we'll surely be drowned in the fall-out."

"Nevertheless, we have to do it," Iverson said. "We have to commit racial suicide, and within three days, because if we don't, they'll do it for us. I can't stand to think of them separating and sending their cells out. The horror alone would be too much for a normal mind to tolerate. If they do it, there won't be a sane or sensible person left in the world within a week. Or we'll all go fast when they find the right men and blow up the bomb stockpiles. We're lost, all right. The whole Earth is lost to man and animal. It belongs to the Zines from now on."

Despite their previous opposition to him, Linc felt the need to encourage them. Yet he could find no encouragement in the threats. The Zines had hemmed them in, and there was nothing to do but surrender up the Earth to the greater power and greater horror of the monsters from space.

"Unless they're bluffing," Collins interjected, "unless they read your mind and are bluffing, and the bombing will kill them, after all."

"How?" Linc asked. "If they can separate their cells and bring them back together again, they can't be killed by an explosion. They heal themselves. We've all seen it. Explode them, and they'll simply gather in their atomized particles and fuse them together again."

"But maybe the bomb would entomb them in the hole, and—"

"You can't entomb them! Not when they can teleport." Linc stood, worn out. "If there was a way to weaken them, to weaken them to the point where they couldn't use their mental powers to full advantage, we'd have a chance. But that's out, too. There's enough radiation on Earth itself to keep them alive and able without our artificial help. We may as well face it. We're going to have to give them their bomb in three days, and then another and another, and that's all there is to it."

As the stark truth settled over the room, he said brief good-byes and left. He had fought and lost. He wanted no more of this struggling for a nonexistent answer. Stanley and Collins didn't need him; they had made that plain before. They didn't like him or need him, and he let resentment take him and lead him home.

Ichabod received him joyously, and he stooped to pat the little dog's head, then set out his dinner. The dog ate like a small wolf, and Linc remembered the way Wes had joked about it, and he said the same joking words aloud in the kitchen, just to fill the silence.

He cooked dinner for himself, then sat despondently in the living room. For the first time in his life he was completely unsure. He had always envisioned himself as invincible, and certainly his past record supported that self-image. Now, suddenly, he was defeated. He was a small man, invincible in small crises; but bring on a big one and he was through.

Two hours passed and the day waned and Ichabod awoke from his nap. His feet clicked on the wood, fell silent on the carpet, and then he was there before Linc, one paw raised and brushing Linc's knee, a high whine in his nose, and his mouth full of rubber rat.

Linc grinned despite his lethargy. "You want me to throw it, old boy?" he asked the spotted dog.

Ichabod immediately dropped the rat, wet and forlorn, on the carpet. Linc picked it up, squeezed it to produce the artificial noise Ichabod dearly loved, and heaved it into the dining room. The dog tore away after it, skidding on the waxed floor. He snuffled it around a bit, then brought it back. Linc repeated the game, once, twice, five times, until Ichabod's fat stomach panted for breath.

"Enough, friend," Linc told him. "You've got to watch your heart. You're too fat."

He straightened, realizing what he was doing. In the deadly silence of the house, in the loneliness, he was talking to the dog as Wes had talked to him, treating Ichabod as someone willing to listen and share. He started to reproach himself, then said, "What the hell," and patted his lap as Wes had always done to coax the dog into it. Ichabod jumped up, turned around and sat down. Linc stroked the hard, springy hair. The smell of the dog was strong, but not unpleasant.

"Whatever you are, I think I'm beginning to understand. You're automatic companion and mind-eraser combined, aren't you?"

Ichabod swiveled his head about and licked Linc's chin.

"Maybe I've missed a lot, ignoring you. But then, you didn't offer much either. It was always and only Wes."

The dark, dog eyes stared into his, partly puzzled, partly sad, like all dog eyes. "I don't blame you for being confused, little dog. I guess you never had such problems thrust upon you. But, you see, I'm in a blind alley, and I haven't found a way out."

The phone bell erupted into the quiet, and Ichabod sat bolt upright. "Pay no attention," Linc quieted him. "We're not going to answer it. Let them consider us evacuated, or dead. Tomorrow we're going to be evacuated. I have enough power of my own left to get both of us out safely. And, by heaven, we're not going to stay here and be irradiated to death."

His voice covered the continued jangling of the phone, and then it stopped and he sat back, his hands on the dog's body. Ichabod was warm and the steady rhythm of his breathing was comforting. Linc cast his doubts aside and accepted friendship where he found it.

During the next hour, the phone rang eight times, and there was one knock on the door. It wasn't late, yet outside it was dark with the early twilight of autumn. Linc didn't put on any lights. Let everyone think him gone. Tomorrow he would be.

When he dozed in the chair with Ichabod, the dog left him to stretch out more comfortably on the carpet. The clock striking eight woke him. No sooner had the last chime faded than another pounding came at his door. After a short wait, a key fitted into the lock, clicked, and the door opened. The lights snapped on, and Kelly stood there, looking anxious.

"For heaven's sake, you're home," she said. "I thought you'd left the dog all alone from the way he was barking."

"No. We've been keeping each other company."

"And not answering phones."

"Were you the one who called?" he asked.

"I called twice. It was time for Ichabod's dinner, and I wanted to be sure you were here to feed him."

"We're a fine pair. The world is coming apart around us, and all we're concerned about is a dog."

"I intend to stay concerned. Ichabod belonged to Wes—I intend to be concerned as long as Ichabod lives."

"If you're concerned about anything else, you've come to the wrong place." As he looked at her, the old guilt came back to stifle him.

"I've come to the only place I have," Kelly said. "To the only person I have left—or care a damn about. I heard about your experience today."

"How did you hear? I imagined it would be top secret."

"Dr. Iverson called me. He's been trying to reach you."

"I suspected as much when the phone wouldn't stop ringing. I have no further business with him."

"He wants you back on the team. He said that whether or not anything was accomplished, he'd like to have you there—that he'd feel more secure with you behind him."

Kelly slipped out of her coat and switched on more lights. "It's too dark and morbid in here."

"You may as well use them all. Before long there won't be any electricity. There won't be any more anything."

She stopped in the middle of a motion, and studied him. Her green eyes were soft and concerned. There was something different about her, although Linc couldn't exactly pinpoint it. All the teasing had gone out of her voice, the flirting from her eyes; she was suddenly more woman than girl—and, he could have sworn, sincere for the first time since he'd known her.

She came toward him slowly, and he swung away. He couldn't face it—not the touch, nor the embrace she obviously intended.

"Don't push me off again," she pleaded. "If we're all either of us have left, why can't we be together? Is it still because you don't trust me?"

Linc shrugged.

"You can trust me now, Linc. In the last few days, I've done a lifetime of growing—growing up, and growing wiser. I've come to my senses, to know myself and you. I realize it sounds trite at this moment, but I love you, Linc. I love you and need you—not as a protector, but as a part of myself."

Linc still avoided direct contact with her.

"You can't deny that you've changed either," she continued. "Those hairs on your coat are dog hairs. You've been holding Ichabod. That tells me a lot. You've come to need, just like everybody else needs. You need to be loved now, and now I can give it to you."

She was saying that the change in him had made it possible for her to find affection where she hadn't before. Could that be true?

"Before, you always had to be the one to give. You wanted to wait on me, to order me. By caring for the little things, you thought you could demand the bigger things. I couldn't face that."

"But that's not true at all," he protested, "I catered to you simply because I knew no other way; I had no other way. I wasn't Wes, who could ply you with poetry and gentleness."

Kelly shook her head, wonderingly. "I never saw it that way. I never understood."

"It doesn't matter now." He tried to put an end to the mutual confession. "All that is done."

"It is not! If we've both changed and become new human beings, then don't deny these new beings a chance. Linc, the guilt is past. What we did is done, and keeping apart will never rectify it. You still have work to do. Despite what you're feeling now, you're the only one who has a prayer of solving this terrible problem. And you can't do it if you're torn, and denying yourself the things you need. Admit them, and then get on with your work."

"I have no work."

"You're simply discouraged. Don't you see, Linc, if there's a hope left in the world, that hope is you. You are the only man to make contact with the Eyes, to ever stand against them and come out alive. No one else can do what you can do. You know things no one else knows. You've experienced things they've only heard secondhand. Yes, and if it comes to it, no one else can even go down swinging as well as you."

He stared at her, absorbing what she said and weighing it. Something stirred in him in answer to her, because she was making such sense. He wanted to express it, but all that came forth was, "You have changed, Kelly...astoundingly."

"That's what I've been trying to tell you." She sat down beside him. He didn't shy away. Her hand covered his, and then her arms were about him, and he was holding her closely and tightly. His sense of guilt ebbed in the embrace. He had paid the debt.

She murmured into his ear," I think we're worthy of each other now. We've grown up, and I had a terrible lot of it to do."

"And I," he answered, "I've discovered my own weaknesses, finally, and surprisingly enough, it hasn't made me vulnerable."

He kissed her, then drew her still closer. All that he had wanted a few weeks before was suddenly his, born out of horror and guilt and despair, but his. And all the sweeter because of it.

"I don't ever want to move again," he said to her.

"No, Linc. We can have tonight. But tomorrow I must give you back to Iverson. Promise that you'll go?"

CHAPTER SEVENTEEN

THE LAB WAS DESERTED, with only a skeleton crew on duty, but this morning it held no loneliness for Linc. He was still discouraged, but not lonely. Kelly had filled that gap.

He wandered the halls, looking in on the reactor, hunting halfheartedly for Iverson, ending up in the artificial-gravity room. This was the actual heart of the lab. The rest was icing, built to support it. Here was Iverson's heart, too. This room was the culmination of years of study, the focus of many lives, and the hope for the future of space travel. Designed to create gravity, it was already partly successful. The principles learned here applied to a space cabin could make men's journey into the stars bearable.

Now, he wondered, would there ever be such a journey to the stars? The stars had come to them and promised to drain the Earth.

A sound at the door turned him around, and Iverson was there, hesitant, not quite sure what to say.

"You, too, Doc?" Linc murmured.

"Me, too? Oh—you mean being drawn to this room. Yes, me, too. I suppose I came to be a morbid witness of the end of this, and everything else we have worked for. I didn't expect to find you."

Linc made one of the few awkward apologies of his life. "If you'll let me, Dr. Iverson. I'd like to come back. Not that I'll be of any help, but I'll be here."

"*Let* you?" Iverson came all the way in, "I tried to reach you six times last night to ask you to return."

"You're not still hoping I can pull us back from disaster?"

"I suppose I was—last night," the old man admitted. "But, looking at you, I see that you have no such hope. Still, I'm glad you're here. And I wouldn't have said that a month ago."

Linc nodded, "I understand. I was a great trouble-shooter, but not much of a human being." He shifted, uneasy with the ground they were on. "What's the program here?"

"The plan stands. Tomorrow the first bomb will be detonated. Washington has given us the go-ahead, and Collins still hopes the explosion will destroy the Eyes."

"It won't."

"I know it. But men don't throwaway their last hope easily. What bothers me is that we can't finish our evacuation. We've withdrawn all controls. People can leave as they wish, but there will be some who won't go, or who have to stay for other reasons."

"And the ones in the hole," Linc added.

Iverson paced the chamber. "This is a hard blow to an old man, Linc. My life is in this room, thirty years of it. I started research into artificial gravity years ago, working on the side, at my own expense, because I couldn't obtain a grant. Then when the goal is in sight, and I finally get total support and even a *RUSH* priority, it all goes up in smoke. It isn't fair, you know?"

Iverson was older in that moment than Linc had ever seen him—wrinkled and lined and moist-eyed.

"I knew I could never go with them," Iverson continued. "I had no dreams of actually going into space, but I did want to send part of myself, and help them get there."

"We're all in the same boat, Doc. We must face the brute fact that no one is needed anymore. The monsters will run our world, and gravity is the last thing they'll need. Earth has too much of it for them."

"Yes—the great slugs. Earth wasn't made for them! Can't they see that? Earth isn't a dead, radioactive world!"

"On the other hand," Linc mused, following his own line of thought, "if the Eyes knew about this room, they might demand use of it. Here, with the mechanism working in reverse, gravity could be lessened, and they'd be comfortable."

"It doesn't work in reverse."

"I know it. But you could fix it so it did. You might salvage your work, after all." He was offering anything he could, to erase the dreadful despair from Iverson's face.

"I wouldn't spend a minute of my effort to accommodate them. I'll go down with the rest of the human race."

Linc no longer heard him. His mind had caught hold of his own words and was busy with their implications. He sat up straighter.

"Doc!" he cried. "Maybe...How many G's can this room create?"

"That's top secret," Iverson replied automatically.

"But can it duplicate any more than Earth normal?"

"It can. And secrets don't apply now, do they? This room can make five G's. It's a side effect. I only wanted Earth normal, but in getting it, I got more than I bargained for."

"Five gravities. That should do it."

"Should do what?"

"Iverson—we have to kill those monsters, right? To be rid of them, we have to kill them, and so far that has seemed impossible."

"It is impossible. They heal themselves."

"They heal, yes. But what is their greatest fear, their greatest worry? Food! And that's how we must kill them, by starving them to death. They can't heal starvation."

"I see your point, and it's finally the right point. But how?"

"We haven't much time, and I'll need help all down the line. I want to use this room. I want to use men. Will you help me?"

"Sight unseen, and unheard?"

"I'll give you the details, but it has to be fast. If this works at all, it will take a lot of equipment and a lot of risk. I'm going to lure those monsters here, where I can control them."

"You mean to say you've come up with a plan?"

"What I've hit upon is an idea. I haven't time to plan it out. I can only play it by ear and pray that it evolves into a plan. Here…" Linc picked up a pencil and scribbled fast on a piece of paper. "I'm writing out your part. Work fast and get it ready, Doc." He handed the paper to Iverson.

"Lead shields?" Iverson grunted. "But why?"

"Just get everything on that list and put it where I've written. Right now I have to get to the hole. If I fail in this part, the whole thing's off. Pray for me."

He didn't wait for objections. Iverson would surely object to his endangering himself when he was the only man who knew the plan. Yet what he had in mind could barely be called a plan. It was a hunch that for the moment rested on lead shields, bait and a tremendous risk. The risk was his.

The approach to the hole hadn't changed. The National Guard was still dug in, though further back. He gave them laurels for their persistence. He drove as close to the pit as possible, then walked the rest of the way.

As he walked, he thought fast. How did you lie to a telepathic mind? It had picked his brain before; but then he had been off guard. Perhaps by using great will power, by covering the truth with layer after layer of sheer will, he could bring it off. It would be a deadly game.

The entrance was astir with moving shadows. Two Eyes rose out of the depths of the earth. He closed his mind as completely as he could and prepared to battle for every second of his life.

He called them, "Can any of you hear me?"

The Eyes watched him but made no swirls in his head. They were leaving him alone, "I have to talk," Linc shouted inside his mind, switching to their level of communication.

The two Eyes parted, making room between them, and out of the hole, sailed a huge one, watery-blue, and although they all looked alike, he recognized it as his one-time prisoner.

"Then you did hear?" he asked.

"I heard. You have disturbed us. Why?"

"I've come with a proposal—another compromise. I must be heard."

"Have you come with your answer? Will the bomb be tested on the third day?"

"If you deny my new proposal, it will. But my compromise is a better way, a surer way. Will you listen?" He was sticking close to the truth, using the truth to conceal the lie, and hoping the lie stayed covered.

"I sense great excitement in you," the Eye whispered. "You are disturbed."

"I'm worried," he answered. "So much depends upon this meeting. It's natural for me to be worried. Please overlook it."

A sense of doubt came into his brain, and he knew he had failed to win the confidence of the creature. He had to win its trust to keep the Eye from searching deeper. He tried the first thing that popped into mind—flattery.

"I've told my people what you said. We realize what we are up against—your greatness, your power. That you crossed the stars, that alone places us in great awe of you. And, of course, we realize the futility of denying you. We're prepared to meet your demands. Only, we've thought of a better way."

The doubting subsided slightly. "How can there be a better way?" the Eye asked. "*We* have thought of this one, so how can there be a better?"

"Forgive me," Linc continued with servility. "I don't mean to question your plan. It's a good plan—for you. But we must consider ourselves, too. You'd think us fools if we didn't. And in the long run, our plan would secure life. Otherwise, your days might still be numbered."

There was a new stirring among the Eyes, and Linc realized that all three of them were listening to him.

"Explain yourself," came the whispered command.

He drew a deep breath to calm his agitation, and said, "I tried to tell you before what radiation would do to my people—even the sporadic radiation you demanded as your compromise. It matters very little whether the bombs are all exploded at once, or one at a time over a long period. The result for us would be the same. To create an atmosphere sufficiently radioactive for you would kill us. And then you would have no one to continue creating the radiation, and ultimately you would die, too."

A mental grunt thrust out at him. "We hadn't considered that point. It is well taken. But what is the alternative?"

"My new proposal." He let concern rise to shield the lie he was about to speak, and pulled bits of truth in to cover it further. "If you will consent to controlled feeding, then we can all be safe. If you allow us to protect ourselves, then we will live to go on feeding you."

"That is logical. But what is this controlled feeding?"

"I want to take you away from here—out of this place—to the laboratory. You know the lab." He looked directly at the watery-blue one. "There we can provide you with all the radiation you need. We create it there. We take ordinary substances and make them violently radioactive, enough to give you food and energy forever."

"And how would you remain safe?" the Eye asked.

"By shielding ourselves. With you in the lab, there would be no need of bombs and fall out. We could protect ourselves against the radiation by staying away while you absorbed your energy. We have equipment to protect us there. You could feast as often as you liked and we could still remain safe and able to prepare you further feasts."

As he blurted out the thoughts, he immediately filled his brain with pleading and worry, blotting out the real truth that threatened to creep forward. He kept his mind vibrating with hope and anxiety. If he slipped just once...just once...

"If you slipped just once in what?" the Eye demanded.

He grew suddenly cold, with a chill that spread down his spine. "If I slip just once in my duty, in my effort to convince you, then I have killed my own people," he covered quickly.

It was obviously good enough, for the Eye dug no deeper.

"What is your answer?" he hurried on before they could question him. "If you agree, I can begin preparations immediately. By tomorrow, you will be with me and enjoying a full diet."

"You understand the amount of radiation we require?" The Eye stressed the point. "We absorb tremendous quantities. The more active we are, the more radiation we need. We will not want to be held down. We do not intend to pass the rest of our existence unable to get about. We will need sufficient energy to nullify your gravity. Can you supply this much without a bomb?"

"Better than with a bomb. It can be concentrated—all for you, not dispersed in the atmosphere."

The Eyes hovered closely together, and he wished that he could read them. But they had shut him out of their thoughts. His thoughts were theirs whenever they wanted them, but they were able to shut him out.

"You must decide quickly," he urged. "This will take longer to prepare than a bomb."

"We see the haste clearly in your mind," the Eye answered. "It almost hides everything else. Why are you so much in a hurry?"

"I've already told you."

"Very well. We believe you. And we have conferred with our brothers. It has been a long journey through space. A long, hungry journey, and the hopes you conjure of our again knowing satiation are too tempting to ignore. We will do it your way—not out of concern for you and your kind, you realize, but because we value you as providers and wish to keep you safe to continue providing."

"I couldn't expect such as you to care for us," Linc said. It was a two-sided thought. They caught the side he had tired to keep for himself.

"You do not like us! You pretend flattery, but do not like us!"

"You are a threat to us. What else can you expect? We stand in awe of you. Isn't that enough for the present? We are offering to supply your needs. Isn't that enough?"

All thought erased from his mind, he waited for the answer, for it would be the final one.

"It is enough," the answer came, "We will wait for you until tomorrow. Come for us, and we will try your proposal, fully confident that if it does not suit us we can change it at any time. We have that ability. You have seen it. You would not dare deceive us, for that would be the signal for us to spread and bring an end to you."

"We would not dare," Linc assured the Eye, "I know that better than anyone else, for I've shared your thoughts. Tomorrow, then. I'll come with men and we'll transport you to the lab. I won't ask you to walk. I realize how difficult our gravity is for you. In the meantime, can we consider it settled, and that you will take no more people from us?"

"We have no need of them. Out of all of them, we found only one who was of help to us. Three others had glimmerings of help, but not enough. It is strange that your kind lives so separately. We expected all to know what one knows."

The Eye was referring to Hendricks—then to Myers, Bennet and Wes. "We don't have your power of mind," Linc said. He wanted to get away now. He was exhausted from the long pretense, the long struggle to keep secrets from them.

"You may go." The Eye read his wish. "Prepare our way. And do it well!"

He retreated from the hole with shivers running down his back where they continued to watch him out of sight. He had carried it off, but he wasn't sure he could relax. This contact had held no shadows or swirls; it had been clean and easy, so he had no way of knowing when it was broken.

As he reached his car, he shrugged his worries off. He had to consider the contact broken, for he needed to think out the plan. What would come of it, he didn't know, but his courage, absent for so many days, was back, and along with it fresh hope and confidence.

CHAPTER EIGHTEEN

THEY LEFT the flat vans parked at the edge of the woods and walked the road together, carrying the great stretchers. They walked the road, clad in the awkwardness of radiation suits, and they were all together—all but Linc. He was apart from them through the necessity of keeping the plan to himself.

These Guardsmen who had volunteered to join Kellroy knew only that they were to transport the Zines to the Lab, and that the creatures would be fed a sumptuous dose of radioactivity. That was all they knew, and therefore all the Eyes could pick from their brains.

Linc knew the truth, and he set in play the emotions he had found effective in jamming the discovery that he was lying. For now the plan was set and he had more to cover than before.

The men halted at the start of the ramp. Kellroy swung to Linc. "Do we go down?"

"We have to," Linc answered. "They can't take a step. But don't let that give you any ideas. They don't need physical strength."

"And I don't need to be told." Kellroy was defensive. Linc paid no attention. He had specifically asked for Kellroy, wanting the man's bravery and level-headedness. "I still don't understand the 'whys' of it," Kellroy complained. "Why should we cater to them?"

"To save ourselves," Linc told him. It was what Kellroy had to believe. "Come on, Lieutenant, order your men down."

The branches were nearly bare about them, the color gone with the wind and morning rain, and these steps down, Linc knew, would demand all the courage these soldiers had in their bodies.

As the order was passed along, and a stiffening was visible among the men, Linc took the first stride onto the ramp.

He knew his way too well. Soon the light would fade and there would be darkness, and that in turn would bloom into the violet glow of the Eyes' radiation. Terror breathed with him as he walked, remembering the other time. The men behind him mustn't see the terror. He had to set the example because he had been here before.

The darkness waxed thick and a stench came to meet him. The stench of dirty human bodies and the special stench of the creatures themselves. It hadn't been so strong before. But the sodden air, heavy from the rain, had crept this way and held it inside the earth.

At the point where the glow should have sprung up to light the way, only a vague dimness met him. And it grew better as he progressed. "The men with lights," he shouted, "turn them on."

Light shafted out from behind him like horizontal pillars. He reached the bottom of the ramp and swung to the right.

In the cavern, he stepped carefully among the people who squatted there, staring at nothing, knowing nothing, vomiting and sighing. Sick, mindless and dying, they screamed at him with their silence to help, to revenge, to retch himself, but he picked his way through them, ignoring them. He had to set the example.

Against the far wall was the semicircle of limbed whales he had witnessed before. Different from before was their faintness of glow. They were weak from lack of radiation, but not dying, he reminded himself. Never dying, these creatures, for the Earth alone could support them, even if uncomfortably. The light of the lamps hit them suddenly and they were horrors.

Giant, bloated things, black and shiny, they watched him come with their now little eyes. Pig eyes—eight inches across, but still pig eyes in the bulk of their bodies.

The men stopped and he couldn't blame them, but couldn't let them spread fear to each other either. "Let's work!" he shouted. Nothing could go wrong now, or Earth was doomed under the promised assault of hypnotizing cells.

A boy grunted close to Kellroy. His head drew back, his mouth opened, and a cry of anguish echoed through the cavern. He fled, and his footsteps were loud as he made for fresh air.

Kellroy was quick to take control. "Get those stretchers spread out and start helping the Zines on. Move!"

The men didn't respond, caught between panic and the need to obey. Linc and Kellroy acted together, grabbing the nearest stretcher and spreading it open by the semicircle of bloated things that waited and watched with their empty, alien eyes. As they did so, the other men spread theirs, too.

Together with three others, Linc and Kellroy reached for one of the creatures. Linc remembered the feel of the Eye he had pushed into the cage, and his hands didn't want to touch the shiny black skin, but he forced them forward. He made contact, and the skin was cold—not slimy, but cold and hard, almost a shell. It was evolved to absorb and withstand the burn of radiation. It would have to be thick and protecting.

They heaved to lift the great form and barely raised it from the ground. As they shifted it to the stretcher, the appendages that were arms and legs flapped against them, and even with the strain of the weight, gooseflesh erupted on Linc's skin. When the Zine was settled, Linc wanted to wipe his hands and shudder. He didn't dare. Instead, he said inside his mind, "Are you comfortable?"

"Fairly," the creature whispered back. "Get on with this. If your plan doesn't work, and soon, we will demand a bomb."

"Right away." Linc mentally bowed and scraped.

He supervised the loading of the others and when it was done, a new problem arose. There was no path through the squatting people, and carrying the weight, the men couldn't pick their way.

"Would you clear a path for us?" Linc asked the shape that housed a watery-blue Eye he thought he recognized.

"Walk over them," was the answer.

He took the chance of angering the thing, and countered, "My men won't do that. Neither will I."

He got no answer, but almost immediately the crowded people rose and shuffled off to the sides. The ones who were too far-gone into idiocy to obey themselves were pulled aside by the others. The path was clear.

"Thank you," Linc said.

"It is of no importance. Get on with your promise."

The men bent down, six to a stretcher, and hefted the Zines into the air, walking in a dirge-like rhythm toward the ramp. The people along the sides of the cavern paid them no attention. Their captors were leaving, but they didn't know. They were free, but they didn't care. They had nothing left to know or to care with.

Bearing the weight of the stretchers was exhausting, but they finally emerged into the sun. In the brightness of day, the creatures looked even more grotesque. Like huge, shiny seals, only lacking their sleekness and grace, but blubbery and bloated, they rode on their stretchers, blinking about with their reinstated eyes. They were obscenities in the forest, for they were not of the Earth, and it was impossible to believe that they were even of God.

One by one the men loaded them, three to a van, then climbed inside the cabs and jammed into the available cars to avoid riding with the things.

Linc found the alien with the blue Eye he had communicated with earlier and clambered into the van. He had to ride with the creatures. He had no choice but to ride along and reassure them, thinking his lie, so they wouldn't come looking for him mentally and unnoticed and catch him thinking the truth.

The ride was interrupted only once, when going over a bump a creature felt discomfort, and emitted a sound that was hair-raising. It was half-roar, half-yelping scream.

The lab, coming into sight, was a great relief. Linc was already worn from the mental battle, but primed himself for his greatest effort, and jumped down.

"You know the room we have prepared for them," he told Kellroy. "See that they're placed there gently. I'll find Iverson and get their feast ready."

"Will it be soon?" a whisper asked.

"Very soon. Don't tax yourselves."

He left quickly and strode the halls to Iverson's office. The old man looked at him warily, wanting to ask, but not daring.

"We'll have to chance it," Linc answered his unspoken question. "I can't tell if they're tuned to me or not, but we'll have to chance it. Have you got the piece of hot stuff?"

"All ready," Iverson bobbed his head. "It's in that shielded box over there. Now be sure you don't stay one second in the room with it, or you're as good as dead. The lead plating is ready. The men are ready. All that remains is for you to say the word."

"I'll say it soon enough. Are you all straight on your part?"

"Straight and eager. It's an unfamiliar feeling. I thought it was gone forever. You'll have your G's when you need them."

"They're all in place," Kellroy called as he stuck his head in.

Linc went to the corner and picked up the lead box by its carrying handle. "Here we go," he muttered softly.

The men he passed on his way to the artificial gravity room where the creatures were housed wore strained faces and clenched fists. The tension was high and tight about him, and it rasped in his own voice as he whispered to them to get set.

He entered the artificial gravity room, keeping all thought of its formal name from his mind. It was full now—full of the shiny, nakedly glowing black bodies with their Eyes.

"I've brought it," he said mentally.

"Only that?" one of them whispered back.

"It's enough. You'll see."

He set the box close to the bulk of one of the Zines.

"Don't touch it yet," he warned. "It's not safe for me, and if you value me at all, you'll let me get clear."

"Get clear? What are your instructions then?"

"Wait until I leave the room and shut the door. Then one of you may open the box. There will be a great flux of radioactivity and you will have your feast. When you're through with this box— have used it up—call, and I'll bring another."

"Very well," came the thought. And Linc caught a mental image of hunger, and salivation, and gluttony.

"We've shielded this room from the outside so none of your radiation can escape and harm us." He began the biggest part of the lie, clouding it over, concentrating on dual thoughts—what he was communicating and joy and relief at being near safety. "By the same token, none of the radiation will be lost. You'll have it all for yourselves. For added protection, we're going to erect more shielding, so if you hear pounding, you'll know what it is. We didn't have time to complete the work this morning."

His lie was accepted, for all he received in response was a hurry-up to get out so the meal could begin.

"When will you close the door so we may safely start?" he was asked, almost in unison.

"Right now. Forgive me for being so slow."

He retreated from the room and closed the door, checking its seal and shielding. The radiation counter they had placed in the room immediately began to sputter. The box was open and the feast was beginning. He smiled. They would gobble it up quickly because they were hungry and thought more was forthcoming. He had carried the mental part off perfectly. Now there only remained the physical.

The men were already moving up to the walls with heavy shields of lead and fastening them into place. In an hour's time the room would be secure against radiation. None would get out—and more importantly, *none would get in.* Not even the background radiation of the Earth would penetrate these walls. The Zines would be cut off entirely from every source of food.

"Good," he called to the men. "Work fast. Make it quick."

As the radiation counter grew less active, indicating that the radiation in the room was dwindling fast, he hurried to Iverson's little control room. The old man was seated before his panel, waiting for the signal.

"Now?" he shouted.

"Now!" Linc cried. "Let them have all five G's!"

The lights blinked, and somewhere buried in the wall machinery started to whir. Inside the room, the gravities piled on top of each other, riveting the Zines to the floor. One, two, three, four, five! And now, Linc figured, it would require effort for them even to breathe. With the energy they'd be expending they would soon use up the effects of their meal and be helpless. Then they would start down the road to starvation, unable to protest, unable to defend themselves. And, he prayed, unable to separate their cells and put through their threatened attack.

He caught Iverson's hand in a hopeful clasp, and went back to help with the lead plates. He lifted one of the pieces into place and was just about to secure it when a cry broke out at his left. He dropped the plate, startled, and looked for its source.

The sight froze him. Sticking through the wall, grasping one of the workmen by the throat, was a bloated arm, one of the shiny, black arms of the Zines. It choked the man into unconsciousness and dropped him with a thud upon the floor. Beside it, an Eye popped through the wall, small and ugly, and expanding. It grew to fill its section of the corridor, and although it wasn't focused on him, Linc could feel its hypnotic power spreading out.

It was fantastic, and the beginning of his worst fears.

What the Eyes had done before, teleporting themselves over the Earth, was nothing compared to this. They had never gone through solid matter. But this proved that they could, and that they hadn't been bluffing in any of their threats.

They were here, in the corridor, and his work crew was being drained as men crumpled to the floor, crushed like dolls by the arms, or shuffled away, hypnotized. And the next step? He shuddered as he realized that the next step would be the appearance of the separate cells, in retaliation and revenge.

His only chance, and Earth's only chance, lay in the hope that the Zines wouldn't realize the full consequences of this situation in time; that they would fight this battle as they had started it, with arms and flying Eyes, and not proceed to the separation into cells. If they did that, then the world was lost.

More arms were coming through. Unattached arms that ended abruptly at the neck, including shoulder muscles for strength. He had to move. He had to do something to protect his men. Where did the Zines get their strength? The gravity should have stopped them.

He grabbed up a length of metal piping and started down the row, banging away at the appendages, making every blow tell. Something grabbed him from behind and pulled him off his feet. It was an arm. He clawed at it, but its grip was beyond his strength. He cried for help, but none came. He was choking in its grasp.

Then Iverson's face was before him, and the old man was hacking away at the arm with a pair of scissors. Watery blood spilled down the front of Linc's shirt and he was free. Together, he and Iverson ran the row, pounding and slashing at the arms and the Eyes, closing their ears to the screams of the dying and the agony that engulfed them. Men were falling. Others were being led away. What had gone wrong?

A staccato barking swung him round. Ichabod was jumping up and down in the hall, his teeth snapping shut on air as he tried for an arm and missed his mark.

"What the devil!" Linc cried out. Before the exclamation was finished, his attention went past Ichabod, and there coming up behind the dog was Kelly, swiveling in stark fear, one hand over her mouth, as she dodged the arms and Eyes that swarmed among the men.

CHAPTER NINETEEN

THEIR EYES MET. Hers showed pure panic, and he started for her, pushing men and Zine arms aside, weaving in and out. A Zine hand emerged from the wall beside him and grabbed for his sleeve, but he slapped it back with a vicious stab of the pipe.

"Linc!" Kelly fell against him. He caught her up, and held her. "I didn't know, Linc! I only wanted to be near you."

"How did you get through the gate?" he demanded. "Didn't the guard—"

"There wasn't any guard." She jerked away from him and screamed, "Ichabod! Stop it! Ichabod!"

The spotted dog had hold of one of the arms and was shaking his head back and forth, growling in his throat. The arm levitated and pulled the animal off his feet. He dangled by his mouth, and the growl changed to a whine. Linc caught him with one hand, and with the other smashed the shiny black claw. It dropped Ichabod into his waiting grasp.

"Now take him and get out!" He thrust the dog at Kelly. "Hurry!" This corridor was pandemonium, and he had to get her to safety.

She obeyed without question, dodging her way toward the door. Halfway down the corridor, an Eye stopped her. It was two feet long, and brown, but there was menace in it.

"Run, Kelly. Don't look at it!" he commanded.

With a taking ahold of herself that was visible even to Linc, Kelly ducked past the Eye and continued for the door. Then an arm, losing its clutch on a workman, arrowed for her and caught her about the shoulders. With a leap Ichabod sank his teeth into it, but it didn't let go.

Linc raced to add his strength to Kelly's struggle. The arm was leathery under his hands, and he tugged and pulled at it with desperate energy. Kelly was growing pale in its grip as it crushed her. Linc put his own teeth to the job, following Ichabod's example, and at the first startled relaxing of the arm, he wrenched it from her. He grabbed up his pipe and struck until it winced and retreated. Then he took Kelly and ran with her to the door, shoving her through.

"Get to the car and stay there!"

She left at a run and he returned to the fight. Half of the workmen were either down or standing stupidly in hypnosis. He had misjudged somewhere. He had counted on the gravity making the Zines use energy so fast that they would be too weak to defend themselves. But he had been wrong, for here they were—parts of them—floating and sailing about the corridor, disembodied and gruesome.

The men who hadn't been attacked by the flying arms concentrated on their work, getting the last of the lead shields in place. But what good would that do if the Eyes weren't subdued?

He went back down the row with his pipe, defending the still working men as best he could. He was exhausted; the muscles in his back and shoulders were like aching sponge, their strength ebbing fast, pain coming up to take them over. Sweat streamed down his face and tears streaked his skin, but he fought on, for this was certainly his doing and he had to make it right.

An Eye settled before him. Before he could attack it, it began to change, and he stepped back. Before his gaze, it shrank. And one of the arms in his field of vision suddenly let go its hold on a workman to hang limply in the air. It faded back into the wall—*back into the wall.*

Just as he started to hope, another arm near him *exploded.* One second it was there and whole, and the next it had disintegrated into particles so small they were nearly invisible; and these, too, exploded until the arm was no longer there.

This was the moment then, and Linc trembled at the immensity of what he had seen. The arm had split into a multitude of separate cells, bent on destruction.

He started to order his men to give up the fight and save themselves, if they could, when a haziness appeared in the empty space where the arm had been. Gradually the space refilled, collecting into larger and larger particles until the arm was again before him. Its shape was whole, but it hung limp and weak. It glided to the wall and seeped slowly through, disappearing back into the room.

All along the corridor, the arms were retreating, tired and spent.

Iverson came up, "What's happening?"

"I think we've made it, Doc. They've finally used up the radiation—all of it—and they're stuck. They tried to make good on their threat too late. They haven't enough energy left to split apart. The gravity took its toll."

Iverson's face was torn with disbelief that ached to turn into acceptance. "Then you think we've won?"

"Not us, Doc. Luck—God—and their own egotism. If they had split sooner, we'd be through now. Pray that they don't rally!"

The workmen halted to watch the weirdness that surrounded them. The last arm was seeping back into the wall, and two of the Eyes followed. The other Eyes hung motionless, something gone out of them—the power and the menace. They shrank, from two feet down to one, and then to eight inches, and they grew dull and off-color. One by one they floated to the wall and slowly, inch by inch, pushed themselves through it, back to their parent horrors, and the sure starvation Linc had planned for them.

The hall was clear and silent.

Iverson, standing beside Linc, was an emaciated caricature of himself, but his face was warm with relief. "You did it," he said to Linc. "*You did it*. And there are no words in the world big enough to thank you."

"There isn't time for that, anyway. There are people still in the hole who need help, and there's a little more lead to put up. Let's not leave them one tiny bit of energy. Let's count the hours until they're gone from the face of the Earth."

The workmen went back to the plates as their vote of thanks. Iverson gripped his hand, then set off to make arrangements for the people in the hole.

Linc walked out of the corridor, out into the fresh, cold air of autumn, and the blast of a horn drew him in the direction of the car. Kelly ran to meet him halfway, Ichabod jumping and barking at her heels.

She threw herself into his arms and caught him so tightly that he grunted in protest. "It's over, isn't it?" she said, "I can tell by your expression. It's over, and we can go home."

"We can." He pushed her back so he could see all the happiness, relief, and promise of her. "I'm transferring my destiny from the monster Zines to Kelly Adams. Do you think it's a fair exchange?"

"You'll find out. You'll have years to find out."

"Well," he teased, turning her to walk with him, "at least I'm sure of Ichabod."

He liked the hard, sure sound of his footsteps on the cement. He was whole again, confident again—more than he had ever been before. He had gone into hell alone, and come out as three: a man, a wife, and a dog. It was the basis of many a life, and he clasped the goodness of it close.

THE END

A PURSUIT ACROSS THE GALAXY...

Heinrich Nge was an interplanetary hoodlum of the worst kind, and when he commandeered one of the Federation's own destroyer-class spaceships, he suddenly shot to the top spot on the Galaxy's list of most wanted criminals.

Raspold, one of the Federation's top agents, was given the grim job of finding and apprehending Heinrich Nge. Little did he know that his chase would lead him to a mysterious planet at the edge of the Galaxy—a planet from which no one had ever returned with their sanity intact. Raspold would soon discover that this taboo world was home to a deathless alien entity— something so powerful that all humanity would tremble before its might...

CAST OF CHARACTERS

RASPOLD
Just like any other agent—he was out to get his man. But time was running out for him, and maybe Earth.

HEINRICH NGE
The most wanted criminal in the galaxy. He had commandeered a Federation destroyer and now he was going to use it!

JIM QUINN
Just a common street peddler on a distant planet. But people paid plenty to know what he knew.

BIG CHUCK WOODWOLF
His sister was a captive of Heinrich Nge. Her freedom was his goal, and nothing could sway him from tracking Nge down.

RICHARD ALI'I
The Boss…the brains…the head of FECAB. He sent Raspold on a suicide mission to the edge of the galaxy.

AGA-OGLU
He was a great space pilot to have along on a dangerous mission—even if he was a former criminal.

SOME FABULOUS YONDER

By
PHILIP JOSE FARMER

ARMCHAIR FICTION
PO Box 4369, Medford, Oregon 97504

*For more information about Armchair Books and products, visit our
website at…*

www.armchairfiction.com

Or email us at…

armchairfiction@yahoo.com

CHAPTER ONE

RASPOLD was in a tavern in Breakneck, capital city of the Federation planet, Wildenwooly. He was drinking, but only in the line of duty. The bartender had some very interesting information for him, and Raspold was elated. He was finally getting some place; the trail, once so cold, was now warmer.

Then, a messenger (from Saxwell Space Links) walked into the tavern and handed him a sealed envelope. He tore it open and read. The message was in code and was to the point.

JOHN CARMODY TURNED HIMSELF IN AND
IS NOW AT JOHN HOPKINS REHABILITATION
CENTER.
REPORT AT ONCE TO ME.
R.A.

Four hours later, Raspold was talking to his chief, Richard Ali'i. He had had to wait at the spaceport of Breakneck for two hours for a scheduled ship. The trip between Wildenwooly and Earth—20,000 light years—took, in wristwatch time, ten minutes. He spent an hour going through Customs and Sanitation. Another hour was consumed in taking various taxis and tubes to the headquarters of the Chief of Federation Extra-Terrestrial Criminal Apprehension Bureau (FECAB). This was deep within the bowels of Under Copenhagen.

Richard Ali'i was a big, handsome man of middle age, dark-skinned, black-haired but with blue eyes (Samoan and Norwegian immediate ancestry).

"Whatever made Carmody surrender?" asked Raspold. "You sure he hasn't got some nasty scheme up his sleeve?"

"Thought of that. But his turning himself in seems to be genuine. Apparently, he was on Dante's Joy. Strange things happen there. Remind me to tell you about it sometime. Now, we've got something that can't wait."

He paused, lit up a Siberian cigar, and said, "It's about No. 2. Rather, I should say, No. 1, now that Carmody's, uh, abdicated."

"Heinrich Nge?"

"Yes. I've had ten agents on his trail for the past four years, as you know. Five of them have disappeared recently. Two were murdered. One is off somewhere. I can't get hold of him; maybe he's been done away with, too. The tenth...well...he was bought."

Raspold was genuinely shocked. "A Fecab?"

"Thoroughly screened. But tests are given by human beings, and human beings are...fallible. The evidence is undeniable. McGrew took a bribe, sold out to Nge. We'd never have known if he hadn't been badly hurt in a drunken brawl in Diveboard. Under drugs, he babbled like a maniac. Not for long. Something in his body exploded, blew him to bits, killed a doctor and a Metro inspector. The explosive must have been surgically implanted. And set off by remote control. McGrew was in no condition to do it himself, even if he'd wanted to."

DIVEBOARD?" said Raspold. "Then Nge, or one of his men, must be on that planet. The bomb must have been set off by radio."

"We think so. However, I'm not through yet. McGrew in his babbling told us something we would never have known otherwise. You remember the disappearance of the Federation destroyer *George A. Custer* two years ago?"

"Between Earth and Aldebaran?"

"Yes. Maiden voyage. Thirty men aboard. Translated from Earth, was supposed to appear above Einstein ten minutes later, ship's time. But she never did, and no one knew what happened. Now, we know Nge highjacked her."

"Highjacked?" Raspold's brows arched in surprise. "If I didn't know you so well, sir, I'd think you were kidding."

"I wish I was. No, Nge did the impossible. Or improbable. With one man. A member of his organization who had contrived, somehow, to become a crew member. He released a deadly gas through the ventilation system of the destroyer, thus killing all the crew except himself. Then, he piloted the bird to a rendezvous at some planet McGrew didn't name, and turned the *Custer* over to Nge. Must have been a damned good pilot. He did the translation all by himself."

"So, what's he going to do with the *Custer*?" said Raspold.

"I don't know. Or didn't. We fed this new data into ATHENA. And ATHENA, after checking this against what it knew about Nge, came up with a reasonable, if astonishing, probability. Maybe not so astonishing, considering Nge."

Raspold wanted to urge Ali'i to continue, kill the suspense. Instead, he waited restlessly.

Ali'i said, "Voittamaton."

"Voittamaton?" Raspold repeated aloud. "Wait a minute! I got it! Fifty years ago...Miika Versinen. Sure...I saw a dramatic re-creation of his life. Ran as a three-part series. And, of course, I read about him when I was a kid."

He looked at Ali'i as if he still thought Ali'i was joking. "You mean Nge's going to use the *Custer* to storm

149

Voittamaton? Even after Versinen failed so miserably and so bloodily?"

Ali'i nodded grimly.

Raspold raised his hands and shrugged his shoulders. "We won't have to worry about him any longer. Or any of the men with him. Why not let him go?"

"Because, in the first place, we don't know for a certainty that this is what Nge plans to do. It's only a high probability. Second, Voittamaton is taboo, off limits. Third, we have to stop Nge now before he hurts innocent people while preparing for the expedition against Voittamaton. Fourth, I want our department to get him—now. There are about ten Federation agencies of Earth alone trying to catch him, and the Great Light alone knows how many from other Fed or non-Fed planets."

Raspold nodded thoughtfully and said, "I'd like to see the blackguard get his comeuppance, which he will, if he tackles Voittamaton."

"That," said Ali'i, "is what we're aiming for and I think you're best qualified to do it."

CHAPTER TWO

TWENTY minutes later, Raspold had sketched his plan, received his authorization and a draft for 5,000 C, and was on his way. It took an hour for him to get back to the port. In the meantime, one of Ali'i's secretaries had arranged for a seat on a nonsked jumper. Because Raspold was going to Diveboard, a non-Federation "open" planet, he had to have a passport. Ali'i's secretary had given him a forged one bearing the name of Dick Ricoletti. Ricoletti was, presumably a subcitizen of the Middle North American Department, Lifelong Limited Privileges Resident of Lesser Laramie. Raspold had spent some time in that city and could speak the dialect quite well. Not that he expected to run across anyone acquired with it but he liked to present a perfect character.

His passport carried his portrait, his fingerprints, retina-prints, earlobe prints, blood type, EKG-patterns, and voiceprint. When Customs and Sanitation took these and matched them against the passports, they would discover nothing wrong. And, when they wired the prints to ATHENA for double-checking, they would receive from ATHENA assurance that the prints belonged to Dick Ricoletti. What Customs and Sanitation did not know was that, when the inquiry about Ricoletti was plugged into ATHENA, it went to a data block that had been inserted by the FECAB.

Raspold leaned against a wall and smoked a cigarette while waiting for this procedure to be completed. He was a tall man, about 12 centimeters above average height (1.7 meter), but looked taller because of his thinness. His broad and thickly muscled arms and shoulders and chest contrasted strangely with the girlish thin waist, narrow hips, and slender legs. He was wearing an auburn wig with a high-piled curly coiffure of the latest fashion. His eyes, normally a deep brown, were now a dark purple. The wig and contact lenses had had to come off during customs inspection, but no one had commented. Almost every passenger wore them.

His features were as Nature had given them; no surgeon's knife or plasti-flesh for him. His forehead was high; his eyebrows, black and thick and meeting over the nose; his nose, big and thick, like a bloodhound's. The lips were medium sized and had only a smudge of lipstick and that red, not the fashionable green flecked with gold. On his left ear, he wore a huge golden ring with a large golden green pendant.

PRESENTLY, he walked out with the other passengers to the *Willowisp*, a twenty-seater craft belonging to a small line. The pilot, however, was a retired Federation Navy navigator. After the passengers were seated, the pilot gave his usual description of the trip they would make; the translation of 180,000 light-years in exactly nothing flat (objective and subjective time), the shorter translations, and the time it would take to fly to Diveboard's spaceport after the final "jump."

Raspold paid no attention; he had heard similar lectures over a hundred times. The passengers demanded his concentration. After examining each in minutest detail, he decided that they were what they seemed to be. A couple of import agents going to Diveboard to set up business, and the rest, emigrants. These mostly came from the subclasses, men and women who could no longer endure the crowded apartments and jammed streets of the great enclosed cities, the low standard of living, the tribute paid from their meager wages to local politicians and their thugs, their ratings as lower class citizens (which their children might escape but not them). They had scraped enough money together to buy the expensive tickets to the far-off sparsely settled planet on the rim of the Galaxy (enticed by TV-shows of life on that planet), agricultural equipment, tools, guns, clothes, and whatever else they thought they might need. Now, they were facing a new life, ill-equipped, most of them, for the strange life on the frontier planet. But they all had dreams of some fabulous yonder, some place where there would be no formal classification of social and economic scale, more than enough fresh air to breathe, silence, trees, grass. And where they would be their own men and women.

Raspold felt sorry for them. They would find that what they had regarded as chains on Earth were, in many ways, walls to protect and guide them. Now, chain-naked, helpless, or inadequate, unsure of how to act. And their life would be hard, hard beyond their powers of conception.

He thought of Versinen. Miika Versinen. Transplanted into English from the Neo-Finnish of the colonial planet Toivo, Micah The Bloody. Versinen was the first and the greatest of the space pirates. A yellow-haired bearded giant who looked like an ancient Viking. He carried a broad axe at his belt, a weapon useless in warfare but quite adequate for splitting his prisoners' skulls in half. He was a madman but a successful one. Until he heard of that dark planet beyond the rim of the Galaxy. The sunless body traveling outwards toward Andromeda. An Earth-sized planet bereft of atmosphere, seemingly devoid of life from its beginnings. Yet, there were mysterious structures on its surface. Over a million of them, pillars with globes on their ends. They glowed; they looked like an army of phantoms.

THE first Federation expedition to attempt to explore—a Naval force of a destroyer, a tender and a laboratory-carrier had failed. Ten kilometers above the surface, the power in all three vessels had been cut off, and the ships crashed. The crews were killed except for a navigator. Finding that the power was now restored, he had escaped in a one-man hopper and succeeded in translating back to Diveboard, the nearest planet.

A second Federation force tried to land. The power of all six vessels was cut off while they were still in orbit. Then, restored. The fleet had left, and the planet was marked off-limits.

But Versinen listened to rumors, to wild tales. The inhabitants of the dark runaway possessed great powers and great riches. The man who conquered them would be the most powerful and the richest being in the Galaxy. Versinen decided he would be that man. Recklessly he brought his fleet of ten vessels out of translation only a kilometer above the surface and dived to the surface before his power could be extinguished. Three of his vessels miscalculated, for the translation drive was not as accurate at that time as it was now. Two crashed. One translated below the surface, and there was an explosion that left a giant crater and thousands of the globed pillars flattened to the ground.

What happened after that is for speculation. Two of the pirate fleet still lie where they landed, several kilometers from the cavern's mouth. The third, the *Kirves*, was located in orbit around Diveboard; its only occupant, Versinen. He was mumbling and nonresistant. For a long while, all he could distinctly say was, *"Voittamaton! Voittamaton!"*

"Unconquerable! Unconquerable!"

Later, at John Hopkins, he quit talking and became catatonic. All efforts to arouse him failed. For ten years, he was a blob. Then, one day, he opened his eyes, and he gave a thin scream.

"I don't want to die!" he cried. "I can't! I must not!"

He muttered, "They're both horrible. But life is better."

A few minutes later, he was dead.

The pilot's voice brought Raspold out of his reverie. They had made the final translation 50 myriameters from Diveboard's surface. From now on, they would proceed by gravitic drive.

CHAPTER THREE

AN hour later, Raspold was through the lax Customs of Diveboard and walking its streets. It was high noon over Copenhagen and almost dusk here.

He walked slowly to give the impression of a man out on a sightseeing tour. He wondered if he should contact the agent Ali'i had told him about. How did he know he could trust Jack Yee? He knew of the man, but he did not know him personally. And, while Ali'i was not likely to make a mistake about a man, he could. Yee might have been all right until Nge got to him and offered him a large attractive bribe. Raspold decided to see what he could do on his own.

He found that, aside from the uneasiness of his situation—and he was not one to be thrown into a sweat easily—he was enjoying his stroll. The city of Diveboard was much like Breakneck, the capital of Wildenwooly. It was built of a medley of log structures, of quick-drying foam shells supported by sprayed beams, a few buildings of native stone: granite, limestone, or pre-stressed concrete, roughly dressed planks, even of paper impregnated with hardo. The streets were the only evidence of planning. These were wide and ran straight and crossed each other at right angles. Some, those nearest the spaceport, were paved with the cheap and quickly laid hardo. The rest were dirt.

The men who thronged the streets were a varied lot. Many were recent immigrants from Earth, but there were also human beings from the colonial and independent planets: Toivo, Tserokia, Novaya, Big Sudan, Po Chui, Heinlein, Maya, Last Chance, Goibniu, and two dozen or more others. A minority among the human beings, but not rare, were oxygen breathing nonhumans. Sinister (to human eyes) Felicentaurs from Capella, the huge Ursucentaurs of Ross 128 III, feathery bipedal Gkuun from Taurus IV, pygmy Flickertails from Van Houden, a big-turbaned Pachydermoid from Puppis. And a near-human type with slanted purple eyes and bulging cheekbones of which Raspold had never heard.

The men who jostled each other on the paved and the dusty streets came from many social classes and professions. Richly dressed merchants and obvious tourists; commercial spacemen in their blue, white, or gold uniforms; poorly dressed farmers or ranchers; buckskin-clad hunters or prospectors; and the nondescript. There were a few gravity-fed units coasting through the streets or high in the air, some electrical fuel cell-powered modes of transportation, and even a nuclear-powered truck. By far the most popular modes of transportation, which gave an archaic air to the scene, were the buggies and wagons drawn by the furry equinoids of Diveboard. Whatever the immigrant could afford to import from Earth, he drove. And, if he didn't have the money for a Terrestrial means of travel, he used the native resources.

RASPOLD saw a chair sitting on a sidewalk. Beside it was a sign in big black letters in Lingo: LEG-PAINTING. ¼ S. A LEG. Below was a name in English: JIM QUINN, PROPRIETOR. Standing beside the chair, his tool of trade on a small table beside the chair, was a medium-sized, chunkily built youth with bright orange hair—his own, judging from the shagginess—and a toothy smile. Raspold said to the youth, "I have long legs. Going to charge extra for them?"

Quinn grinned and said, "No, sir. Anything I lose on you, I'll make up when a fellow with short legs comes along."

Raspold sat down and placed his right foot on the short stool provided. Quinn took a bottle of clear liquid from his table and squeezed a shot of the liquid into a cloth in his other hand. Then he began rubbing Raspold's right leg with the damp cloth. The red, white, and blue barber-pole stripes painted on Raspold's limb ran together. After Quinn had wet a large area, he took a dry cloth and began to rub the area. The pale flesh beneath began to show.

"Earth?" said Raspold.

"Middle Dublin, 3rd Sector, sir," said Quinn. "My parents were second-class C, although my old man got First before he died. Played the bassoon in the Greater Dublin Symphony for twenty years. Me, I have no musical talent. Back to second C for me until I was a majority. Then, to third. But my mother taught me to read and write. And you know there's lots a second-C that can't do that. Finally, got tired of no money, being shoved around. And cube-happy. Couldn't stand being crowded all the time, couldn't breathe any more. Then, luck, pure blind dumb luck! Stepped into a public bath and found a dead man. Some old guy that musta been slumming; he had some M's in his purse, so he couldn't have come from the Middle Sector. Musta had heart failure. No one else in the place. I took the M's and runned. Used some of the credits to find out where I could get hold of an outlaw jumper. Paid most of my M's to the agent and the pilot and took the jump to here with ten others. Landed with just enough money to buy me this chair, stool, table, and leg-painting tools. But I'm doing O.K. now. Someday, I'll be a big man on Diveboard. And I can breathe, I can breathe."

"You don't miss the big city and all its refinements?"

"Sometimes. You know, the gang, the girls. But I wouldn't ever have amounted to anything; I'da always been a drunken C. Here, things get tough, rough, you gotta fight like hell sometimes. But what the hell, you had to back on Earth."

RASPOLD examined his legs and said, "You're doing a good job. Paint them black. Solid. No stars or crescents."

Quinn looked up, winked, and said, "You dint really need a paint job, sir. What's on your mind?"

"You must get around, hear a lot," said Raspold. "There's two S for this job if you can give me a little information."

"I come happy for two S," said Quinn, grinning bucktoothedly. "Yeah, I hear, see. But it might cost you."

"There are people in this city who have money. Where do their women—wives or what have you?—go to buy their clothes, get their wigs cleaned and curled, get a sono?"

"Rene Gautier's," said Quinn. "Best place in town. Only place, in fact."

"You just earned 3 S," said Raspold. "Now, you've probably set up your business near Gautier's…"

"Yeah," said Quinn, grinning. "He's my only competitor. But not really a competitor, because only the full purses can afford him. But I place my chair near him a lot, because I like to see the dangoes that waltz in and out. Some pretty good lookers."

"That's what I want to know," said Raspold. "Has one of Gautier's customers ever been a beautiful woman who uses Erector Set Perfume?"

"What's that?"

"A natural perfume from Umchawa. Used to be, anyway. It's been synthesized but is still by far the most expensive. The man who smells it has an immediate erotic reaction, if he's at all capable of one."

Quinn hawhawed. "Yeah, I smelled it twice, both times when I was working in front of Gautier's. The first time, I didn't think anything of it, the woman was such a dish.

Second time, I was painting a customer's legs when she went by, and he told me what it was. I couldn't figure out why a woman would be wanting to have it on her when she was walking on the streets. You'd think she'd cause a riot...get... Say! Maybe she *was* walking the streets! Naw, she dint have to, she was too beautiful, too well dressed."

"How tall was she?"

"Oh, about an inch or two higher than I am."

"Lots of jewelry?"

"Loaded."

"She comes to Gautier's regularly?"

"Not that I know. I saw her last Thirdsday and a Secondday two weeks before. Say, that's enough. I've given you more'n 3 S' worth."

"Five S now. Tell me a little more, and it's six. Was she alone?"

"Once. Other time, she had another woman with her. A blast-off, too, but she wasn't wearing that Erector Set stuff."

RASPOLD took six S out of his purse and handed it to Quinn. He said, "You're an intelligent man, and, therefore, curious. You must have asked around about this woman."

"What for? What chance would I stand with a woman like that? Maybe someday, after I make my pile... Yeah, I asked around. Nobody knows her name, and Gautier sure isn't going to give out any information. The tightlipped little fairy. But I can tell you one thing that'll be at least worth a half-S. Haw, haw! She don't live in town."

"Half it is," said Raspold. "What does she ride in?"

"Believe it or not, a horse and buggy," said Quinn. "A Diveboard horse, not one of the Earth kind. She drives like a maniac. But it ain't hers. She rents it from Tak Alvarez; he's got a livery stable out at the edge of town. I painted his legs a coupla days ago. He says she walks in from the forest, from nowhere, and rents the outfit. Then, coming back from Gautier's, she leaves the horse and buggy with Tak, and walks off into the forest. So…"

Somebody could be waiting for her in a grav, thought Raspold. He said, "Many people live in the country around here?"

"More every day. Diveboard's population has doubled in the last ten months. Mostly poor would-be farmers or hunters or prospectors."

"Any rich ones?"

"A few. There're two nobody knows much about. Word is that they're big-shot criminals who've piled it and want to take it easy. Which they can do. Earth can't touch them; this's a Free Planet."

"I know. Now, what're the names of these so-called criminals?"

"Nobody knows the name of one of them. The other calls himself Gottfried von Fulka."

Quinn knew no more than that about von Fulka. Except that his house—mansion, rather—was on an island in a lake about 80 kilometers north of the capital. The house was built about two years ago; von Fulka had not moved in until a year later.

"Alvarez' livery? It's on the north side of town?"

"South."

Raspold rose and examined the paint on his legs. "Very good," he said. "You'll go far in your profession—whatever it may be in the future."

"Another S-worth of advice," said Quinn, squinting shrewdly at him. "If you're thinking of hanging around Gautier's until this chick shows up, forget it. Gautier goes to her now."

Raspold's brows, thick and black, rose and he said, "You earned it. How do you know this?"

SOME FABULOUS YONDER

"Oh, I get around."

"Details, please," said Raspold, holding out, not an S but an Un with a large M on it.

QUINN'S eyes widened, and he said, "Gautier drives a long red Wang. He's easy to spot, even late at night, especially here where lotsa people stay up all night for one reason or another. He's driven out on the North Road twice about two in the morning and didn't show up until the next night. Where'd he go? That road ain't passable for a sport car once you get ten km. outta town. And he ain't shacking up with no farmer's daughter. If he was, everybody in town'd know it. No, he parks his car someplace, and somebody picks him up. The Erector Set chick hasn't shown after she made those two trips, so..."

"The mountain goes to Mohammed. Or vice versa."

"More advice. Gautier may be one of the boys, but he's a hard nut to crack; he came here because he got into some trouble on Earth."

Raspold handed him the M and said, "Part of that is for silence. And loyalty in the future. I want you to work for me. More where that came from."

"How do you know you can trust me?" said Quinn. "I want to get ahead, and I know I need money for that. Suppose..."

Raspold shrugged. "I'm taking a chance. But those who betray me..."

"I'll hitch my wagon to your star, mister...?"

"Call me Dick Ricoletti for the present," said Raspold. "It wouldn't be good for either of us if you knew my real name. And I warn you, even talking to me as you have been doing may be very dangerous."

"If I scared easily, I wouldn't be here," said Quinn.

Raspold asked where the best restaurant in town was and then walked off. He strolled through the bustling colorful noisy streets, following Quinn's directions, until he came to The Soulful Cow. This establishment, a two-story building of rough-hewn logs of a reddish wood, was a combination tavern and eating place. A blast of chatter and laughter blew from out the open doorway, with a mixed odor of tobacco, beer, and frying steaks. Raspold stepped into a huge room filled with people and smoke. The great dark-red beams overhead were festooned with heads of native animals and signs in various alphabets, ideograms, and syllabaries. A bar, cement-topped, ran the length of the northern side of the building. Men stood two or three deep along it, and over a dozen bartenders sweated to keep their customers from dying of thirst. At the rear was the kitchen, open to view, and here were the cooks, their helpers, and waiters, preparing the only course The Soulful Cow served; steaks, potatoes, butter, beans, and a dark bread.

RASPOLD's mouth watered. He had had steak on Wildenwooly, but it had been his first in an Earth month. On Earth, he could rarely afford true meat, but here where cattle was one of the chief industries, and transportation from the plains to the city was not so expensive, he could have all the steak he wanted.

Raspold found an empty seat at one of the long plank tables. The waitress came over and he ordered a stein of native dark beer with his meal.

While waiting Raspold took special note of a man who sat directly across from him. This fellow was easily the biggest human being in the place. Also the broadest. His forearms looked as thick as Raspold's thighs. His chest looked like two drums of muscle. His hair was black and straight, and the handsome face was brown. His eyes were a light green. He sat brooding, his huge right hand almost completely enfolding the stein of beer.

From time to time, he took a swallow from the stein. As he did so, his green eyes looked at—and through—Raspold. Yet Raspold was sure that the big man had taken in every detail of Raspold's face and dress.

Presently, a youth came in and bent down by the big man and whispered into his ear.

Raspold was startled, for the youth was the red-haired leg-painter, Quinn.

Quinn, straightening up, gave Raspold a wink and a grin, and he walked away. Raspold wondered if Quinn meant these for a friendly greeting or a signal that this man had something to do with his quest.

RASPOLD rose and strode after Quinn. He caught him just outside the tavern, out of sight of anyone sitting within it.

"You working for that dark giant?" he said.

"Sorry," said Quinn. "I don't tell one of my clients another's business. It ain't ethical. It also ain't healthy."

"How much?" said Raspold.

Quinn's face, lit by a lamp above and to one side of him, darkened.

"You haven't got enough," he said.

Raspold laughed and said, "That tells me a lot about you. Maybe I can trust you, after all. O.K. I'll find out for myself. But you can do something for me. There's a Q in it for you. You know a man of Terran Chinese descent named Jack Yee? I don't know where he lives just now; he moves around a lot."

Quinn nodded, and Raspold took a notebook and a pen from his purse, tore out a leaf, and began writing. Finished, he handed the leaf to Quinn.

"I could get into contact with him right now, but I don't want to use the waves. And I've got some business to take care of first. When you see him, don't say a word. Just hand him this paper. Got it?"

"His place might be bugged?"

"Right. And don't bother trying to read this. It's in code."

"You must be on Heinrich Nge's trail," said Quinn.

Raspold had trained himself to keep a poker face, but he could not help betraying some surprise. "How do you figure that?"

"I hear a lot, see some. Word's around that he's here somewhere on Diveboard. A coupla his men seen in town last few months. And the word also is that Raspold's in town, hot on Nge's trail."

Raspold smiled slightly and said, "Communications engineers ought to investigate the possibility of the grapevine. For swiftness, it beats the speed of light. Well, now you know you're in hot water up to your neck, and you're likely to get drowned. Want to back out?"

"It's exciting," said Quinn. "And I got a chance to make a big profit."

"I don't think you mean a profit from Nge," said Raspold. "As soon as you've delivered the message to Yee, come back here and wait for me."

Quinn walked off, and Raspold returned to his seat at the table. By then, his dinner was before him, and he ate it with great pleasure. His enjoyment was not a bit tempered by the hard stares the big man across the table was giving him. When Raspold had paid his bill and rose to leave, the big man also stood up. Raspold walked out of the tavern, aware that he was being followed.

CHAPTER FOUR

DIVEBOARD'S moon, almost as large as Earth's, shone fitfully through a half-clouded sky.

"Mister," said a rumbling voice behind him. "A word."

Raspold turned around, noting that the man was keeping his distance. If he intended to attack, he meant to do it with a weapon. Raspold idly fingered the pendant on his earring.

The fellow spoke in Lingo but used strange phonetic values that showed he had not learned it as an infant along with his native tongue but in later life.

"My name is Big Chuck Woodwolf," he said, not offering his hand. "I'm a Tserokian."

Raspold said, "I've been to Tserokia."

Woodwolf flashed a smile and said, "You speak my language?"

"Regretfully, no. My name is Ricoletti. What do you want?"

"O.K. We'll use that name, though I think I know who you really are. Listen, you heard of the big raid that Heinrich Nge made on Sequoyah a year ago?"

Raspold nodded. Sequoyah was the capital city of Tserokia, a T-type planet colonized seventy years before (when interstellar travel had first started) by several thousand Cherokees. Since then, the population had expanded to thirty million, largely through the immigration of other racial groups and nationalities. The immigrants had become naturalized or, as the Tserokians phrased it, "adopted," and had learned to speak Cherokee. But that tongue was now dying out, replaced by the standard Federation speech, Lingo. The racial continuity of the original colonists (already half-white) had been broken. Big Chuck himself was probably descended from at least three races and two dozen nationalities. But he thought of himself as Cherokee.

Two years ago, six months after the destroyer *Custer* had been highjacked, a fleet of ten vessels had appeared over Sequoyah. The *Custer* was one of them. Before anyone knew what was happening, the fleet had landed, looted the planetary treasury, the government art museum, and had also kidnapped a number of Tserokian women. There was no doubt about the identity of the leader of the pirates. Heinrich Nge. He had left a letter saying that he had enjoyed his visit there, thanked them for their gracious hospitality, and promised to return when their treasury was refilled. Also, complimented them on the beauty of their women. The letter bore the image of the scorpion (*Nge* was Swahili for *scorpion*).

"My sister, Tuli, was one of the girls taken by the pirates," said Woodwolf. "She's the most beautiful woman I've ever seen; she was to marry the richest man on Tserokia. He's dead now; killed by the pirates during the raid. I loved my sister."

"Why tell me this?"

"Because I figure you're looking for Nge, too. You know some things I don't. I know some things you don't. If we work together…"

Raspold considered. Woodwolf might be an agent of Nge. He could be approaching him with this story with the intent of capturing him. If so, he might give Raspold a chance to find Nge.

"Would you be willing to submit to questioning under *chalarocheil?*" said Raspold. "I'm not one to take unnecessary chances."

"Yes."

"In that case, it may not be necessary. Let's go some place else and talk."

RASPOLD merely walked across the street and stopped before the dark front of a farm equipment store. They were outside the illumination area cast by the nearest lamp, and he could watch the door to The Soulful Cow. Big Chuck Woodwolf began talking at once.

"I went to Wildenwooly, Diveboard, Peregrino, Liang, Krona, all the 'free' planets. I figured that Nge might be found in a place where the Feds could not legally touch him. Then I went to Earth several times and also visited a dozen non-human planets. No luck at all.

"Then, instead of just running around, sniffing here and there like a dumb hound trying to find a lost trace, I sat down and did some thinking. If I were Nge, where would I go? And why? Nge wants to be the biggest man in the Galaxy. He wants power and wealth. How can he best do this? By looting the biggest treasury in the Galaxy, that's how. And what is that? Voittamaton, if you believe all you hear.

"But Voittamaton is well-nigh invulnerable. So, if Nge needs men, ships, weapons to take Voittamaton, he will steal the ships and rob some place to give him the money to buy men and weapons. So, he highjacks the *Custer*, and he loots Sequoyah. He now has money and firepower. But he also needs a base of operations. What inhabited 'free' planet is closest to Voittamaton? Diveboard, on the rim of the Galaxy, and only ten light-years from Voittamaton."

Raspold smiled. This man, using the little mass of gray matter within his skull, had come to the same conclusion as the skyscraper-tall computer, ATHENA.

"I came back here. I hang around taverns, the market-places, find out who knows the most, tap into the grapevine. I even became partner in some small robberies here to get the confidence of the underworld. I'll repay the men I robbed after this is over. I got a conscience.

"One night, while I was hanging around the Twelfth Street Tavern, a man I recognized entered. I didn't know his name, but I couldn't forget that face; we'd blazed away at each other during the raid on Sequoyah from opposite ends of a hall. He wounded me with his rifle, almost killed me. Now, I could reach out and get his neck between my hands and squeeze once. Instead I buddied up to him. Pretended I was a planet-picker who'd tried to keep a planet to himself and been cashiered out of Federation Service. Down on my luck. He was cagey at first, but he got drunk, and he said he might possibly have something for me to do—if I was made of strong stuff. Wouldn't say any more, and I figured that he wasn't likely to. I knew that the little device in his body might be transmitting our conversation to some monitor who only had to press a button and blow both of us to kingdom come. He knew it, too.

SO, I told him that The Soulful Cow was a better place for steaks, drinks, and women, and we staggered out into the street. When we came opposite the entrance to an alley, I chopped him alongside the neck and dragged him back into the dark end. When he came to, he was bound tight and had a gag over his mouth. I used my little flash to show him what I'd written on a piece of paper. It told him what I wanted to know. What was his name? Where was my sister? Where was Nge?

"He had one hand free so he could write an answer. He wasn't about to try to speak. If his speech was being monitored, he wouldn't live more than a minute. Neither, probably, would I, but I had to take the chance. I had also written that, in return for the information, I'd let him loose. I knew he wouldn't say anything to Nge, because Nge would kill him. He wrote his answer. *'Go to hell.'*

"Brave talk. But I took his sandal off and ignited my cigarette lighter and held the hot wire between his toes. He didn't dare scream. I took the wire away and gestured to him to write. He must have made up his mind then, for he began to scribble. He let the paper fall, I picked it up and read.

"My sister was still alive; Nge had taken her for one of his mistresses. She was pregnant. She was at Fulka's place. He didn't know where Nge was, for Nge often took off for visits elsewhere.

"I asked him some more, by paper, of course. Where Fulka's place was? Who was Fulka? Did Nge intend to attack Voittamaton? He wrote that Nge was Fulka."

Woodwolf stopped talking. He was breathing heavily.

"So what happened?" said Raspold coolly.

"I'd promised to let him go free," said Woodwolf. "And I did. I untied him, after relieving him of a knife and a gun and knocking him out again. Then, I phoned the police but didn't give my name, of course. Told them that I'd seen Howard Guy and another man at the end of that alley. Guy was tied up; the other man was writing something on a piece of paper and showing it to Guy, and Guy was doing the same for him. I even told them about the hot wire between Guy's toes."

"You said that you'd let him go free," said Raspold. "Was that...?"

"I'm not through talking yet. The police didn't get hold of Guy; I knew they wouldn't. I kept my word. It wasn't three minutes after the call that a big explosion took place right in the middle of Twelfth Street. Fortunately, nobody but Guy was involved.

"You see, I know, like everybody else, that Nge has his contacts in the local police force. Maybe the one I called up.

The contact must have radioed Nge, and Nge wasn't taking any chances on Guy spilling anything."

THEY started to walk down the street. But, hearing the frenzied barks of a dog and the equally frenzied cries of a man, they turned. Two blocks behind them, a youth ran as fast as he could, shouting for help. Several yards behind him bounded the dog, a large black mongrel that looked as if he had a heavy dash of German shepherd in him.

"Looks like Quinn," said Raspold.

"Yeah," said Woodwolf. "And that dog…"

He broke the magnetic clasps of his shirt with his left hand and with his right reached under the shirt. Raspold, having previously noted the bulge under his left armpit, was not surprised to see the hand emerge clutching a pistol.

"Damn, damn!" groaned Woodwolf. "Quinn's in the way."

"What's the matter?" said Raspold.

"Has to be one of Nge's dogs," said Woodwolf. "Nge must have stolen some piece of clothing from Quinn and set the dog to track down the owner."

Raspold saw the picture. He drew his gun, a .32 Weckel, and ran diagonally across the street. He shouted, "Quinn, out of the way!"

Quinn saw them and must have understood. He sprinted for the sidewalk nearest him, which was Woodwolf's side of the street. Raspold, arming carefully, pressed the trigger.

The gun bucked twice, and the dog went whirling sidewise in the dust. Quinn kept on running. Meanwhile, Big Chuck Woodwolf had run into the middle of the street, and he fired immediately after Raspold. The dog, crumpled in a heap, moved a few inches under the impact of the .45. Quinn dived into an alley between two buildings. Woodwolf, only a few meters from the dog, threw himself flat on the dirt.

Raspold, suddenly realizing his vulnerable position, did the same.

He was deafened, and the ground trembled under him. Dust swirled into the street; the plastic sheet of the store window near the dog blew inwards in a solid sheet, and the crash of objects falling off the store shelves was in the ears of the three as they rose and sped down the street.

After running for several blocks, they stopped beside the side of a building. "Don't your citizens get nervous with all these explosions?" said Raspold, gasping for breath.

"They love excitement," said Quinn. Then, "That was close! But I'm O.K. Listen, Mister Ricoletti, I couldn't deliver your note! Your friend Jack Yee was dead! I went to his room, on the second story of Krishna's Hotel, and I knocked. There wasn't any answer. The door was unlocked. I hollered again, 'cause I dint want my head blown off. Still no answer. I pushed the door, it swung in, and there was Yee on the floor. He was dead but from what I don't know. Poison, maybe, or gas. So, I got to hell out of there with your note still in my hand."

"Nge must have discovered his identity," said Raspold. Now, as far as he knew, he was the only FECAB agent on Diveboard.

CHAPTER FIVE

I WAS walking back," said Quinn, "when a car drove by. It stopped, and a door opened, and the dog jumped out. He stood there a moment, whining and sniffing. Then, like a hound out of hell, he ran for me, barking. I ran, and the dog came after me. Something told me I better not stop and try to talk to him. You showed up, and..."

He paused, then wailed, "Nge's after me, too!"

"He won't get you unless he gets us, too," said Raspold. He was considering every aspect swiftly. He could take a jumper back to Earth, talk to Ali'i, get a crew of FECAB, and return. But he couldn't take a legal ship, for Nge's men would be watching the spaceport. Moreover, the police, if working with Nge, could arrest him and turn him over to Nge. If he hired an illegal jumper, he might fall into Nge's hands just as easily as if he tried the legal route. Nge might have the word around among the underworld that he wanted Raspold. Even if he got to Earth, Nge would be gone by the time he returned. He might already have left Diveboard on the expedition against Voittamaton.

"Any place in town that rents cars or gravs?" he said to Quinn.

"Yeah. Jock Barry. But he's as crooked as a pretzel. He could be a stoolie for Nge."

"We won't rent one from him. We'll steal it," said Raspold.

They walked to Barry's place, a single-story foam structure on the edge of town. It was three in the morning; the building was dark. Raspold shot the lock off the front door. He and Quinn entered and picked out a Bluebolt four-seater gravity-drive. Unfortunately, there were no keys available. He stuck the muzzle of the pistol against Barry's ribs as Barry came charging out of his rooms in the rear. Barry did not argue; he handed over the gun in his hand and the keys. Raspold, wanting to make sure that Barry would not contact Nge—if he had intended to do so—took him along in the Bluebolt.

Big Chuck took over the controls and lifted the runabout just above treetop level. He steered it northwards, toward Fulka's house on the island 80 kilometers away. About half way there he landed the Bluebolt in an open space. Raspold, after making sure that Barry had no wrister or other means of wireless communication on his person, told Barry to start walking back home.

TEN minutes later, the big Tserokian slowed the Bluebolt. The lake was in sight. It sparkled in the light of Diveboard's full moon. The house on the island in the middle of the lake gleamed whitely. No lights came from its windows.

Big Chuck, following Raspold's orders, slid the Bluebolt down the bank, into the lake, and under the surface. The car spurted forward in the darkness of the waters until it struck the shallow mud of the island. The Tserokian lifted it slowly above the surface. They were on the beach, just outside the thick forest surrounding the house. There were no roads to the house. Raspold debated with himself whether they should proceed on foot, then decided against it. Big Chuck lifted the Bluebolt to a position level with the tops of the trees. The car, bending the treetops before it, moved toward the house. When they came to the clearing around the house, they stopped.

"I don't see how they could be expecting us," said Raspold. "But, with Nge, you never know. If it's a trap, we go into it."

A thick stone-and-cement wall about ten meters high surrounded the house, which was about sixty meters from the wall. The house was a two-story structure also built of native rocks and cement. It looked as if it had from ten to twelve rooms. Against the northern wall stood a stone garage.

Raspold had Big Chuck guide the Bluebolt completely around the house. He was well aware that anyone looking out of the dark windows could see the glint of moonlight on the silvery Bluebolt. At any moment, he thought, guns will start firing and we'll know where we stand.

"There are windows but no doors," he said. "They must get to the rooftop via grav and go down through a trapdoor. So will we."

"Nge isn't the man to sleep without guards of some kind," said Big Chuck. "That is, if he is in there. We don't even know that. Something's in there."

"Wait a minute," said Raspold. "You have to think about one thing. Nge's the greatest booby-trapper in the world. If he's left that house for keeps, he'll likely trigger it. If he knew I was coming to it, he wouldn't, for he's sworn to take me alive. But maybe he doesn't know I've tracked him this far."

HE told big Chuck to take the Bluebolt back across the forest-top to the beach. Here the car descended, and they slid a few feet above the beach around the island until Raspold saw what he was looking for. A log washed up by the waves, a log about one decimeter in diameter and two meters long. The three got out of the car, picked up the log, and laid it at right angles to the front and back seats. Quinn and Raspold held the log steady while Woodwolf piloted the car to a height of 20 meters.

The car moved until it was over the house, still silent and white in the moonlight. Woodwolf locked the controls and rose from the pilot's seat to help them. With his strength added to theirs, one end of the log rose easily and was held vertically by the side of the car.

Raspold said, "Let her loose," and the log dropped. They sat down quickly, strapped themselves with the safety belts, and Big Chuck rolled the car fifty degrees along its longitudinal axis so that they could get a good view over the side.

The log, black in the silver moonlight, was almost on its target by the time they were ready to look. When it struck, it was horizontal, and the roof received the impact of the full length.

A bright flash appeared. Big Chuck slammed the Bluebolt into sudden flight, and the occupants were pressed back against the seat. For a moment, they were deafened.

Raspold looked back and saw planks and stones and other objects flying up higher than the car. If they had stayed, they would have been hit.

"I think," said Raspold, when he felt the others could hear him, "the mere opening of the rooftop door would have set off that mine. Anyway, we know one thing. Nge, if he was there, has left. Probably for Voittamaton. If he really dares."

THEY shot back to the city. Raspold went to the Terrestrial Consul and identified himself. After telling part of his story to the Consul, he had no trouble getting passports for himself and Woodwolf. Quinn decided to stay on Diveboard and continue in business. The passports gave the two immunity from police seizure (such a right has been granted in the contract with Earth ten years previously). He and the big Tserokian took a nonsked to Earth. An hour after getting through Customs, Raspold stood in the office of Ali'i.

"If your surmises are correct," said Ali'i, puffing away on a big cigar, "and if what I've read of Voittamaton is true, we can forget about Nge. He's as good as dead."

"We can't know for sure," said Raspold. "I want permission for myself, Woodwolf, and a pilot to go to Voittamaton. A small ship might be undetected by Nge. But if a big force showed up, we'd just scare him. He'd go into translation, and we'd have to start the chase all over again."

"Woodwolf?"

"Swear him in as a temporary agent with limited powers and under my supervision," said Raspold. "If you don't, the damn fool will go to Voittamaton by himself. And he might get in the way, cause God-knows-what kind of mess. He's a good man, and he knows Nge's history, his behavior patterns."

"You'll have to take full responsibility for him and his actions," said Ali'i. He pressed a button and spoke into the box on his desk.

"Miss Petersen, show Mr. Woodwolf in."

Raspold and Big Chuck spent two hours with Ali'i, and then they went off to sleep for two hours while Ali'i made arrangements. Waking up completely refreshed, they removed the Morpheus electrodes from their temples and went to eat breakfast. Afterwards, Ali'i introduced them to their pilot.

Raspold recognized him at once.

"Glad to see you're on the team," he said. "We couldn't have a better man."

He introduced Big Chuck to Aga-Oglu, a tall broad-shouldered man with a narrow face, a big curved nose, and deeply sunken eyes. Later, when Raspold was alone with the Tserokian, he said, "He's a native of Kagan. Was a member of the Baudelairean Gang. I was the one who arrested him. About three years ago. He was rehabilitated and discharged from John Hopkins a year ago. Now, like a lot of rehabs, his experience with the criminal world is being used to good advantage by FECAB."

"You aren't a rehab?" said Big Chuck.

"If I'd been a criminal," said Raspold, "I'd never have been caught." He smiled to soften the egotism of the statement, but Big Chuck was not sure that Raspold was at all facetious.

Aga-Oglu called them, and they boarded the ship. Their take-off time was 13:47.22; to be delayed a second meant that new data would have to be fed into the ship's computer and a new translation period arranged for.

AN hour later, subjective time, they were in a wide orbit about thirty thousand myriameters from Voittamaton. The nearest star was the sun of Diveboard, some ten light-years away. The rim of the Galaxy was so far away that it looked like a rough luminous humpbacked disc seen edge on. And there was so little light that the planet, relatively close, was invisible.

"There it is," said Aga-Oglu, indicating the ghostly white circle on the screen before him. The image faded out and strengthened in 45-degree sectors, and on each side of the circle were little bursts of whiteness.

"Those little flashes are too big to be vessels," said Aga-Oglu. "Orbital debris; asteroidlets, maybe."

He flicked off the active scanner and turned on the passive.

"Now what?"

"We land," said Raspold.

Aga-Oglu shrugged and said, "I'll set the computer to land us in thirty minutes. We ought to be in our suits, have everything else ready by then, okay?"

Raspold nodded, and the three began to prepare for the landing. Twenty minutes later they were in their space suits and strapped to their seats. Aga-Oglu had turned the scanner on for another two minutes, long enough for the computer to receive all necessary data. Then, three minutes before the translator was to go into action, he turned the scanner on again. The computer rechecked their position and verified the setting of the translator "gauge".

"We make it in one big jump," said the pilot. "A series of small translations might allow Nge or whatever is on that planet to detect us between jumps. I've set the translator for minimum tolerance. We won't materialize any closer than one kilometer. We could try within that distance, but we'd run the risk of materializing under the surface."

Raspold's hands were tightly clenched around the arms of his seat, and they remained tight when Aga-Oglu went into action. He switched the controls to manual and rammed two control sticks forward. The vessel accelerated, and the occupants felt themselves pressed back against their seats. The window in front of them suddenly cleared; they were automatically on visual now. They clamped their jaws to keep from crying out. The surface was rushing toward them; they were going to crash!

But Aga-Oglu knew what he was doing. He had shot the craft downward as swiftly as he dared after coming out of translation so that he could get on the surface before their power was mysteriously cut off. Twenty seconds later they had landed.

CHAPTER SIX

THE entire upper half of their ship was transparent, and they could see the surface of the planet. Rather, could see what the darkness permitted.

It was more than they had expected. Something gleamed outside. Somethings. Tall and white, apparently casting a self-generated and feeble glow. Everywhere around them. So close they pressed against the vessel. Aga-Oglu had, with magnificent skill, landed them—wedged them—in an aisle of the phantom objects.

Raspold examined the closest one. It was a slender round pillar, which rose to a height of five meters. At its top was a globe approximately two meters in diameter. This was only partially white; it bore irregular blackish blotches. The globe on the stele next to it also had the patches, but these were of a different pattern. And, on each stele, running from top to bottom, were characters. Alphabetical letters?

Raspold turned away from them. "How close are we to The Mouth?" he said, describing the opening in the mountain.

Aga-Oglu, looking at a card in his hand, said, "We were supposed to make a final translation within at least ten kilometers of The Mouth. The scanner took a fix while we were landing. We're just nine kilometers away. Straight North. How's that, huh?"

"Did it pick up any of Nge's ships?"

"No. How could it? If his fleet landed in this forest..."

Aga-Oglu read two other cards, and he said, "No more atmosphere than the Moon. Funny, too, when you're on a planet only a little smaller than Earth. Should at least be a frozen atmosphere, gas-snow."

Raspold considered. They could lift the ship above the globed steles and make a dash for The Mouth in it. Or two could get into each of the one-man "hoppers" stored in the rear of the bigger ship and advance between the aisles of the steles and beneath the cover of the globes. That meant that the Kagan would have to remain in the ship.

Aga-Oglu protested.

"If we have to come running," said Raspold, "I want everything triggered to go the moment we drive into the hopper-port. And if we don't return within two hours, you are to leave without us, at once, and report to Ali'i. That's an order."

He made sure his watch synchronized with Woodwolf's and Aga-Oglu's, shook hands with the Kagan, and walked to the hoppers. These were small rugged craft much used by spacers in asteroid mining. The two in the port had been especially beefed up for service on a large planet; they were capable of speeds up to six hundred kilometers an hour and could cruise at one hundred kilometers an hour for six hours before needing refueling. Each was armed with two .45 machine guns located in the forward end of the thick runners (like a sled's) placed at the under part of the craft.

RASPOLD rotated the hopper so that it faced the north and lifted it over the *Pulex* and down into the aisle in front of it. Woodwolf's craft followed him.

Raspold began to increase his speed swiftly. But, after several seconds, while the tall white pillars and their globes shot by him, he lifted his hand in signal to Woodwolf. And he slowed the craft, looking in the rearview mirror to make sure that the big Tserokian wasn't going to hit him. When he had come to a halt, he lifted the hopper level with the globes.

He examined the nearest ones. Shaking his head, he proceeded slowly enough to allow himself a good look at those passing on his right. He crawled past them for a minute. Then, as if making up his mind, he lifted his hand again, and shot the hopper forward, reaching one hundred kilometers per hour in five seconds. Again, the white and silent aisle sped by in a blur; the huge hole at the base of the mountain—outlined on the scanner—expanded before him. He stopped the hopper two kilometers from it, and Woodwolf landed directly behind him. Raspold flipped the switch that would put them in tight-beam communication. "I slowed down because there was something familiar about the patterns of the dark patches on the globes. Did they not look to you as if they represented continents? As if the globes were supposed to be planets, and the white portions are seas?"

"I didn't think so," said Big Chuck. "But, now that you point it out..."

"You don't suppose they do represent planets?" said Raspold. "Markers? Markers for what? Possessions?"

"This place gives me the spooks," said the Tserokian. "It looks like one big graveyard. The biggest in the world."

The hairs on the back of Raspold's neck rose. He said, "Maybe it is."

"What do you mean?"

Raspold shrugged and said, "I really don't know. But the whole thing is curious. A thousand square miles of nothing but globes on steles. For what purpose?"

"Maybe somebody in there has the answer?"

"If he—it—does," said Raspold, "I hope he feels like talking."

He reached for the controls, then stopped. Above and ahead of him, above the mountain, a luminous round object had appeared. It was, at first, a pale globe, dinner plate sized.

Which meant that, at this distance from him, it must be at least fifty meters in diameter. It could have been hanging, undetected, all this time; now, it had started to pour out light. And, in a few seconds, the light had strengthened, had become as bright as the Earthly sun.

"What the hell's going on?" said Woodwolf.

"Something just came out of the cave mouth," said Raspold. "It flew up the mountainside, went over the top."

HE sat for several seconds, rigid in his seat, before speaking. "Maybe it's a decoy. But let's go after it, anyway."

He shut off the beam and shot the hopper at an angle, which would take it just above the sharp point of the mountain. Woodwolf followed him. Raspold, clearing the peak, saw that the mountain was part of a range of similar jagged cones. And he risked a quick look behind him and saw that the monuments were white as bleached bones under a desert sun. And that nowhere in the illuminated area was a sign of Nge's fleet. Perhaps, he thought, Nge had taken his ships into the cavern mouth. Or, he had never reached the surface.

His mother ship, the *Pulex,* was still sitting wedged in the aisle. He could imagine Aga-Oglu's frantic reaction to the light, and he hoped the man would stay where he was, as ordered.

The hopper almost struck the top peak, then it was by. And Raspold saw the thing that had flown from the cave. It was not more than thirty meters from him and was hanging in space, facing him, as if waiting for him.

It was the strangest creature that Raspold had ever seen, and he had seen many. It had a long reddish-brown body roughly centaur-shaped. The lower torso gave a bi-lobed impression; there was a deep groove running its length where a spine would be in any other creature and where one might be in this. Six spindly and grotesquely long limbs hung downward from the lower torso and ended in something like a human foot. The upper torso had narrow shoulders and a neck and a head and two arms as spindly and overly long as the "legs." These ended in enormous hands with fingers that made Raspold think of spider legs.

The face was that of a demon's. Humanoid, it had a chin, acromegalically developed. A nose that looked like a parrot's beak. Great forward leaning ears. Two long independently moving fleshy strips sprouting from each cheek. The forehead was very low; the skull was hairless. The eyes were set in fleshy slants.

It was the tail that startled Raspold the most. A thick pillar, almost as long as the body, it ended in a thick oval four-lobed pad.

The creature was a nightmare, something out of an opium smoker's dreams. It had no right to exist, to be unprotected by a spacesuit, to have limbs where limbs were not needed to move, to have a nose where no air was, to have ears where sound had no medium through which to travel, to have a mouth where it could not talk.

It moved, seemingly by a biologically generated control of gravity. It lived without artificial devices where nothing could live naturally.

Raspold decided to break the silence between the hoppers; he activated the radio. With all the maneuvering they might have to do, they could not afford to jockey around until lined up for tight-beam transmission.

"Watch that tail!" he said to Woodwolf. "It looks dangerous."

"Here come four more," said Woodwolf's voice.

Raspold spun the hopper around so he could see past the Tserokian's craft. Four similar creatures were just coming over the peak.

A SHADOW appeared above him; he looked upward and at the same time placed the hopper into a reverse motion so savage that the upper part of his body strained against the belts holding him. The thing—which he mentally termed the "space scorpion," darted after him, its long arms held out toward him.

He stopped the hopper and threw it forward, intending to ram the creature. But the scorpion shot off at an angle.

Woodwolf's hopper darted towards Raspold's. It tilted upward, and flame appeared at the open end of one of the runners beneath the hopper.

The scorpion, struck by a series of .45 slugs, turned end over end, its legs and arms flailing. Then, as if it had suddenly lost its power over gravity, it began to fall straight down.

Raspold steered his hopper at the four scorpions. These scattered, increasing the gap between them, some going up and some down. He had lost his chance to get all of them with one sweep of the machine-guns. But he did center one and gave it a burst. It was hurled backward, cart wheeling, and then began to fall swiftly.

There was a thud, and he looked upward to see a face upside down, pressed against the port on his left. The scorpion was clinging to the top of the hopper and was peering down at him.

For several seconds, he looked into the eyes above the falcon's beak. They were black, innocent of white of pupil or any other color. A ball of jet.

Then, he turned his hopper over and over in a violent maneuver to throw the creatures away, but the thing clung tightly, and the four-lobed pad on the end of its tail came down against the right port and pressed against it.

Immediately, the irradiated plastic began to melt.

Raspold snatched the .45 automatic from its holster by the edge of his seat. He fired twice into the window, the muzzle centered on the pad. Normally, the bullets would have come flying back from the plastic. But, weakened by the melting, the plastic was no obstacle. The bullets plunged into the fleshy looking pad, and the pad jerked away.

Woodwolf's hopper suddenly appeared, the ends of its runners on a level with the top of Raspold's craft. Flame shot out from the open end; the scorpion's face disappeared. And reappeared on the other side of Raspold's hopper as it fell away.

That left two. No, one. For another had attacked Woodwolf, and to do so it had to pass by Raspold. He fired, knocked it spinning away, followed, dived after it, gave it four more bursts, and saw it fall toward the peak.

NOW, the two men maneuvered their hoppers to herd the scorpion and catch it in a crossfire. But the creature turned and fled. Its speed must have been at least three hundred kilometers an hour; it went over the peak and disappeared, presumably toward the cavern mouth.

Raspold checked the hole in the plastic port. It was about the size of his hand, but he didn't worry about it. The cabin had no air in it; the access ports had been closed for protection against micrometeorites.

"If we go into the cavern," said Raspold, "we may encounter thousands of these. You know how little chance we'd have then."

"Yeah," said Big Chuck. "Maybe most of them were too busy with Nge to bother us. And what about Aga-Oglu? We'd better check on him before we do anything else."

Raspold looked out of the corner of his eyes at the bright-as-the-sun globe above him. He was sure that the scorpions were not responsible for that. Whoever had released them against the two Terrans had placed that globe there.

"We'll check on Aga-Oglu," he said. "Keep silence unless it's necessary to break it."

They dipped at an angle to the peak and stopped just above it. The rows on rows of globes and pillars were as before, ghostly, chill, white. The *Pulex* lay where it had been. The Kagan, Raspold knew, would see them when they came down along the face of the mountain. He'd know they were all right.

They dropped down the almost vertical face of the peak. But, before they reached the great opening below them, they were in darkness again. The globe had been extinguished.

Raspold felt cold. They were being watched. How? By whom? He did not know. But he assumed that he would soon find out. Probably not to his pleasure.

Just below the top of the cavern, he stopped. Why go on? Why not be sane, be discreet? Return to Earth, tell them what had happened. It was more than likely that Nge had met defeat at the hands of whatever lived in the bowels of Voittamaton. If the Federation wanted to, it could send a fleet back, a fleet that could land as they had and could shoot missiles with thermonuclear warheads into the cave. Get rid of the menace once and for all. Or, if Voittamaton were truly invincible, then Nge could be marked off the books and the planet would be left alone forever.

He sighed. The old proverb was true. Curiosity killed the cat, and Raspold had a cat's curiosity. He could not endure not knowing what had happened to Nge. What was the power within this dark planet?

He broke the silence and said to Woodwolf, "I'm going on in, but you don't have to be stupid, too. Go back to the *Pulex*."

"I hope you're not ordering me to return," said the Tserokian. "I don't want to be guilty of insubordination. But if I have to, I will. I swore I'd find my sister or find out what happened to her. And I swore I'd get Nge."

"It's your neck," said Raspold.

CHAPTER SEVEN

HE directed the craft into the cave, just beneath the arch of rock. And he stopped almost at once. He had expected to be surprised but not so soon.

Below him, at least five hundred meters below, was the floor of the cave. He could see it easily because it glowed with a light. A strange light that illuminated only the area of the floor and cast no glow above a definite demarcation. The ships of Nge's fleet were clearly illuminated by the light. They rested on the floor in ranks of six, the stolen destroyer *George A. Custer* and the largest ships in the front rank and the others, graded according to size, behind them. All had various ports open, the ports out of which the pirates must have proceeded on foot or in hoppers. The front ranks were by the wall at the far end of the cave, the wall that had stopped further progress on their part. And the personnel of the vessels must have gone through an opening of the wall, an opening large enough for ten men abreast but too small for the ships.

Raspold wondered where the light came from. Then, as he dropped down two hundred meters for a closer look, he saw that the surface of the lighted area had a shiny appearance. It was almost as if the entire floor of the cave had been covered with a thick plastic which trapped light issuing from some unseen source.

He gasped and dropped down again and then paled.

The floor *was* solid with some clear material. The ships were caught in it, embedded like insects in amber!

Raspold almost turned back at this point. If the power within Voittamaton could spring a trap like this, could release some gluey or flowing plastic substance and imprison big ships like this, then light it up for display purposes, what chance did two men have? Who knew but what the light was for his benefit?

The ports were open. Therefore, the men who had left the fleet must have gone on through that archway in the far wall. But the men that must have been left behind in the ships were trapped. Doomed to die of starvation.

He thought, why didn't they just translate? The plastic could not hold them if they used the drive.

The answer was obvious. They did not have the power. It must have been cut off by an outside agency, just as the power in that Federation expedition had been cut off. So, the men would not die of starvation. They would die choking as soon as they used up the air in the ships and then that in their spacesuits.

He had a thought, one, which did not please him. If the plastic material also filled up the entrance to the next chamber or cave, he would be forced to turn back.

He guided the hopper over the embedded ships and to the archway. And found that the luminous material stopped several meters short of it. There was more then enough room for the hoppers to pass through.

THE entranceway did not lead immediately to another cave, as he had expected. It was the opening for a tunnel, cut out of solid rock, that curved not quite imperceptibly to the left and led gently downward. Raspold had turned on the searchbeam so that he could see where he was going; the light splashed off an oily blackness of hard-seeming stone. Then, a bright glow was ahead, the tunnel ceased, and they were in another cavern.

This was so huge that it looked like the interior of a pocket world. It was well lighted from an invisible source—

nothing new in Raspold's technology—and the floor, polished granitoid stone, held thousands of objects. These were arranged in rows; the aisles between were broad enough for five hoppers abreast. The objects were in groups and stood on black metal platforms about two meters high. It became evident, as they advanced down the aisle that they were in a museum. The objects consisted of paintings, stone and wooden sculptures, wood and stone and metal weapons, furniture, models of dwellings: tents, houses, temples, castles, and boats, wagons, chariots. And, standing stiffly and silently beside the artifacts, the makers of the artifacts.

These looked at first like wax dummies. Raspold lifted his hopper and went closer. And he was sure that the statues were stuffed specimens, superb examples of taxidermy. They were members of some centauroid species with which he was unfamiliar.

After a while, they came to an aisle that crossed the one they were on at right angles, and Raspold decided to turn onto that. He drove for several kilometers until he met another aisle, which continued in the same direction as the aisle he had originally been on. Turning down this, he at once saw that another type of sentience was represented on the platforms. These were bipedal, humanoid, their legs from the knees downward incased in tubes of clear plastic-like material. As he passed the platforms, he saw that the groups were arranged to show the stages of physical and cultural evolution of the various subspecies among the bipeds. Near the end of the aisle, they were passing platforms with highly developed artifacts, artistically and technologically.

They crossed an aisle at right angles to this one, and started down it and found that this represented the same progress in evolution for a centauroid race of quite a different type than the first they had seen.

Raspold lifted the hopper until he could see far across the gigantic chamber. There, barely within the limits of his vision, was what he had expected. He gestured to Big Chuck and shot over the heads of the thousands of silent figures until he was at the desired aisle.

He did not need to break silence to tell Woodwolf what these represented. The subhuman figures were familiar enough to both of them, from their schoolbooks. After a minute, they were going by inescapably recognizable sentients. Homo Sapiens.

RASPOLD sped down the aisle while the prehistory and history of man flashed by. Ten kilometers, and he was at the end. Beyond, a sea of empty platforms.

He did not turn then and go down the aisle that ran at ninety degrees to this. He knew that if he did he would see the present development of all the extra-Terrestrial sentients he knew and many many more he did not know. How far that aisle extended was a matter of conjecture. It went so far it passed the horizon, out of sight. But he was willing to bet with any taker that every sentient group that presently inhabited this Galaxy was represented. Presently? Probably many that had existed but did no longer. When he had risen high to take a look, he had seen quite a few rows that had ended long before the others, that had empty platforms at the end of their lines.

Did the vast prairie of empties before him wait for further steps in evolution of the human race? Or did the curator of this museum consider that Homo Sapiens was through, and the empties were to be filled with new sentients?

Raspold shivered, and lifted the hopper high. He rose to the top of the chamber, over two kilometers high, and looked for doorways. He found one, an entrance that looked small from where he was. But, when he came close to it, it was huge. An archway a hundred meters high and two hundred broad. And it was a thousand meters thick.

On emerging from the entrance, they found themselves in another cavern as Brobdingnagian as the last. And their eyes widened and their lips parted with gasps of wonder as they gazed upon mountain after mountain of piled-up jewels. Diamonds, emeralds, rubies, topazes, every precious stone that they knew of and many more they did not. The twinkling glittering masses, heaped higher than three-story buildings, were composed of cut jewels of every size, from thumbnail dimensions to diamonds taller than a man.

Raspold wondered why Nge had not stopped here, taken all he could carry, and returned to his fleet. Perhaps, he had, and found his fleet trapped forever and had come back to find the possessor of these treasures and either kill him in revenge or force him to unspring the trap.

More likely, though, he had not retraced his steps. Nge might be tempted to grab and run but he would resist it. More than a share of this, he would want the knowledge and the power of the owners of this world. If he had those, he could easily be the most powerful man—being—in the Galaxy. And he could take whatever he wanted.

Or so Nge would reason, thought Raspold. *I think like a criminal, and that is how I would think.*

If even a portion of these were dumped on the market, they would be very cheap. Maybe not. There were a thousand worlds in the Galaxy that he knew of and a probable ninety-nine thousand more to be found. These could be spread out very thin.

HE repressed the impulse to take several of the larger jewels with him and sped as swiftly as discretion allowed toward the opposite wall of the cavern. Here he found another archway just like the last one, but he paused before it.

Big Chuck maneuvered directly behind him, and they established tight-beam transmission.

"It's still not too late," said Raspold. "We'd not be criticized at all if we return to Earth. We've invaluable information. The discovery of a form of life that can live in airless space, biologically control gravity and generate a plastic-melting heat is enough to justify us. Especially, if we pick up several of the bodies of the scorpions we shot down and give them to the scientists for dissection. And we can take some of the jewels. They're not stolen from Federation people, not as far as we know. We'd be entitled to keep them. You could buy the biggest ranch on Tserokia; I could resign from the FECAB, set up my own agency.

"But there are stronger factors. I believe that we're as helpless before the inhabitants of Voittamaton as newborn kittens before a hungry wolf. From what I've seen, we don't have a chance."

"I'm going on ahead," said the Tserokian.

Raspold sighed and drove the hopper down the archway. This was even longer than the previous ones. And, as they neared its opposite end, they saw that it was obscured, flickering, like a flawed sheet of plastic on which light was playing.

But Raspold's hopper went through it as if it did not exist. They were inside another cavern. The hopper lost the two decimeters of height above the floor. Raspold was startled, but he saw at once that every light on his instrument panel had gone out and all dials indicated zero. His power was cut off.

Shadows fell on his hopper, and resolved into dozens of the scorpions. They grabbed his hopper and rose with it to a height of fifty meters before he could decide what action to take. By then, he knew that he could do nothing except go along for the ride. If he shot the scorpions, he'd be dropped and killed.

Besides, he knew that the inhabitants of Voittamaton had finally taken action against him, that they had been waiting for him, and had sprung the trap. At least the tension of waiting for attack was gone. Behind him, Woodwolf's hopper was also being carried.

CHAPTER EIGHT

RASPOLD looked through the spaces between the cloud of brown bodies around his craft. This chamber was even more fantastic. Its walls were plated with gold, and the gold was set with patterns of jewels. There were niches in which were set statues and paintings. The artwork, however, differed from that he had seen in the first chamber. This, it was evident, was all of a piece. The work of one group of sentients. The paintings were bizarre, many almost incomprehensible. And the statuary represented beings he had never seen before. Creatures that could only be termed dracocentaurs. Except that they had six lower limbs. The upper torso was scaled, and the arms were long but humanoid. The face looked like an intelligent dragon's.

Abruptly, the hopper fell as those carrying it let themselves drop. For a few seconds, he wondered if he were to be killed as an eagle kills a tortoise, by dropping it and breaking its shell. But the scorpions applied deceleration, and he was gently lowered onto the floor. Immediately, the plastic ports shattered, fell outward, and huge hands with spidery finger's reached in and took his automatic from him. He was dragged out of the craft and set on his feet.

The visor to his helmet was opened, and it was then he knew that the chamber had atmosphere. When he was whirled around, he saw that Nge and his men had also been caught. They were standing in orderly rows, unarmed and as naked as the day they were born. Two hundred or so men and women in twenty rows of ten each.

Behind him, Woodwolf cried out, "Tuli! Tuli!" and he spoke long string of phrases in his native tongue.

So, Woodwolf's sister was one of the women. That part of his quest was ended, anyway.

And he recognized Heinrich Nge. The man was standing in the first row, half a pace ahead of the others. The giant's massively muscled body was beautiful, shining copper in the golden light. The face—high browed, aquiline-nosed, thick-lipped, was set in scowling lines; he looked like a statue of an ancient Pharaoh carved from a polished close-grained dark-red stone. His hands, like those of everybody in the ranks, were free. But his feet could not move, and, as Raspold was carried closer, he saw why. Every human being had his legs embedded inside a block of some transparent material.

Shocked, he thought of the stuffed beings in the museum. Their legs, also, were set inside similar cubes.

Carried horizontally, looking upward, Raspold saw that the ceiling of the gigantic chamber was covered with scorpions hanging upside down or else drifting slowly near the top. He turned his head to both sides and saw that, behind the human beings and on both sides, the floor was packed with the creatures.

Perhaps the most terrible aspect of the scene was that they uttered not a sound.

HE and Woodwolf were carried before the front row of the prisoners, also silent, and there the suits were swiftly removed from them. Their underclothes were stripped off, and scorpions carried in two metallic boxes. Inside the boxes was a clear liquid. The feet of each man were thrust into a box despite their struggles, and a scorpion dropped a tiny red pellet into the liquid in each box. Within a few seconds, the liquid had become a jelly. In half a minute, the jelly had become a solid. The men and the boxes were lifted into the air, and the boxes were slid from the material. And the men were set back on their feet. Raspold found that he could stay upright without any difficulty; his feet were far enough apart.

Before, he had been too occupied with what was happening to him to take a good look at the thing—things—about ten meters in front of the human beings. Now, he saw that a ball of some glassy stuff hung in the air at a level with his head. The ball had a diameter of about thirty meters and colors played inside the sphere as if a hundred living rainbows were chasing each other. On top of the ball, sitting or lying in a depression, was a dracocentaur.

It was about twenty meters long, exclusive of the long scaled, and barbed tail which hung down on the other side of the ball but now and then rose into the air and waved about like a cat's tail. The upper torso reared into the air, propped up by the elbows of the long arms. The face was huge and frightening; the eyes were enormous. From each cheek hung a long tendril of pale flesh. The mouth, when opened, revealed quite human teeth, teeth that looked grotesque in that mouth, in the half-human, half-dragon face.

The eyes were completely black. They looked ancient beyond the scope of his mind. Their blackness was that of interstellar space itself. No, that of extra Galactic space, frightening, the emptiness and foreverness.

Raspold stood humble and quaking and silent, like some suppliant before the greatest of all kings. Behind him, the others were silent, too.

FINALLY, the dracocentaur opened its mouth, and the black and flexible lips spoke. They spoke in Lingo, but with phonetic values strange to Raspold's ears, so that he thought first that it was an entirely foreign language.

"You came through the Place of Dead Worlds before you entered my home!" it said in a loud roaring voice. "Did not that make you think? Think that you could do nothing against one who has seen those globes form out of the primeval gas and become balls of flaming gas and then cool off and give birth to brainless life and then to creatures that can talk and then give death as the parent sun cooled or became a nova? Nothing against one who may see this Galaxy die? And see another rise from the ashes?"

Raspold felt as if his bones had crystallized into ice. So that was what the globes on the steles represented? He had passed through the greatest graveyard in the world, the graveyard of planets long dead. But what sort of creature was this that could mark the passing of a world by setting up a monument? And wait eons for another to die and set up another marker? How long, how immeasurably long, since the first stele and globe?

The dracocentaur stopped talking and looked at them for several minutes. Then, it said, "No. You would not stop to think. You would not dare to stop. Your greed blinded you. As it has every creature that has tried to storm this world. Long before your ancestors were even one-celled sea creatures."

Raspold did not think he had the courage. Yet, he spoke. And, afterward, he thought it was the bravest act of his life.

"You are wrong! I did not come here to steal. Neither did my companion. And some among the others did not come of their own free will. They were brought along as prisoners. And my friend and I came only because we hoped to catch these criminals."

The being on the sphere opened its mouth. Its eyes focused on Raspold. It said, "I know."

There was another silence while the brain that had outlived mountains of granite considered them.

Then, "I cannot worry about your petty problems—how petty you cannot guess—of good and evil. You are all one to me. Would you distinguish between the moral characters of a swarm of gnats?"

"I would," said Raspold boldly. After all, what did he have to lose? Moreover, would a being as powerful, as ancient as this, be irritated by a being like himself?

Perhaps. A lion will swat at a fly.

"One insect considers another," said the dracocentaur.

"I talked to your predecessor, Versinen," said the being. "He went mad. Rather, more mad. Because I showed him what awaited him when he died."

IT paused and seemed to stare through them, the walls of stone, the mountain, and out to the stars. Or beyond the stars.

"What waits for us all," it said. "What terrifies even me."

Now, for the first time since Raspold had entered, Nge spoke. He bellowed, "You are lying! After death, there is nothing. Nothing! You are trying to frighten us! You do not know! You do not know!"

The dracocentaur waited until the echoes of Nge's frenzied cries had ceased. Then, it said, "I know."

Again, it fell silent, and the brain within considered thoughts beyond the scope of man. It said, "The one who came before Versinen was a creature whose kind you do not know. They perished some hundreds of thousands of years ago—your Earth years, that is. He came seeking knowledge, not treasure to loot. I showed him what waited for him, for us all. He left crazy. Not as insane as Versinen, because he had greater stability. But he returned to his planet and told what he knew. I think that his revelation had something to do with their swift decline and death."

"What do you intend to do to us?" asked Woodwolf. "I only came here to get my sister and to make Nge pay for what he has done."

"During which, you injured some of my children," said the being. (Raspold thought of him now as Voittamaton; man must name everything).

"Your children? These? said Woodwolf, gesturing at the scorpions.

"Yes. For much longer than you can ever conceive, I was alone here. You see, my people have been practically immortal for a—to you—immeasurably long time. We were scattered over this Galaxy and others. Then, one by one, we died. Some by accident, for we are not truly immortal. Most by suicide. They had lived too long. Only I am left. I would have killed myself, too, but I lived long enough to find out what waits for us after death. And then I dared not.

"But one of the things that made life intolerable was that we quit having children. We quit because we saw that life was, in the end, only futility. Moreover, after eons, we lost the desire to mate. You people have found out how to prolong your lives. And you are just beginning to encounter the numerous problems immortality brings. Wait until you are semi-immortal, like us. Then...

"However, recently—about a thousand of your years ago—I thought, why not have children? They will be some companionship. Not much. Some. So, I removed several million eggcells from suspended animation, and changed their structure somewhat so that they can live and operate in space as well as in atmosphere of any type. They are also the only truly omnivorous sentients in the Galaxy. They can eat anything: rocks, trees, plants, animals. They can survive on radiant energy, too, though this is only enough to keep the spark of life from going out. Naturally, they derive the most benefit from eating flesh.

THESE you see now are preadolescents. They have been developing for several hundreds of your years. Soon, they will be adolescent and will be reproducing. Then, when this planet is too crowded, they will be venturing into the stellar-systems in your Galaxy. Look out then!

"But these do not represent the greatest danger to you. There is a storm gathering on the Galaxy nearest to this, beings who are far more dangerous than my young. But you need not worry about them for a century or more.

"However, you may be able to fight these youngsters. They are intelligent but ignorant. Savages. I will teach them nothing. It will be interesting, I hope, to see how they develop, but I doubt it. Interest dies as immortality grows."

"What about us?" shouted Nge. "We are not immortal! We want to live as long as we can! We cannot hurt you, and it will cost you nothing to let us loose…"

"You plead for your lives? Beg?"

"I beg for nothing," said Nge. "I will not go down on my knees to you and whine for my life! I do not want to die. But, if I have to kiss your scaly tail, I will die first! I do say that we can be no danger to you. So, why not let us go? Especially if what you say is true about the afterlife? Why condemn us to something you cannot face yourself?"

A horrible rictus opened Voittamaton's mouth. He said, "So! You do not believe what I told you about death. You are only using what I said to argue with me. I will not argue."

He was silent again for a while. Then, "I admire courage and the will to live. Even if I know they mean nothing. Perhaps, that is why I brought my young to life."

He gave a quite human shrug of his shoulders, and…

Raspold did not at first grasp what had happened. Seemingly, between the blink of his eyes, he had been transported from the chamber of Voittamaton to the interior of a spaceship. He was in the lounge (he had seen enough of these to know) and stars hung outside the transparent viewport of the lounge. Whether the transition had been instantaneous or he had been made unconscious and transported here, he didn't know and would never know.

The important thing was that Nge and his crew and Tuli and Chuck Woodwolf and himself were here. They were standing on a great heap of jewels, a layer of diamonds and other precious stones at least a foot thick.

Beyond the lounge was the open doorway to a corridor. And, far down the corridor, another open door. The entrance to the bridge. The pilot's chair was empty; nobody was at the controls.

NGE and his crew still had their feet encased in the transparent blocks. But the blocks were gone from the legs of Raspold, Woodwolf, and a woman who must be Woodwolf's sister.

Raspold, the shock clearing, saw the situation as arranged by Voittamaton. The ship was accelerating or the gravitic field was on. Otherwise, they'd have been floating in free fall. The way to control of the ship lay open. Raspold shouted, "To the bridge, Woodwolf!" Then he was in the pilot's seat and there, dead ahead, looming so hugely it looked as if it would crush them, was the bulk of a planet. It filled the screen except for one corner cut by an arc.

Raspold was too old a spacehand to be alarmed by its seeming proximity. Instead, he located and found the transceiver controls. And, within a minute, he was in contact. The planet was Diveboard.

THE END

If you've enjoyed this book, you will not want to miss these terrific titles…

ARMCHAIR SCI-FI, FANTASY, & HORROR DOUBLE NOVELS, $12.95 each

D-1 **THE GALAXY RAIDERS** by William P. McGivern
    SPACE STATION #1 by Frank Belknap Long

D-2 **THE PROGRAMMED PEOPLE** by Jack Sharkey
    SLAVES OF THE CRYSTAL BRAIN by William Carter Sawtelle

D-3 **YOU'RE ALL ALONE** by Fritz Leiber
    THE LIQUID MAN by Bernard C. Gilford

D-4 **CITADEL OF THE STAR LORDS** by Edmund Hamilton
    VOYAGE TO ETERNITY by Milton Lesser

D-5 **IRON MEN OF VENUS** by Don Wilcox
    THE MAN WITH ABSOLUTE MOTION by Noel Loomis

D-6 **WHO SOWS THE WIND...** by Rog Phillips
    THE PUZZLE PLANET by Robert A. W. Lowndes

D-7 **PLANET OF DREAD** by Murray Leinster
    TWICE UPON A TIME by Charles L. Fontenay

D-8 **THE TERROR OUT OF SPACE** by Dwight V. Swain
    QUEST OF THE GOLDEN APE by Ivar Jorgensen and Adam Chase

D-9 **SECRET OF MARRACOTT DEEP** by Henry Slesar
    PAWN OF THE BLACK FLEET by Mark Clifton.

D-10 **BEYOND THE RINGS OF SATURN** by Robert Moore Williams
    A MAN OBSESSED by Alan E. Nourse

ARMCHAIR SCIENCE FICTION CLASSICS, $12.95 each

C-1 **THE GREEN MAN**
    by Harold M. Sherman

C-2 **A TRACE OF MEMORY**
    By Keith Laumer

C-3 **INTO PLUTONIAN DEPTHS**
    by Stanton A. Coblentz

ARMCHAIR MASTERS OF SCIENCE FICTION SERIES, $16.95 each

M-1 **MASTERS OF SCIENCE FICTION, Vol. One**
    Bryce Walton—"Dark of the Moon" and other tales

M-2 **MASTERS OF SCIENCE FICTION, Vol. Two**
    Jerome Bixby: "One Way Street" and other tales

If you've enjoyed this book, you will not want to miss these terrific titles…

ARMCHAIR SCI-FI & HORROR DOUBLE NOVELS, $12.95 each

D-11 **PERIL OF THE STARMEN** by Kris Neville
THE STRANGE INVASION by Murray Leinster

D-12 **THE STAR LORD** by Boyd Ellanby
CAPTIVES OF THE FLAME by Samuel R. Delaney

D-13 **MEN OF THE MORNING STAR** by Edmund Hamilton
PLANET FOR PLUNDER by Hal Clement and Sam Merwin, Jr.

D-14 **ICE CITY OF THE GORGON** by Chester S. Geier and Richard Shaver
WHEN THE WORLD TOTTERED by Lester Del Rey

D-15 **WORLDS WITHOUT END** by Clifford D. Simak
THE LAVENDER VINE OF DEATH by Don Wilcox

D-16 **SHADOW ON THE MOON** by Joe Gibson
ARMAGEDDON EARTH by Geoff St. Reynard

D-17 **THE GIRL WHO LOVED DEATH** by Paul W. Fairman
SLAVE PLANET by Laurence M. Janifer

D-18 **SECOND CHANCE** by J. F. Bone
MISSION TO A DISTANT STAR by Frank Belknap Long

D-19 **THE SYNDIC** by C. M. Kornbluth
FLIGHT TO FOREVER by Poul Anderson

D-20 **SOMEWHERE I'LL FIND YOU** by Milton Lesser
THE TIME ARMADA by Fox B. Holden

ARMCHAIR SCIENCE FICTION CLASSICS, $12.95 each

C-4 **CORPUS EARTHLING**
by Louis Charbonneau

C-5 **THE TIME DISSOLVER**
by Jerry Sohl

C-6 **WEST OF THE SUN**
by Edgar Pangborn

ARMCHAIR SCIENCE FICTION & HORROR GEMS SERIES, $12.95 each

G-1 **SCIENCE FICTION GEMS, Vol. One**
Isaac Asimov and others

G-2 **HORROR GEMS, Vol. One**
Carl Jacobi and others

If you've enjoyed this book, you will not want to miss these terrific titles…

ARMCHAIR SCI-FI, FANTASY, & HORROR DOUBLE NOVELS, $12.95 each

D-21   **EMPIRE OF EVIL** by Robert Arnette
THE SIGN OF THE TIGER by Alan E. Nourse & J. A. Meyer

D-22   **OPERATION SQUARE PEG** by Frank Belknap Long
ENCHANTRESS OF VENUS by Leigh Brackett

D-23   **THE LIFE WATCH** by Lester Del Rey
CREATURES OF THE ABYSS by Murray Leinster

D-24   **LEGION OF LAZARUS** by Edmond Hamilton
STAR HUNTER   by Andre Norton

D-25   **EMPIRE OF WOMEN** by John Fletcher
ONE OF OUR CITIES IS MISSING by Irving Cox

D-26   **THE WRONG SIDE OF PARADISE** by Raymond F. Jones
THE INVOLUNTARY IMMORTALS by Rog Phillips

D-27   **EARTH QUARTER** by Damon Knight
ENVOY TO NEW WORLDS by Keith Laumer

D-28   **SLAVES TO THE METAL HORDE** by Milton Lesser
HUNTERS OUT OF TIME by Joseph E. Kelleam

D-29   **RX JUPITER SAVE US** by Ward Moore
BEWARE THE USURPERS by Geoff St. Reynard

D-30   **SECRET OF THE SERPENT** by Don Wilcox
CRUSADE ACROSS THE VOID by Dwight V. Swain

ARMCHAIR SCIENCE FICTION CLASSICS, $12.95 each

C-7   **THE SHAVER MYSTERY, pt. 1**
by Richard S. Shaver

C-8   **THE SHAVER MYSTERY, pt. 2**
by Richard S. Shaver

C-9   **MURDER IN SPACE** by David V. Reed
by David V. Reed

ARMCHAIR MASTERS OF SCIENCE FICTION SERIES, $16.95 each

M-3   **MASTERS OF SCIENCE FICTION, Vol. Three**
Robert Sheckley, "The Perfect Woman" and other tales

M-4   **MASTERS OF SCIENCE FICTION, Vol. Four**
Mack Reynolds, "Stowaway" and other tales

If you've enjoyed this book, you will not want to miss these terrific titles…

ARMCHAIR SCI-FI & HORROR DOUBLE NOVELS, $12.95 each

D-31 **A HOAX IN TIME** by Keith Laumer
INSIDE EARTH by Poul Anderson

D-32 **TERROR STATION** by Dwight V. Swain
THE WEAPON FROM ETERNITY by Dwight V. Swain

D-33 **THE SHIP FROM INFINITY** by Edmond Hamilton
TAKEOFF by C. M. Kornbluth

D-34 **THE METAL DOOM** by David H. Keller
TWELVE TIMES ZERO by Howard Browne

D-35 **HUNTERS OUT OF SPACE** by Joseph Kelleam
INVASION FROM THE DEEP by Paul W. Fairman,

D-36 **THE BEES OF DEATH** by Robert Moore Williams
A PLAGUE OF PYTHONS by Frederik Pohl

D-37 **THE LORDS OF QUARMALL** by Fritz Leiber and Harry Fischer
BEACON TO ELSEWHERE by James H. Schmitz

D-38 **BEYOND PLUTO** by John S. Campbell
ARTERY OF FIRE by Thomas N. Scortia

D-39 **SPECIAL DELIVERY** by Kris Neville
NO TIME FOR TOFFEE by Charles F. Meyers

D-40 **RECALLED TO LIFE** by Robert Silverberg
JUNGLE IN THE SKY by Milton Lesser

ARMCHAIR SCIENCE FICTION CLASSICS, $12.95 each

C-10 **MARS IS MY DESTINATION**
by Frank Belknap Long

C-11 **SPACE PLAGUE**
by George O. Smith

C-12 **SO SHALL YE REAP**
by Rog Phillips

ARMCHAIR SCIENCE FICTION & HORROR GEMS SERIES, $12.95 each

G-3 **SCIENCE FICTION GEMS, Vol. Two**
James Blish and others

G-4 **HORROR GEMS, Vol. Two**
Joseph Payne Brennan and others

If you've enjoyed this book, you will not want to miss these terrific titles…

ARMCHAIR SCI-FI & HORROR DOUBLE NOVELS, $12.95 each

D-41   **FULL CYCLE** by Clifford D. Simak
            IT WAS THE DAY OF THE ROBOT by Frank Belknap Long

D-42   **REIGN OF THE TELEPUPPETS** by Daniel Galouye
            THIS CROWDED EARTH by Robert Bloch

D-43   **THE CRISPIN AFFAIR** by Jack Sharkey
            THE RED HELL OF JUPITER by Paul Ernst

D-44   **PLANET OF DREAD** by Dwight V. Swain
            WE THE MACHINE by Gerald Vance

D-45   **THE STAR HUNTER** by Edmond Hamilton
            THE ALIEN by Raymond F. Jones

D-46   **WORLD OF IF** by Rog Phillips
            SLAVE RAIDERS FROM MERCURY by Don Wilcox

D-47   **THE ULTIMATE PERIL** by Robert Abernathy
            PLANET OF SHAME by Bruce Elliot

D-48   **THE FLYING EYES** by J. Hunter Holly
            SOME FABULOUS YONDER by Phillip Jose Farmer

D-49   **THE COSMIC BUNGLARS** by Geoff St. Reynard
            THE BUTTONED SKY by Geoff St. Reynard

D-50   **TYRANTS OF TIME** by Milton Lesser
            PARIAH PLANET by Murray Leinster

ARMCHAIR SCIENCE FICTION CLASSICS, $12.95 each

C-13   **SUNKEN WORLD**
            by Stanton A. Coblentz

C-14   **THE LAST VIAL**
            by Sam McClatchie, M. D.

C-15   **WE WHO SURVIVED (THE FIFTH ICE AGE)**
            by Sterling Noel

ARMCHAIR MASTERS OF SCIENCE FICTION SERIES, $16.95 each

MS-5   **MASTERS OF SCIENCE FICTION, Vol. Five**
            Winston K. Marks—Test Colony and other classics

MS-6   **MASTERS OF SCIENCE FICTION, Vol. Six**
            Fritz Leiber—Deadly Moon and other classics

Made in United States
North Haven, CT
12 January 2023

30951165R00125